MW01268524

a fine excess

Sarabande Books
Louisville, Kentucky

a fine excess

contemporary literature at play

EDITED BY

KIRBY GANN & KRISTIN HERBERT

FIRST EDITION

Managing Editor
Sarabande Books, Inc.
2234 Dundee Road, Suite 200
Louisville, KY 40205

Cover: *Evening Raga,* by Francesco Clemente.
Courtesy of the artist and the Gagosian Gallery.

Cover and text design by P. Dean Pearson.

Manufactured in the United States of America.
This book is printed on acid-free paper.

Sarabande Books is a nonprofit literary organization.

LIBRARY OF CONGRESS CATALOGING-IN-PUBLICATION DATA
A fine excess : contemporary literature at play / edited by Kirby Gann and Kristin Herbert.
p. cm.
ISBN 1-889330-51-5 (alk. paper)
1. American literature—20th century. 2. Experimental literature, American.
I. Gann, Kirby, 1968– II. Herbert, Kristin, 1968–
PS536.2 .F56 2000
810.8'005—dc21

00-029162
CIP

To Sarah and Jeffrey, with gratitude

contents

9 *Introduction* Kirby Gann and Kristin Herbert

21 William Gass *The Music of Prose*

36 Lynn Emanuel *inside gertrude stein*
38 *Who Is She Kidding*

40 Dean Young *Ready-Made Bouquet*

44 Sharon McDermott *Feast*

46 Sunetra Gupta from *Memories of Rain*

67 Heather McHugh *Language Lesson 1976*

68 Marjorie Maddox *The Other Hand*

70 C.K. Williams *My Mother's Lips*

73 Gabriel Gudding *One Petition Lofted into the Gingkos*
75 *The Parenthesis Inserts Itself into the Transcripts of the Committee on Un-American Activities*

77 Rick Moody *The Mansion on the Hill*

121 Jeffrey McDaniel *Hunting for Cherubs*
122 *The Jerk*

124 Kristina McGrath from *A Scribbler's Life*

139 Barbara Edelman *Geometry Problem*

141 Jack Heflin *Local Hope*

143 Mike Newirth *Give the Millionaire a Drink*

150 Amy Gerstler *Lucky You*

152 Belle Waring *Baltazar Beats His Tutor at Scrabble*

154 PETER LA SALLE *The Latin Ice Kings*

176 SUSAN MITCHELL *The Hotel by the Sea*

179 MICHAEL GRABER *Furry Lewis Ponders Life and Death as a Blues Man*

181 JOHN DREXEL *Music Survives, Composing Her Own Sphere*

183 TERRANCE HAYES *Boxcar*

185 EDMUND WHITE *Record Time*

197 CONNIE VOISINE *Psalm*

200 SEAN THOMAS DOUGHERTY *Labor Day*

201 ALICE FULTON *Babies*

203 VALERIE WOHLFELD *The Blank Notebook*

207 E.E. CUMMINGS *67*

208 TIMOTHY GEIGER *A Note on the Type*

209 MAGGIE ANDERSON *Country Wisdoms*

211 PATRICK CHAMOISEAU *The Eighteen Dream-Words That Afoukal Gave Him*

221 YUSEF KOMUNYAKAA *False Leads*
223 *Venus's-flytraps*

224 A.E. STALLINGS *The Man Who Wouldn't Plant Willow Trees*

225 JOHN HAWKES *The Martyr of La Violaine*

242 BILLY COLLINS *Consolation*

244 WILLIAM KISTLER *And Then There Were the Feet*

245 *Biographical Notes*

254 *Acknowledgments*

256 *The Editors*

introduction

The Prose

COLERIDGE WROTE OFTEN ABOUT THE ACT OF READING, and the different responses a text could, or should, inspire. He demanded a significant responsibility of the reader, recognizing that what we bring to the act of perception can be just as important as what we perceive: "We receive," Coleridge wrote, "what we give." He approached the task of reading in the same way a miner must approach a tract of diamonds: the greater effort and care taken in the extraction, the greater amount of jewels end up on the surface for the world to enjoy. For Coleridge, the diamonds to be gleaned from a text amount to the intensity of pleasures infused in the reader.

And yet his exhortation makes for a two-way track down into the mine—to be trammed by the writer, too, for the responsibility of exacting pleasure from a text cannot lie with the reader alone; there must be a richness on the page that can be brought out; the tract must be laden with ore.

Unfortunately, much contemporary reading reveals a good deal of sedimentary rock.

As a reader, I get excited by the buzz created around a new book, the praise heaped on its moving narrative voice, the precision and clarity of its language, the sincerity of its prose. I rush out to see for myself—only to be disappointed to learn that "sincere prose" refers to a monosyllabic style, that the lauded "precision" must refer to the text's lack of idiosyncrasy—perhaps even originality—and that if there's a richness to be found in the work, it is one that this reader must bring to it entirely on his own. I find a transparent, functional language, constructed for the simple transmission of data, that often belies any perceptive curiosity on the author's part at all. The experience of such books has become common enough to be labeled a trend.

It began with the appearance in fiction of what Bill Buford called "Dirty Realism," and which Tom Wolfe went on to identify more efficiently as "K-Mart Realism," an evocative phrase that gets closer to the heart of the matter: a style that refers to a flat form of writing, weighted with obvious details and heavily concerned with objects and goods, a utilitarian style that depends on the plain surprise of the banal for its effectiveness. We have our masters of the form, and I do not mean to imply that it does not hold any interest or value; however, its pervasiveness is disappointing, as is its lack of diversity. The condition at its heart reflects an austerity of words. Or, often, a casual attitude toward language, as though writers have succumbed to a dreadful stylistic democracy: writing in bald, tempered language, making it difficult beyond the title page to remember the author's name. The telling of the story becomes an act of efficiently reporting the information that relates the tale, and nothing more; the story's events take precedence over all else. Hemingway's influence has been blamed for this "anti-style"; others critical of it point to the decline of reading in general (even by authors), which may be true; or perhaps it reflects the general rushed climate we live in these days, when we find it so difficult to concentrate for more than a few minutes at a time.

Yet concentration is fundamental to writing imaginative work. The writer's task is to do so much more than relate manageable, functional worlds, as our earliest masters—Rabelais, Cervantes, Boccaccio—proved long ago: at its most essential level, the task is to *write* the story, to exercise the mind of the reader through the gymnastic throws in the mind of the writer. William Matthews once compared the act of writing as not much different than children playing with mudpies; Humbert Humbert lamented, "Oh, Lolita! I have only words to play with!"—but what an awesome playmate they made for him, as he molded his singular, colloquially baroque style. All literature rests in Humbert's lament, as words are all we have to express what is sometimes beyond words, and playing with them is often the best route to get to what seems inexpressible. Hence the subtitle of this anthology: *Contemporary Literature at Play.*

But what exactly does "play" mean in this context? How does one go about using the word in relation to literature without making the works sound as though they are merely lighthearted, whimsical riffs?

A glance at the dictionary can help; there are the expected definitions first: *to occupy oneself in amusement, sport, or recreation; fun or jest, as opposed to earnest; a dramatic performance on a stage.* These aren't particularly helpful toward the aesthetic we're trying to define. But look further: *to gamble; to perform on an instrument; to move or operate freely within a bounded space. Elusive change: to cause to move rapidly, lightly, or irregularly—"to play lights over the dance floor."* These definitions get closer. We've sought writers whose styles reflect this approach; whose language isn't strict or merely sober, but comes at the world in its most intense states, in reverie, in revelry, in fine excess; writers who must have, as Paul West once termed it, "the world written *up*." For how else can the artist appropriately reflect our moments of incandescence, our sensuality, our elegiac memories? To go back to my original metaphor of the mine: we have selected writers whose acts of perception have discovered rich, heavily laden tracts of expressive ore. These are writers who show creative delight, who explore the possibilities within the compound sentence, within composed phrases. These are minds unmistakably alive on the page: some tend to frolic, others waltz, but each writes with a level of veracity and intensity that is unique, difficult to forget. The bounded space they move within is the form of their choosing—in the case of these prose selections, story or essay—and there they move freely, in particular, musical fashion, often making unlikely connections, sometimes jutting their sentences into odd and disproportionate rhythms, creating a vivid sensory whole. One could call the anthology a collection of prose dances.

The opening essay by William Gass, for example, is something of a glove thrown down, a challenge that raises the bar of what's expected of the works to come, as he outlines the value of a musical prose while embodying the aesthetic by his own sonorous example.

Rick Moody's "The Mansion on the Hill" is the epitome of literature at play. Moody gives us the story of a loser, a man who makes his living wearing a chicken mask before getting the job as the virtual whipping boy of a power-mad wedding director. Taking these absurd details as unlikely starting points, Moody manages to infuse the character, and thus the story, with a delicate pathos that slowly overwhelms the reader, through a gradual unveiling of information. Though the story is comprised of bizarre happenings, half-jokes, and painfully funny observations, what Moody has accomplished by the end is a deep insight into the nature of understanding a loved one's death. He keeps the reader in playful expectation, wondering what this narrator will fall into next, all the while exploring the prospect of death, love, and their consequences.

Kristina McGrath's excerpt from her novel *A Scribbler's Life* takes a different approach. Here, the playfulness is in structure and language; the puns aren't in events, as in Moody's piece, but in a more Nabokovian fashion: throughout literature. Her sentences and situations rhyme with a history of other works, identified in her use of footnotes: one finds here an unexpected filiation to the works of Austen and Brontë, among others, shedding light on our century by bringing fire from the one previous. McGrath uses a raised, formal language, almost baroque, yet one that dances, that reflects a super-keen sensibility. Examples abound throughout the piece: mice don't merely run amok in the narrator's home at Tenoaks, but "have ruin through the musty walls"; rain doesn't drip through the fissures in a rotting ceiling—"drizzle issues from a wizened crack," as, the narrator adds, "the thoughts from my head."

We don't talk like this, but what if we did? The vivid richness of the language—an almost archaic dialect that has fallen out of fashion—reinvents itself and thus the world. For how much more vivid is the world of this text, with its wizened cracks, its author in petticoats who "consult[s] with only the pillows," than the daily mundane world in which we live? And yet McGrath's textual world is rooted in our more habitual one; she has snatched details the less careful eye and ear may miss and, in presenting them before us, dramatizes a singular way of seeing and feeling.

Patrick Chamoiseau moves from yet a different direction. His story "The Eighteen Dream-Words That Afoukal Gave Him" is formally innovative but not difficult; an experiment in eclecticism, "Afoukal" combines different linguistic and literary traditions (oral storytelling and literary writing; creole slang with formal French) that cross cultures and ideologies, forging a verbal music that still comes through in English. His use of "dream-words" is a jubilant act of imagination, a device he employs to cross generational time to inspect the life of Caribbean slaves; the fact that the dream-words themselves are not listed (if they exist) only adds to the mystery of a lost time and the paradox of living as a slave and finding oneself suddenly, unaccountably free.

The wild variety of works selected here demonstrates that the idea of literature-as-play is an inexhaustible one. Mike Newirth has written a story of social hyperrealism, a stab at a social class devoid of morality or even purpose, a class that is often hailed as the reward at the center of the American Dream. Newirth captures the feel of summer in the Hamptons with no conventional plot line or central character, but through snippets of dialogue and interwoven half-scenes, a braiding of glimpses that create an incandescent milieu. Driven by intense language that scores in its imagery: a "distinguished anesthesiologist" is described as "lean, leathery, hair varnished like a helmet"; the "practiced repose" of geeky options traders is disturbed by the "intrusion of china cups and pale sandwiches," which "flusters their paid-for vacation hoohrah." In just a sentence, Newirth precisely evokes a time, place, and mood. It's as though he is attempting minimalist form and infusing it with maximalist language.

Valerie Wohlfeld creates a kind of metaphysical portrait of the sea, a rhapsody to what the sea symbolizes and suggests to the mind. With poetic logic she lists the many influences the sea has had on world-views, from the Greeks to Goya to the present, unnamed narrator. The language is loaded and maximal, as rich as its subject. Her long periodic sentences are stuffed with metaphor and simile, bordering the overwritten, the purple, moving languorously but powerfully, much like the sea itself. Then, the language reins itself in at the last possible instant, capturing the sensation that being alone with the sea can bring: a *reverie.*

Edmund White explores the subject of adolescent loneliness as "a full state," giving us a portrait of the artist's developing sensibility in a language of playful alliteration; John Hawkes creates a dreamlike world rife with seductions and betrayals; Sunetra Gupta combines a torrent of prose with the precise stanzas of Tagore's poetry. The works selected here comprise a mine of the editors' choosing; here you'll find the *word,* along with the world, written *up.* Tram your way in.

—Kirby Gann

The Poetry

The poems in this anthology pulse with the charge of invention that Benjamin Franklin must have felt when he "discovered" electricity by flying a kite. Stirred by such a current, the heart leaps, as if out of the body, to meet it. To handle this voltage—to be electrified without being electrocuted—demands courage and conviction as well as restraint, a balance that is, as Keats put it, *a fine excess*. The poets whose work appears here stretch language beyond the expected, use sound and rhythm, the logic of dreams and intuition. Freed from their usual parameters, words make sense outside of sentences; phrases extend and end unexpectedly—fractured, fragmented, bent but unbroken. These are poems that test preconceived, prefabricated ideas about what a poem is, does, includes. Invention presides over convention. Humor, too, is irreverently employed—puns, jokes, and riddles—as wordplay satisfies the human craving for surprise, a relief from our everyday perspectives.

Belle Waring and Jeffrey McDaniel are playfully inventive at a formal level as well as through the music and rhythms they create. With "forms" from everyday life—word problems, a Scrabble game—they pose and ponder unanswerable questions. Belle Waring's poem, "Baltazar Beats His Tutor at Scrabble," springs from a word problem opening ("If Myra counts fifteen cows and Alfredo counts nine, . . .") and uses the metaphor of a board game to spell out the particular life of a thirteen-year-old whose dad beat him up. The conceit is clever and the linguistic jump-cuts quite fantastic, and Waring manages to ground such playful invention with insights that are, by turns, sobering and luminous. McDaniel's prose poem "Hunting for Cherubs" reads like a word problem in a class devoted to ethical math. Both absurd and profound, the poem is determined to provoke thought and in so doing, injects an odd humor. These poems are good examples of process-oriented thinking, the value of which lies in provoking thought rather than in answers or resolutions. In this kind of play, the object is to surprise the consciousness into thinking beyond the expected, in the moment the game goes off the board.

Humor is a subversive tool: the jokes of any culture are a clue to its taboos: sex, religion, politics, death. We euphemize and joke about what is most difficult to discuss. Amy Gerstler's "Lucky You" is an excellent example of how a poem can play, linguistically, without compromising the tragedy it recounts.

The writers collected here have found ways to make language un-vanish, to awaken us to the fresh, lush, delectables of English, to let the reader in on the fun. And when writers play with language, the stakes are high. Not serious, necessarily, but sacred nonetheless. Poets, in particular, have much to say about their medium. In these poems, literary theory is afoot: the same debates that rage in critical and scholarly prose are here, in lively debate.

Emanuel's "Who Is She Kidding," from her collection, *The Dig,* undercuts the notion of narrative transparency and debates the common reading of autobiography as truth: "We may faint dead away before she's/going to tell us what the truth is." Emanuel uses this witty, cantankerous voice to deconstruct the more traditional "I" that conflates the speaker with the poet, herself, because ". . . honey, you can't fit a girl like that/into the straitjacket of a book of poems."

With his subtle sonnet, "A Note on the Type," Timothy Geiger creates a theoretical alternative to the either/or thinking that animates scholarly debates around L=A=N=G=U=A=G=E poetry. Though certainly a testament to the literal presence of language, this poem celebrates the letter as a form that creates space. Starting with the intellectual necessity of the alphabet, Geiger lingers on the beauty of the symbol and its utterance. But what makes this sonnet most compelling is the mystery it amplifies: "Lao-tzu called the space inside the vessel/its usefulness. What of the alphabet?" Our efforts to convey ideas through language rely, in large part, on hypothesis: words themselves are metaphors. In the space held open by language, thought can extend beyond all boundaries, regardless of natural and social laws, beyond the confines of mortality itself.

"Feast" by Sharon McDermott celebrates words as flesh. "Can you smell the yeasty rise of bread/in a choice bite of syllables?/I smell tang of lemon and/the hands that slice it./. . . *Plum* is fleshy—/pit deep in sour-sweet skin. /*Hunger* hinges on the deep/guttural *ung* that desires to be filled."

The impulse to stretch language beyond its everyday use is evident in the work of Terrance Hayes and Jack Heflin, both of whom work with vernacular and idiomatic expression, using rhythm, musicality, and linguistic enjambment or incantation to great effect.

Rather than reveling in such pleasurable excesses of language, Heather McHugh, Maggie Anderson, and Yusef Komunyakaa play within the economy imposed by everyday diction, illuminating the richness of slang, cliché, euphemism, and idiomatic, colloquial, and vernacular expressions. In so doing, these poets teach us to listen differently, to mint fresh meaning from the deflated currency of common speech by paying attention.

McHugh's "Language Lesson 1976" illuminates vernacular phrases, delighting in double entendre: "Hold is forget,/in American. . . . / The language is a game as well,/in which love can mean nothing, //doubletalk mean lie. I'm saying/doubletalk with me . . . . //Make nothing without words//and let me be/the one you never hold."

In her poem "Country Wisdoms," Anderson works with the rich images and rhythms of rural idioms to portray a certain hardscrabble attitude that is distinctly American. This poem, at first glance, could almost seem "found." Indeed, Anderson's selection of phrases and her shaping of them is remarkable, in terms of both music and logic. But even more potent is the poem's subtle impact, one that relies on the phrases themselves and the reader's attention. The language is held up, as if in quotation marks, for examination: "They say these things." Though no direct commentary is made, the implication is that these expressions, if we listen, speak for themselves: "Then they say, Bootstraps./Pull yourself up."

Yusef Komunyakaa uses colloquialisms quite musically in "False Leads" to give voice to "Slick Sam/the Freight Train Hopper," whose language snaps with fakes and dodges. Here is proof that play can be dead serious. Slick Sam, an escaped slave, outwits Mister Bloodhound Boss by laying a false trail. Not only is the texture of this language playful, it renders a high-stakes game in which the speaker, Slick Sam, bets his own life.

All three of these poems are doubly clever in that they play with the paradox of language—awakening us to notice both what it veils and what it reveals. As in jokes, there is a twist and an insistence that the reader be involved enough to get it. They require a mental double take, telling just enough but refusing to explain themselves away.

The thrill of art—and of play—is the opportunity it offers to shift perspective. Witness Dean Young's "Ready-Made Bouquet." The poem is rife with unexpected combinations and takes utterly unpredictable turns. The abstraction of love, for instance, is particularized by paraphrasing Magritte's surreal images—a tuba on fire, a bottle with breasts. And its counterpoint, the despair of loving, "may lead to long plane rides with/little leg room, may lead to a penis full/of fish, a burning chicken, a room filled//with a single, pink rose." Young jousts with the notion of symbolic language, using humor without losing the poem's more somber undertones of emotional turbulence. ("Don't piss while in the river is a native saying //he thinks at first is symbolic.") Finally, the poem ends by drawing the reader's attention to perspective: to how we see the rose and the room it overwhelms: "Funny, how/we think of it as a giant rose,/not a tiny room."

—Kristin Herbert

the music of prose

William Gass

To speak of the music of prose is to speak in metaphor. It is to speak in metaphor because prose cannot make any actual music. The music of prose has the most modest of inscriptions. Its notes, if we could imagine sounding them, do not have any preassigned place in an aural system. Hence they do not automatically find themselves pinned to the lines of a staff, or confined in a sequence of pitches. Nor is prose's music made of sounds set aside and protected from ordinary use as ancient kings conserved the virginity of their daughters. In the first place, prose often has difficulty in getting itself pronounced at all. In addition, any tongue can try out any line; any accent is apparently okay; any intonation is allowed; almost any pace is put up with. For prose, there are no violins fashioned with love and care and played by persons devoted to the artful rubbing of their strings. There are no tubes to transform the breath more magically than the loon can by calling out across a lake. The producers of prose do not play scales or improve their skills by repeating passages of De Quincey or Sir Thomas Browne, although that might be a good idea. They do not work at *Miss iss ip pi* until they get it right. The sound of a word may be arbitrary and irrelevant to its meaning, but the associations created by incessant use are strong, so that you cannot make the sound *m o o n* without seeming to mean "moon." By the time the noun has become a verb, its pronunciation will feel perfectly appropriate to the mood one is in when one moons, say, over a girl, and the "moo" in the mooning will add all its features without feeling the least discomfort. In music, however, the notes are allowed to have their own way and fill the listeners' attention with themselves and their progress. Nonmusical associations (thinking of money when you hear do-re-me played) are considered irrelevant and dispensable.

In sum, prose has no notes, no scale, no consistency or purity of sound, and only actors roll its *r*'s, prolong its vowels, or pop its *p*'s with any sense of purpose.

Yet no prose can pretend to greatness if its music is not also great; if it does not, indeed, construct a surround of sound to house its meaning the way flesh was once felt to embody the soul, at least till the dismal day of the soul's eviction and the flesh's decay.

For prose has a pace; it is dotted with stops and pauses, frequent rests; inflections rise and fall like a low range of hills; certain tones are prolonged; there are patterns of stress and harmonious measures; there is a proper method of pronunciation, even if it is rarely observed; alliteration will trouble the tongue, consonance ease its sounds out, so that any mouth making that music will feel its performance even to the back of the teeth and to the glottal's stop; mellifluousness is not impossible, and harshness is easy; drum roll and clangor can be confidently called for—lisp, slur, and growl; so there will be a syllabic beat in imitation of the heart, while rhyme will recall a word we passed perhaps too indifferently; vowels will open and consonants close like blooming plants; repetitive schemes will act as refrains, and there will be phrases—little motifs—to return to, like the tonic; clauses will be balanced by other clauses the way a waiter carries trays; parallel lines will nevertheless meet in their common subject; clots of concepts will dissolve and then recombine, so we shall find endless variations on the same theme; a central idea, along with its many modifications, like soloist and chorus, will take their turns until, suddenly, all sing at once the same sound.

Since the music of prose depends upon its performance by a voice, and since, when we read, we have been taught to maintain a library's silence, so that not even the lips are allowed to move, most of the music of the word will be that heard only by the head and, dampened by decorum, will be timorous and hesitant. That is the hall, though, the hall of the head, where, if at all, prose (and poetry, too, now) is given its little oral due. There we may say, without allowing its noise to go out of doors, a sentence of Robert South's, for instance: "This is the doom of fallen man, to labour in the fire, to seek truth *in profundo,* to exhaust his time and impair his health and perhaps to spin out his days, and himself, into one pitiful, controverted conclusion"; holding it all in the hush of our inner life, where every imagined sound we make is gray and no more material than smoke, and where the syllables are shaped so deeply in our throats nothing but a figment emerges, an *eidolon,* a shadow, the secondhand substance of speech.

Nevertheless, we can still follow the form of South's sentence as we say it to ourselves: "This is the doom of fallen man. . . ." What is?

	. . . to labour in the fire . . .
	. . . to seek truth *in profundo* . . .
	. . . to exhaust his time . . .
and	. . . [to] impair his health . . .
and perhaps	. . . to spin out his days . . .
and	. . . [to spin out] himself . . .

"into one pitiful, controverted conclusion." That is, we return again and again to the infinitive—"to"—as well as to the pileup of "his" and "him," and if we straighten the prepositions out, all the hidden repeats become evident:

. . . to labour into one pitiful, controverted conclusion . . .
. . . to seek truth in one pitiful, controverted conclusion . . .
. . . to exhaust his time in one pitiful, controverted conclusion . . .

... [to] impair his health [obtaining] one pitiful, controverted conclusion ...

... to spin out his days into one pitiful, controverted conclusion ...

... [to spin out] himself into one pitiful, controverted ...

To labour, seek, exhaust, impair, spin out ... what? Work, truth, time, health, days, himself. Much of this tune, said sotto voce in any case, doesn't even get played on any instrument, but lies inside the shadow of the sentence's sound like still another shadow.

So South's prose has a shape which its enunciation allows us to perceive. That shape is an imitation of its sense, for the forepart is like the handle of a ladle, the midsections comprise the losses the ladle pours, and the ending is like a splashdown.

This is the doom of fallen man, to labour in the fire,
to seek truth *in profundo,*
to exhaust his time
and impair his health
and perhaps to spin out his days,
and himself,
into one pitiful, controverted conclusion.

In short, one wants South to say: "pour out his days . . ." "in two one pit eee full, conn trow verr ted conn clue zeeunn . . ." so as to emphasize the filling of the pit. However, "spin" does anticipate the shroud which will wrap around and signify "the doom of fallen man."

In short, in this case, and in a manner that Handel, his contemporary, would approve, the sound (by revealing the spindle "to" around which the sentence turns and the action that it represents is wound) certainly enhances the sense.

However, South will not disappoint us, for he plays all the right cards, following our sample with this development: "There was then no pouring, no struggling with memory, no straining for invention. . . ." We get "pour" after all, and "straining" in addition. The pit is more than full; it runneth over.

Often a little diction and a lot of form will achieve the decided lilt and accent of a nation or a race. Joyce writes "Irish" throughout *Finnegans Wake,* and Flann O'Brien's musical arrangements also dance a jig. Here, in O'Brien's *At Swim-Two-Birds,* Mr. Shanahan is extolling the virtues of his favorite poet, that man of the pick and people, Jem Casey:

> "Yes, I've seen his pomes and read them and . . . do you know what I'm going to tell you, I have loved them. I'm not ashamed to sit here and say it, Mr. Furriskey. I've known the man and I've known his pomes and by God I have loved the two of them and loved them well, too. Do you understand what I'm saying, Mr. Lamont? You, Mr. Furriskey?
>
> Oh that's right.
>
> Do you know what it is, I've met the others, the whole lot of them. I've met them all and know them all. I have seen them and I have read their pomes. I have heard them recited by men that know how to use their tongues, men that couldn't be beaten at their own game. I have seen whole books filled up with their stuff, books as thick as that table there and I'm telling you no lie. But by God, at the heel of the hunt, there was only one poet for me."

Although any "Jem" has to sparkle if we're to believe in it, and even though his initials, "JC," are suspicious, I am not going to suggest that "Casey" is a pun on the Knights of Columbus.

> "No 'Sir,' no 'Mister,' no nothing. Jem Casey, Poet of the Pick, that's all. A labouring man, Mr. Lamont, but as sweet a

singer in his own way as you'll find in the bloody trees there of a spring day, and that's a fact. Jem Casey, an ignorant Godfearing upstanding labouring man, a bloody navvy. Do you know what I'm going to tell you, I don't believe he ever lifted the latch of a school door. Would you believe that now?"

The first paragraph rings the changes on "known" and "loved," while the second proceeds from "know" and "met" to "seen" and "heard," in a shuffle of sentences of the simplest kind, full of doubled vowels, repeated phrases, plain talk, and far-from-subtle rhyme, characteristics that lead it to resemble the medieval preacher's rhythmic prose of persuasion. It is the speech, of course, of the barroom bore and alcoholic hyperbolist, a bit bullyish and know-it-all, even if as empty of idea as a washed glass, out of which O'Brien forms an amusing though powerful song of cultural resentment.

It is sometimes said that just as you cannot walk without stepping on wood, earth, or stone, you cannot write without symbolizing, willy-nilly, a series of clicks, trills, and moans; so there will be music wherever prose goes. This expresses an attitude both too generous and too indifferent to be appropriate. The sentence with which Dreiser begins his novel *The Financier,* "The Philadelphia into which Frank Algernon Cowperwood was born was at his very birth already a city of two hundred and fifty thousand and more," certainly makes noise enough, and, in addition to the lovely "Philadelphia," there are "Algernon" and "Cowperwood," which most people might feel make a mouthful; but the words, here, merely stumble through their recital of facts, happy, their job done, to reach an end, however lame it is. Under different circumstances, the doubling of "was" around "born" might have promised much (as in Joyce's paradisal phrase "when all that was was fair"); however, here it is simply awkward, and followed unnecessarily by another "birth," the reason, no doubt, for Dreiser's mumpering on about the population. After another sentence distinguished only by the ineptness of its enumeration ("It was set with handsome parks, notable buildings, and crowded with historic memories"), the author adds fatuousness to his list of achievements: "Many of the things that we and he knew later were not then in existence—the telegraph, telephone, express company, ocean steamer, or city delivery of mails." "We and he" do ding-dong all right, but rather tinnily. Then Dreiser suffers a moment of expansiveness ("There were no postage-stamps or registered letters") before plunging us into a tepid bath of banality whose humor escapes even his unconscious: "The street-car had not arrived, and in its place were hosts of omnibuses, and for longer travel, the slowly developing railroad system still largely connected with canals." It makes for a surreal image, though: those stretches of track bridged by boats; an image whose contemplation we may enjoy while waiting for the streetcar to arrive.

"Bath of banality" is a bit sheepish itself, and brings to mind all the complaints about the artificiality of alliteration, the inappropriateness of rhyme in prose, the unpleasant result of pronounced regular rhythms in that workaday place, the lack of high seriousness to be found in all such effects: in short, the belief that "grand" if not "good" writing undercuts its serious and sober message when it plays around with shape and the shape of its sounds; because, while poetry may be permitted to break wind and allow its leaves to waltz upon an anal breeze, prose should never suggest it had eaten beans, but retain the serious, no-nonsense demeanor of the laboring man in *At Swim-Two-Birds.*

Some tunes are rinky-dink indeed, and confined to the carnival, but I get the impression that most of these complaints about the music of prose are simply the fears of lead-eared moralists and message gatherers, who want us to believe that a man like Dreiser, who can't get through three minutes of high tea without blowing his nose on his sleeve, ought to model our manners for us, and tell us truths as blunt and insensitive, but honest and used, as worn shoes.

What they wish us to forget is another kind of truth: that language is not the lowborn, gawky servant of thought and feeling; it is need, thought, feeling, and perception itself. The shape of the sentence, the song in its syllables, the rhythm of its movement, is the movement of the imagination too; it is the allocation of the things of the world to their place in the world of the word; it is the configuration of its concepts—not to neglect them—like the stars, which are alleged to determine the fate of we poor creatures who bear their names, suffer their severities, enjoy their presence of mind and the sight of their light in our night ... *all right* ... *all right* ... *okay*: the glow of their light in our darkness.

Let's remind ourselves of the moment in *Orlando* when the queen (who has, old as she is, taken Orlando up as if he were a perfumed hanky, held him close to her cleavage, and made plans to house him between the hills of her hope) sees something other than her own ancient figure in her household mirror:

> Meanwhile, the long winter months drew on. Every tree in the Park was lined with frost. The river ran sluggishly. One day when the snow was on the ground and the dark panelled rooms were full of shadows and the stags were barking in the Park, she saw in the mirror, which she kept for fear of spies always by her, through the door, which she kept for fear of murderers always open, a boy—could it be Orlando?—kissing a girl—who in the Devil's name was the brazen hussy? Snatching at her golden-hilted sword she struck violently at the mirror. The glass crashed; people came running; she was lifted and set in her chair again; but she was stricken after that and groaned much, as her days wore to an end, of man's treachery.

Where shall we begin our praise of this passage, which, in *Orlando,* is merely its norm? And what shall we observe first among its beauties? Perhaps, in that simple opening sentence, the way the heavy stresses which fall on "mean," "while" (and equally on the comma's strong pause), "long," "win-," "months," "drew" and finally "on" again, make those months do just that (the three *on*'s, the many *m*'s and *n*'s don't hurt, nor does the vowel modulation: een, ile, ong, in, on, ou, on), or the way the river, whose flow was rapid enough reaching "ran," turns sluggish suddenly in the middle of the guggle in that word. Or maybe we should admire the two *and*'s which breathlessly connect a cold, snowy ground with shadowy rooms and barking stags; and then, with confidently contrasting symmetry, how the three semicolons trepidate crashing, running, lifting, while enclosing their two *and*'s in response. Or should we examine, instead, the complex central image of the figure in the glass, and the way the two clauses beginning with "which" are diabolically placed? Or the consequent vibration of the sentence from the public scene of Orlando in embrace to the queen's personal shock at what she's seen out the open door, thanks to her "magic" mirror. Nor should the subtle way, through word order mainly, that Virginia Woolf salts her prose with a sense of the era—her intention quite serious but her touch kept light in order to recall the Elizabethan period without parody—be neglected by our applause.

It is precisely the queen's fear of spies and murderers which places the mirror where it can peer down the corridor to the cause of her dismay—that is the irony—but it is the placement of the reasons ("which she kept for fear of spies always by her," etc.) between the fragments of the perceptions ("through the door," "a boy," and so on) that convinces the reader of the reality of it. It is not enough to have a handful of ideas, a few perceptions, a metaphor of some originality, on your stove, the writer must also know when to release these meanings; against what they shall lean their newly arrived weight; how, in retrospect, their influence shall be felt; how the lonely trope will combine with some distant noun to create a new flavor.

What is said, what is sounded, what is put in print like a full plate in front of the reader's hungry eye, must be weighed against what is kept back, out of view, suggested, implied. The queen, in her disappointed rage, has fallen to the floor, but we are told only that she was lifted and put back in her chair again. And nothing will henceforth be the same in the last, morose moments of her life. On account of a kiss caught by a mirror through a door kept ajar out of fear of another sort of assault.

In music, sounds form phrases; in prose, phrases form sounds. The sentence fragment almost immediately above was written to demonstrate this, for it naturally breaks into units: "On account of a kiss/caught by a mirror/through a door kept ajar/out of fear of another/sort of assault." These shards, in turn, can be subdivided further: "On account/of a kiss. . . ." Certain pieces of the pattern act like hinges: "kiss/caught" "door/kept," for instance, while possessives play their part, and the grammatical form that consists of an article and a noun ("a count/a kiss/a mirror/a door/a jar /a nother/a sault") stamps on the sentence its special rhythm.

Words have their own auditory character. We all know this, but the writer must revel in it. Some open and close with vowels whose prolongation can give them expressive possibilities ("Ohio," for instance); others are simply vowel heavy (like "aeolian"); still others open wide but then close sharply ("ought"), or are as tight-lipped as "tip," as unending as "too," or as fully middled as "balloon." Some words look long but are said short (such as "rough" and "sleight"); some seem small enough but are actually huge ("otiose" and "nay"). A few words "whisper," "tintinnabulate," or "murmur," as if they were made of their meanings, while "Philadelphia" (already admired) is like a low range of hills. Some words rock, and are jokey, like "okeydokey." Or they clump, like "lump" and "hump" and "rump" and "stump," or dash noisily away in a rash of "ash/mash/bash" or "brash/crash/smash/flash" or "gnash/lash/hash/stash/cash" or "clash/trash/splash/potash/succotash." Vowel changes are equally significant, whether between "ring," "rang," and "rung," "scat" and "scoot," "pet" and "pat," "pit" and "pot," or "squish" and "squooze."

The Latinate measures of the great organist Henry James find an additional function for the music of prose. Here all it takes is a parade of the past tense ("he had") down a street paved with negations.

> He had not been a man of numerous passions, and even in all these years no sense had grown stronger with him than the sense of being bereft. He had needed no priest and no altar to make him for ever widowed. He had done many things in the world—he had done almost all but one: he had never, never forgotten. He had tried to put into his existence whatever else might take up room in it, but had failed to make it more than a house of which the mistress was eternally absent.

If some men are has-beens, poor Stransom (in James's judgment) is a had-not-been. The passage is crammed with loss: "bereft," "widowed," "failed," "absent," in addition to the doubling of "sense," "no," "never," in succeeding sentences, and the gloomy repetition of the past tense, particularly "been" and "done." Our hero, we cannot help but hear, is a transom. He only looks on. But the music of the passage ties terms together more firmly than its syntax: "being," for instance, with "bereft," "done" with "one," "never" with "ever," and "what-" with "ever" as well. Each sentence, all clauses, commence with poor Stransom's pronoun, or imply its presence: "he had, he had, he had" trochee along like a mourning gong.

Musical form creates another syntax, which overlaps the grammatical and reinforces that set of directions sometimes, or adds another dimension by suggesting that two words, when they alliterate or rhyme, thereby modify each other, even if they are not in any normally modifying position. Everything a sentence is is made manifest by its music. As Gertrude Stein writes:

> Papa dozes mamma blows her noses.
> We cannot say this the other way.

Music makes the space it takes place in. I do not mean the baroque chamber, where a quartet once competed against the slide of satin, the sniff of snuff, or the rustle of lace cuffs; or the long symphonic hall full of coughing, whispered asides, and program rattle; or the opera house, where the plot unfolding on the stage plays poorly against the ogling in the boxes and the distractions in the stalls; or even the family's music room, where heavy metal will one day leave its scratches like chalk screech on the windowpanes—none of these former or future pollutions of our pleasure; but again in that hall of the head (it holds so much!) where, when the first note sounds behind the lids, no late arrivals are allowed to enter, and when the first note sounds as if the piano were putting a single star down in a dark sky, and then, over there, in that darkness, another, the way, for instance, the 1926 sonata of Bartok begins, or a nocturne of Chopin's, slowly, so we can observe its creation, its establishment of relation; because we do see what we hear, and the music rises and falls or feels far away or comes from close by like from the lobe of the ear, and is bright or dim, wide or thin, or forms chains or cascades, sometimes as obvious as a cartoon of Disney's, splashy and catchy, and sometimes as continuous and broad and full as an ocean; while at other times there is only a ding here and a ping there in a dense, pitchlike lack of action, and one waits for the sounds to come back and fill the abyss with clangor, as if life were all that is.

And when we hear, *we* hear; when we see, and say: "Ah! Sport!" *we* see; our consciousness of objects is *ours,* don't philosophers love to say? and though we share a world, it is, from the point of view of consciousness, an overlapping one: I see the dog with delight, you with fear; I see its deep, moist eyes, you its cruel wet mouth; I hear its happy panting, you its threatening growl; and I remember my own loyal pooch, and you the time a pug pursued you down the street; so we say the same word, "dog," yet I to welcome and you to warn, I to greet and you to cringe; and even when we think of what our experience means and ponder the place of pets in the human scheme, thus sharing a subject, as we have our encounter, we will pursue our problem differently, organize it in dissimilar ways, and doubtless arrive at opposite ends.

But I can shape and sound a sentence in such a way my sight of things, my feeling for what I've seen, my thoughts about it all, are as fully present as the ideas and objects my words by themselves bear. D. H. Lawrence, for instance, in that great chapter of *Sea and Sardinia* called "The Spinner and the Monks," does not simply tell us he saw two monks walking in a garden.

> And then, just below me, I saw two monks walking in their garden between the naked, bony vines, walking in their wintry garden of bony vines and olive trees, their brown cassocks passing between the brown vine-stocks, their heads bare to the sunshine, sometimes a glint of light as their feet strode from under their skirts.

Anyone can put a pair of monks in a garden and even hang around to watch their no-doubt sandaled feet flash, but Lawrence is a whole person when he perceives, when he repeats, when he plans his patterns; so that, just as he himself says, it is as if he hears them speaking to each other.

> They marched with the peculiar march of monks, a long, loping stride, their heads together, their skirts swaying slowly, two brown monks with hidden hands, sliding under the bony vines and beside the cabbages, their heads always together in hidden converse. It was as if I were attending with my dark soul to their inaudible undertone. All the time I sat still in silence, I was one with them, a partaker, though I could hear no sound of their voices. I went with the long stride of their skirted feet, that slid springless and noiseless from end to end of the garden, and back again. Their hands were kept down at their sides, hidden in the long sleeves and the skirts of their robes. They did not touch each other, nor gesticulate as they walked. There was no motion save the long, furtive stride and the heads leaning together. Yet there was an eagerness in their conversation. Almost like shadow-creatures ventured out of their cold, obscure element, they went backward and forwards in their wintry garden, thinking nobody could see them.

And we go to and fro here, too, as the sentences do, passing between vowel and idea, perception and measure, moving as the syllables move in our mouth, admiring the moment, realizing how well the world has been realized through Lawrence's richly sensuous point of view.

They clothe a consciousness, these sounds and patterns do, the consciousness the words refer to, with its monks and vines, its stilled observant soul, its sense of hearing them speak as well as seeing them striding along together, the quality of mystery and community the passage presents by putting them in the light of a late winter afternoon.

> And I noticed that up above the snow, frail in the bluish sky, a frail moon had put forth, like a thin, scalloped film of ice floated out on the slow current of the coming night. And a bell sounded.

A beautiful, precise image, translucent itself, is carried forward by an arrangement of *f*'s and *l*'s, *o*'s and *u*'s, with such security their reader has to feel he's heard that bell even before it sounds.

Suddenly the mind and its view have a body, because such sentences breathe, and the writer's blood runs through them, too, and they are virile or comely, promising sweetness or cruelty, as bodies do, and they allow the mind they contain to move, and the scene it sees to have an eye.

The soul, when it loves, has a body it must use. Consequently, neither must neglect the other, for the hand that holds your hand must belong to a feeling being, else you are caressing a corpse; and that loving self, unless it can fill a few fingers with its admiration and concern, will pass no more of its passion to another than might a dead, dry stick.

The music of prose, elementary as it is, limited as it is in its effects, is nonetheless far from frivolous decoration; it embodies Being; consequently, it is essential that that body be in eloquent shape: to watch the mimsy paddle and the fat picnic, the snoozers burn and crybabies bellow . . . well, we didn't go to the beach for that.

inside gertrude stein

Lynn Emanuel

Right now as I am talking to you and as you are being talked to, without let up, it is becoming clear that gertrude stein has hijacked me and that this feeling that you are having now as you read this, that this is what it feels like to be inside gertrude stein. This is what it feels like to be a huge typewriter in a dress. Yes, I feel we have gotten inside gertrude stein, and of course it is dark inside the enormous gertrude, it is like being locked up in a refrigerator lit only by a smiling rind of cheese. Being inside gertrude is like being inside a monument made of a cloud which is always moving across the sky which is also always moving. Gertrude is a huge galleon of cloud anchored to the ground by one small tether, yes, I see it down there, do you see that tiny snail glued to the tackboard of the landscape? That is alice. So, I am inside gertrude; we belong to each other, she and I, and it is so wonderful because I have always been a thin woman inside of whom a big woman is screaming to get out, and she's out now and if a river could type this is how it would sound, pure and complicated and enormous. Now we are lilting across the country-side, and we are talking, and if the wind could type it would sound like this, ongoing and repetitious, abstracting and stylizing everything, like our famous haircut painted by Picasso. Because when you are inside our haircut you understand that all the flotsam and jetsam of hairdo have been cleared away (like the forests from the New World) so that the skull can show through grinning and feasting on the alarm it has created. I am now, alarmingly, inside gertrude's head and I am thinking that I may only be a thought she has had when she imagined that she and alice were dead and gone and someone had to carry on the work of being gertrude stein, and so I am receiving, from beyond the grave, radioactive isotopes of her genius saying, take up my work, become gertrude stein.

who is she kidding

Who is she kidding? Who is she,
anyway, talking as though she knew
when, I can tell you, honey, she never
even saw an artichoke until she was
eighteen and went to Italy and got laid
for the first time on the beach outside
Talamone, and even then
that girl didn't know how to spell
artichoke until she was twenty-three.
But honey, you can't fit a girl like that
into the straitjacket of a book of poems.
I mean no book of poems in the world
is big enough to explain how she got
from Ely, Nevada, to Talamone getting
laid, so she just moves along as though
poetry were an interstate and here we are
passing Ely, here we are copulating
with Marco, all the little stitches
of explaining have been cut.
We may faint dead away before she's
going to tell us what the truth is,
but honey, I'll tell you one thing, life's
like its cooking and Ely was spinach
untinned by Grandma directly onto
the plate so that its brackish

backwash broke into waves and,
leaking, weeping, flooded the hominy.
It dripped off the china the way
Columbus thought the sea dripped
off the lip at the end of the world.
Whole ships rode off into its darkness,
the coffers of nations were squandered.
Artichoke, my god, this one could sell
snow to the Eskimos; this is America,
honey, we don't need any damned artichokes.

ready-made bouquet

Dean Young

It's supposed to be spring but the sky
might as well be a huge rock floating
in the sky. I'm the guy who always forgets

to turn his oven off pre-heat but I might
as well be the one with the apple in front
of his face or the one with Botticelli's
Flora hovering at his back, scattering

her unlikely flowers. Which is worse?
To have your vision forever blocked or
forever to miss what everyone else can
see, the beautiful *Kick me* sign hanging
from your back? Is there anything more

ridiculous than choosing between despairs?
Part of me is still standing in the falling

snow with my burning chicken. In a black slip,
a woman despairs in front of her closet
five minutes before the guests arrive.
In the tub, a man sobs, trying to reread
a letter that's turning to mush. Despair

of rotten fruit, bruised fruit. Despair
of having a bad cat, garbage strewn over
your shoes, sofa in shreds. Despair of saying,
You bet I hate to get rid of him but I'm
joining the Peace Corps, to the girl who
calls about the ad. The despair of realizing

despair may be a necessary precondition
of joy which complicates your every thought
just as someone screaming in the hall, Get
away from me, complicates the lecture on
Wallace Stevens. Ghostlier demarcations,
keener sounds. Wallace Stevens causes despair

for anyone trying to write poems or a book
called *Wallace Stevens and the Interpersonal.*
Sometimes interpersonal despair may lead to
a lengthy critical project's completion but how

could Jessica leave me in 1973 after pledging
those things in bed, after the afternoon looking
at Magrittes? The tuba on fire. The bottle with
breasts. Didn't I wander the streets half the night,

hanging out at the wharf, afraid of getting beat up
just to forget that one kiss in front of the bio-
morphic shape with the sign saying *Sky* in French?
The stone table and stone loaf of bread. The room

filled with a rose. Loving someone who doesn't
love you may lead to writing impenetrable poems

and/or staying awake until dawn, drawn to airy,
azure behaviors of gulls and spaceships.
Some despairs may be relieved by other despairs

as in not knowing how to pay for psychoanalysis,
as in wrecking your car, as in this poem. Please
pass me another quart of kerosene. A cygnet
is a baby swan. Hatrack, cheesecake, mold.
The despair of wading through a river at night

toward a cruel lover is powerfully evoked
in Chekhov's story "Agafya." The heart seems
designed for despair especially if you study
embryology while being in love with your lab
partner who lets you kiss her under the charts
of organelles but doesn't respond although

later you think she didn't not respond either
which fills you with idiotic hope very like
despair just as a cloud can be very like
a cannon, the way it starts out as a simple
tube then ties itself into a knot. The heart,
I mean. It seems, for Magritte, many things

that are not cannons may be called cannons
to great effect. David's despair is ongoing
and a lot like his father's, currently treated
with drugs that may cause disorientation and

hair loss. Men in white coats run from
the burning asylum. No, wait, it's not burning,

it's not an asylum, it's a parking lot
in sunset and they want you to pay. Sometimes
Rick thinks Nancy joined the Peace Corps just

to get away from him so later he joins the Peace Corps
to get away from someone else, himself it turns out,
and wades into a river where tiny, spiny fish
dart up your penis if you piss while in the river.
Don't piss while in the river is a native saying

he thinks at first is symbolic. The despair
of loving may lead to long plane rides with
little leg room, may lead to a penis full
of fish, a burning chicken, a room filled

with a single, pink rose. Funny, how
we think of it as a giant rose,
not a tiny room.

feast

Sharon McDermott

Somewhere the moon as full as a breast,
  or so I render it—pearl
skin, liquid as silk. I like the play
of language, its puzzling limits,
  the growl from the pit
  of a blues man's gut,
the fork and strike of words, metallic
or viscous as honey drizzled onto a biscuit.

Can you smell the yeasty rise of bread
in a choice bite of syllables?
I smell tang of lemon and
the hands that slice it.
  Peel can be sexual
or rend an orange in sections,
succulent, juicy.
Plum is fleshy—
pit deep in sour-sweet skin.
  Hunger hinges on the deep
  guttural *ung* that desires to be filled.

We long for the hot stoops
  of summer, the neighbors'
  whoops and whistles,
  fat conversation:

our own voice quivering to its feet,
    the rhythmic chants of girls
    within a thrumming rope,
    the thrust and parry of sweet talk
    like the smooth hand of a lover
    thumbing nipples to hard seeds.

With words, I am
stepping out. Language
is the sidewalk in August,
    the hiss and sashay
of vowels, strut
of heels, phrases
playing between the cracks.

from memories of rain

Sunetra Gupta

SHE SAW, THAT AFTERNOON, ON OXFORD STREET, a woman crushing ice cream cones with her heels to feed the pigeons. She saw her fish out from a polythene bag a plastic tub that she filled with water for the pigeons, water that they would not be able to drink, for pigeons, her grandmother had told her many years ago, can only quench their thirst by opening their beaks to drops of rain. And she remembered a baby starling that, in the exhilaration of her first English spring, she had reached to hold, her hands sheathed in yellow kitchen gloves, for within her, as her husband had once observed, compassion had always been mingled with disgust.

Even he, the first time she ever set eyes upon him, had disgusted and fascinated her, the dark hairs plastered to his chalk-white legs, for this was in the flood of '78, and he had just waded through knee-deep water, he and her brother, all the way from the Academy of Fine Arts to their house in Ballygunge. He had rolled up his jeans revealing his alabaster calves which dripped the sewage of Calcutta onto the floor of their veranda, and that was what caused her to tremble in excitement and loathing as she pushed aside the curtain with a tray of tea and toast, his large, corpse-white, muck-rinded toes pushed against the bamboo table, soiling the mats she had crocheted in school. She set down the tea, her brother did not bother to introduce her, but Anthony asked, is this your sister? And she had nodded vaguely and smiled, picked up the book that she had been reading all afternoon, there on the veranda, all afternoon, watching the rain. In her room, which she shared with her grandmother, the moldy smell of a deep, long rain was settling in, compounded by the muddy strokes of the maid, who had picked this unlikely hour to wash the floors. She treaded gingerly across and flung open the shutters, letting in a spray of rain. Her grandmother, coming in with the sewing machine, pleaded with her to shut them, her old bones would freeze, she said, so she drew them in again and switched on the much-despised fluorescent light, and lay with her face toward the damp wall, lulled by the whirr of the sewing machine, and the ever loudening beat of the raindrops, until the lights went out, as they did every night, and every morning—the inevitable power rationing—and she was summoned to take out to her brother and his white friend a kerosene light. And so she appeared to him a second time, lantern-lit, in the damp darkness, a phantom of beauty, and his eyes roamed for a time after she had disappeared inside, the ghost of light that her presence had left, there beside him, in the rain-swollen dark. He saw her again at dinner, candlelit, their first dinner, and she sat well back in the darkness, so that he could only gaze upon the flames that danced upon her delicate fingers, the drapes of her sari that fell upon the formica tabletop, and as they were being served yogurt, the lights came on again, the house sprang into action, the fans whipped up the clammy cold air, the water pump revived, Beethoven resumed on the record player. I'd rather you didn't leave the player on during load shedding, said their father, their grandmother shivered, the rain will go on for a few days now, she said, I can feel it in my bones, those poor villagers.

She noticed he had changed into some clothes of her brother's, the long punjabi shirts that he wore over jeans or loose pajama pantaloons, which together with his thick beard (gnat-infested, I'm sure, she would tease him, a veritable ecosystem, their ornithologist uncle called it) set him apart as a man of letters, reaffirmed his association with an experimental theater group. Last year her brother had visited her in London, he had been touring in Germany, and he had sat all day in his hideous check jacket which he always kept on, in front of the television, smelling of alcohol, Anthony had had no patience with him, they were glad when he left. And yet, the first evening that he was here, the two of them had sat and argued late into the night, and she had felt again the soggy wind of that first rain-filled evening upon her limbs, as she folded clothes in the laundry room, their voices drifting toward her, the quivering ring of heat around the edges of the iron. Later as she lay upstairs staring through the bedroom curtains at the haze of the streetlights, their voices rose in thin wisps to edge the darkness, as they had done that moldy evening, when all of Calcutta was one large sea of mud and dung, and floating water-logged Ambassador cars, and children disappeared on their way home from school into open manholes, their covers wrenched off and sold long ago, to drown in the city's choked sewers, on a night like this, he had come to dinner, and been forced to stay, she had been ordered to spread clean sheets on her brother's bed in the living room, which during the day they called the divan, and make one up on the floor for her brother, and so she heard them talk, wide-eyed in the dark of her own bedroom, heard their laughter amid the gentle snores of her grandmother, the vacillating rain. She heard her brother's footsteps, the corridor light came on, she heard him rummaging at his desk, which lay in an alcove in the corridor where, as children, they had kept their toys, the little red tricycle that they rode together on the roof terrace, the silver-haired dolls her aunt sent from Canada. She emerged cautiously from her bedroom to meet his excited eyes.

"You're not asleep yet!" he exclaimed.

"You woke me up," she retorted, but he brushed by her without a rejoinder, she struggled with the heavy latch on the bathroom door until it slid down suddenly, as it always did, and once within, she stood in the mossy darkness, and heard through the thin walls her brother translating to his English friend a play that he had just finished writing last week, his first (there, he had said to her, a week ago, after an afternoon of furious scribbling, what do you think, do you think your brother will make it as a playwright, tell me, Moni, if this isn't better than most of the crap that they call theater, and she had put down her Agatha Christie novel to pick up with her calm fingers the foolscap booklet that he had flung on the bed, at her feet), the play was set in rural West Bengal, where, her brother had wanted to show, the peasantry were still as oppressed as they had been the past thousand years under feudalism, you must take me out there, she heard Anthony say, you must acquaint me with rural Bengal, that was what she had heard him say, her cheeks pressed against the damp bathroom walls, on a night of mad thunder and rains that swept away half the peasantry of their land, left them without the mud walls within which they had sheltered their grains, their diseased children, their voracious appetites, and their stubborn ignorance. For she had come to this island, this demi-paradise, from a bizarre and wonderful land, so Anthony's friends called it, was it true, they asked, that they still burn their wives, bury alive their female children? And she would nod numbly, although she had known only of those children that had escaped death, whether deliberate or from disease, those that had been sent out to serve tea in tall grimy glasses in roadside stalls, or to pluck the gray hairs of obese turmeric-stained metropolitan housewives, fill the gentleman's hookah, blow, blow until the green flame gushes, while the mother, helpless domestic, watches silently and trembles. And even these were often graven images, culled from film and fiction. From such a land Anthony had rescued her, a land where the rain poured from the skies not to purify the earth, but to spite it, to churn the parched fields into festering wounds, rinse the choked city sewers onto the streets, sprinkle the pillows with the nausea of mold, and yet the poet had pleaded with the deep green shadows of the rain clouds not to abandon him, the very same poet who wrote,

> You, who stand before my door in this darkness
> Who is it that you seek?
> It has been many years since that spring day, when there came a young wanderer
> And immersed my parched soul in an endless sea of joy;
> Today, I sit in the rain-filled darkness, in my crumbling shack
> A wet wind snuffs my candle, I sit alone, awake;
> Oh, unknown visitor, your song fills me with sweet awe
> I feel I will follow you to the depths of uncharted dark.

But it was not this song, not yet, that ran through her rain-ravaged mind as the grandfather clock in the living room struck two, interrupting the awkward flow of her brother's translation, the grammatical mistakes she shivered at, why was his English so terrible, and she stood in the bathroom, splashed icy cold water out of the drum onto her feet, she caught a ghost of herself in the cracked mirror, and a sudden embarrassment overcame her, she switched on the lights and took in the cracked plaster, the dilapidated water closet, long since choked with lime, suspended over the Turkish toilet, the cracked mirror, the shelf cluttered with bottles of coconut oil, toothpaste tubes, rusty razor blades, and she compared it to the bathrooms at Amrita's, where she knew Anthony was staying, marbled to the ceiling, with Western commodes and bathtubs, he cannot be used to any of this, she thought, and now as she luxuriated in the lavender-scented heat of her bath, she would wonder how she had ever been used to it either. Yet, for many years, that bathroom had been her only refuge, here she had soaped the corners of her growing body, watched her breasts bud, shampooed the grime of the city out of her long black hair, memorized poems with her face to the knife-edged drops of water from the shower, and that night, before she drew back the latch and stepped into the corridor, she whispered to herself from Keats's "Ode on Melancholy," which they had dissected that afternoon in her Special Paper class, and saw in her mind's eye Anthony, crushing grapes with his strenuous tongue against his palate fine: his soul shall taste the sadness of her might, and be among her cloudy trophies hung.

She was jerked awake in the morning by her mother, it was still raining, the floodwater lapped at the outside walls, but somehow, even in all this, her father had managed to procure a whole chicken on his daily morning excursion to the market. On her way to the bathroom, she glimpsed the sleeping form of her brother, one dark arm grazing the floor, and for once, she shared the indignation of her uncles that it was still her father who went to the market every morning while he slept off his late nights, but let the boy sleep, their father would protest, I go for my morning walk anyway, it doesn't hurt me to stop by the bazaar, besides he is the artistic type, he does not comprehend life's practicalities. So who does the shopping now, who braves the early-morning sun to haggle over fish, fish smeared with goat blood to simulate freshness, you shake the flies from your face and palpate the aubergines, the king prawns are a hundred rupees a kilo today, but nothing is too good for my daughter's wedding, even if she is marrying an Englishman, they will still have it done the traditional way, that was all her father had asked of her. You alone are to blame for the ruin of your children, her uncles would tell him later, you indulged them, and now as you sit paralyzed in your grandfather's rocking chair, your son lies sodden with drink at the Press Club and your daughter is lost to you, over the seas.

And yet that rain-laden morning, her mother had allowed her to wander through the living room in her nightdress, which she never would have tolerated if any other friend of her brother's had been asleep on the moist floor, but he, this white man, was too remote to be a threat, there was no need for modesty, and so she looked upon him, as he slept, the dark eyebrows, deep-set eyes, closed now, the sunburned chin, he did not look quite so European as those Germans that had been here last year, he could almost pass for a North Indian, but for that peculiar papery texture of his scorched skin. She brought in tea, and her brother sat up suddenly rubbing his eyes, but Anthony rolled over, turned his face to the wall, and continued to sleep the sleep of the dead, as he would later in the face of her despair, gray mornings through pale curtains, the finality of his striped pajama back.

"So what should I do with his tea?" she asked her brother.

"Leave it; if he doesn't get up I'll drink it."

The roar of thunder drowns the faint tinkle of rickshaw bells. Thick wet footsteps on the veranda, an umbrella shaken and opened out to dry, the smell of betel juice drifts through the damp air, her music tutor has arrived, on a morning like this, he picks his muddy way past the white man, glances at him with disgust, she leads him into the bedroom, pulls out the grass mat, all smells are magnified in this grand penetrating wetness. She drags out the harmonium from under the bed, the keys are moist with condensation, the notes slice through the damp air, her brother slams the bathroom door. She pulls out the heavy volume of Tagore songs, opens it to the right page, it is a song of rain that she has been learning these past few weeks, she has almost mastered it, but for a few delicate folds in the final phrases. Her tutor runs a gnarled finger across the lines, who but the poet could have captured the sorrow of the rain so well? he asks, as if she might have dared to suggest otherwise.

And so he woke, a strange chill in his limbs, to the sound of her windy voice, unfamiliar halftones, words he would never understand,

> in the dense obsession of this deep dark rain
> you tread secret, silent, like the night, past all eyes.

Her voice rises, she is immersed in the words he cannot understand, although they come to him like the wet morning wind:

> the heavy eyelids of dawn are lowered to the futile wail of the
>   winds
> clotted clouds shroud the impenitent sky
> birdless fields
> barred doors upon your desolate path.

He sits up, a weak cup of tea is pushed toward him, her voice rises again,

> oh beloved wanderer, I have hung open my doors to the
>   storm
> do not pass me by like the shadow of a dream.

Many years later, huddled in a deserted tin mine on the Cornish coast, she translated the same song for him, staring into the sheets of rain that ran by like frozen phantoms across the crumbling entrance, and he sat back against the moldy walls, paying only half heed to her eager, nervous translations, mesmerized instead by the duet of the storm and the sea, until, like the sudden spray, it hit her that he was not listening, he was not listening at all, but they had been rescued, then, by the sudden urge to see their child, the girl left behind at his mother's, was she staring glumly into the rain, her little elbows on the white sill, or was she wrapped up in her grandmother's lap, rocking back and forth to a story, her cold toes digging into the old woman's wrinkled palms. Wedged between two Swedish cars on the Cornish moorland motorway, she had watched the rhythm of her breath as it condensed on the car window, while he had mused of his afternoon with Anna, a curious half-smile flitting across his face from time to time, for he had long come to terms with his infidelity, he implored her silently, ever, to accept it, to reconcile the poetry of his passion for

Anna with his deep affection for her and for her child, as he had done, after many evenings of gentle agony, desperately curling the child's hair in his agitated fingers, the unbearable stillness of a rare summer evening, her regular breathing, a child asleep on a summer evening, sun-warmed sheets billowing in the garden. The doorbell rings, she staggers in with the shopping, her face flushed, he holds her in his sad embrace, I will make dinner, you sit down and rest, and as they eat their scrambled eggs, he looks across at her in the dying light, that beloved darkness in the hollows of her eyes, perhaps she was what really held them together, Anna and himself, without her, there would be no substance to their relationship, he remembers a night, drenched with lavender, in the hills of Provence, where, among the olive groves, he had first kissed Anna's warm lips, he remembers his sad exhilaration grappling with an emotion long forgotten, an emotion that is there but in faint wisps, on the winding path back to the rented cottage he is divided between an excruciating guilt and an insane desire to preserve the passion that having climaxed in that one painful kiss seems now to be melting away. In the distance, he can hear Moni singing, she sits by the window, her song drifting toward them with the spiced winds, her foreign lament, was it sad, was it joyful, it was her song that had hypnotized them then, infused them with a gentle sustained lust, that was, perhaps, their doom,

> in this moonlit night, they have all gone wandering in the forest
> in this mad springtime wind, in this moonlit night

for the lush warmth of the South of France had taken her back to moonlit college picnics by broad tropical rivers, the spell of her song webbed across the wide fields,

I will not go into the inebriated spring winds
I will sit alone, content, in this corner
I will not go forth into the drunken winds

—the inscrutable elation of the poet, who shall not sip of the wild honey of spring, for he awaits a sterner intoxication, and he must remain watchful, lest those that wander in the forest should choke upon the spring breezes and the moonlight, the poet must remain awake,

in this moonlit night, they have gone wandering in the forest
drunk with the young wind of springtime.

She turns around to face them, dense shadows in the doorway, a shadow shifts and sighs, Anna is beside her, the moonlight fringes her wet lashes, and Anthony moves quietly to her other side, they have surrounded her, for one perfect moment she is an integral part of their passion, they are circled by love. And it had become clear to her, as they picked their way through the gorges of the Ardèche, where the butterflies swirled like pieces of burnt paper, that this was no temporary lust, no flitting desire worked by the lavender breezes and the moonlight, no mild weekend enchantment that he would work off by listening to Mozart all day, these she had grown to tolerate, but here, among the charred butterflies, like a thin stream of blood in her mouth, came the first taste of her long tryst with fear. How would it happen, she wondered, would he seat her down gently, and explain, stroking with a kind hand, her long black hair, his other hand strumming on an airplane ticket, and how could she ever go home, home to the wild grief of her parents, the snickers of the neighbors, her brother's pity, his smugness—but no, how could he be smug, he who turned away his cloudy eyes at the airport, think of what you will miss, Moni, think of what you are giving up, how can you desert us like this, Moni? For he had been so terribly proud of her, her voice, her talents, his friends' roving eyes as she served them tea, her refinement, he had molded her, told her what to read, how to appreciate it, taken her with him to plays and films, the right films, forbidden her to accompany her girlfriends to the trashy commercial films they all went giggling to see, not that he needed to, she and her group of close friends preferred English films anyway, he would drag her off to the film societies to see French and German films, Russian films, and now, she would surprise a group of Anthony's friends with a shy, yes, I have seen that, amid conversations where her only other contribution was her smile. A moment of silence, all eyes upon her, someone would ask kindly, how did you like it, trying to draw her into the conversation. Anthony would smile encouragingly, and she would voice some simple opinion and if they were in the mood they would try and tease some more out of her, but soon enough a rapid and incomprehensible debate would erupt, and she would get up to make the coffee. She did not mind it this way, indeed this was what she had been used to at home, among her brother's friends, opinionated, enthusiastic, they were terrifying, the stern, beautiful Amrita, the rotund Gayatri who always played the mother with her glorious, deep voice, the men, all in beards, blur in her mind now, she would sit among them, as she did here, now, among Anthony's friends, silent, smiling, absorbing their life, their determination, their warmth. Would she have become like them, like Amrita, confident and eloquent, had she stayed there? Had she been arrested in her development, remained the passive, attentive child, by crossing the seas to an unfamiliar country, where, despite her half-finished honors degree in English, she could not find the right words, the right expressions, to voice her opinions, to participate but in the most banal of conversations, or was she merely passive by nature, content to sit and listen? Might she have burgeoned, shed the role of the adolescent sister, nurtured by their admiration, their respect? In the summer months before Anthony came to Calcutta, they had invited her to sing a few Tagore songs, offstage, for one of their plays, it was her entrance to their world, she loved the smoky school hall where they rehearsed in North Calcutta, she would look out of the tall windows onto the narrow gutter-lined streets where the little boys played cricket, square-cutting balls into the gutter, to be fished out gingerly and washed under the burst hydrants, the mossy courtyards where their mothers waited with glasses of milk that they gulped and ran out again like a shot to join the game, and then some gentle hand would fall upon her shoulder, could you sing "Je ratey mor duarguli" for us now? Pull out the off-key harmonium, Ranjan fiddles with the tabla, knocking about with a hammer, all right then, Polash has the tape recorder ready, you may begin, Moni,

On the night that my doors broke with the storm
How was I to know that you would appear at my door?
A blackness surrounded me, my light died
I reached towards the sky, who knows why?

Her voice echoes through the old school hall, which creaks every morning under hundreds of fidgety feet, identically shod, the sound of fluttering hymn books, corners that have been creased a century ago by careless sunburned fingers. Later, when they are all eating lunch, spicy meat in earthenware containers, with paper-thin rumali roti, "handkerchief bread," she tries out the old piano, we should have used this rather than that wretched harmonium, she remarks. Gayatri, swinging her legs from the stage, asks her to eat something, but she shakes her head, she suspects that the meat is beef, she knows that they all eat beef, and that the food has been bought from the Muslim restaurant down the road. Her brother teases her about her conservative Brahmanic habits, and embarrassed, she retires to a corner of the vast hall, where behind heavy dust-smothered curtains there are worn gym horses, benches and bars, instruments of torture in the hands of some terrifying gym mistress, her heart floods with sympathy, and yet she feels detached, she is part of another world.

And now on Oxford Street watching a woman crush ice cream cones to feed the pigeons, she is seized by an overwhelming desire to return to that world, although she knows it is there for her no longer, that the experimental theater group has long been dissolved, that her brother squanders his meager journalist's income on alcohol, her mother arranges with her tired hands the disused limbs of her father over the divan in the living room, the divan which used to serve as her brother's bed, the same divan that had been offered to Anthony on that first night of incessant rain. But somehow he had ended up on the floor, perhaps the divan was not long enough to contain his vast frame, and that was where he had woken up to the rain-swollen syllables of her song, buried his face in the clammy pillow to drown his sudden burning desire to smell the rain vapor on her young skin, to run his hands through her moist cloud-black hair, there was a sound of wet feet on the floor beside him, he raised his face from the pillow to find her closing the front door, quietly, so as not to disturb him, and then to check that she had not woken him up, she turned, and so he looked upon her in the leaden morning light, tried to hide his naked desire with a smile, that she did not return, but ran past him, confused, and bumped into her brother, coming out of the bathroom.

"What's your hurry," he asked her. "I can't believe that bohonkus of a music teacher made it in this weather."

"You had better telephone Amrita," he told Anthony in English, toweling his hair as he came into the living room. "I don't think you can go back in this."

And so he had stayed, shared their midday meal of chicken and rice after showering in death-cold water, and during the thunder-filled afternoon, they had played cards on the living room floor, two young cousins had turned up, soaked to their waists, grinning proudly, they had walked all the way from Dhakuria, and they had produced from their sodden shoulder bags several packs of cards. They played rummy, until hypnotized by the rain, they drifted off, one by one, into a leaden monsoon slumber, only he and Moni were too conscious of each other to submit to the torpor of the ponderous rain. She brought pillows for them all, and for one painful moment, he was afraid she would leave, but she sat down to finish the game. For a while, a silence between them deepened with the slap of well-worn cards on the cold damp floor, the delicate snores of the two boys, the heavy wheeze of her brother whose oily hair grazed Anthony's toes. She was across from him, leaning against an armchair, her coal-black hair spread out over the chintz seat, lifted high on either arm, a valley of hair. She had wrapped her arms in her sari, faded print flowers pushed against her chin, and from there his eyes traveled up to her overflowing lips, her remarkable eyes under dark brows,

I heard you singing this morning, he said, you have a lovely voice.

He finds out from her that she is in her second year at college, he is strangely pleased that she is studying English, he leans back against the dank pillow and asks her what she likes to read.

Oh, everything, really—poetry, novels. She likes Thomas Hardy, and Keats. They are reading Keats, now. "Ode on Melancholy."

Boldly, he begins to recite, No, no! go not to Lethe, neither twist wolf's bane, tight-rooted . . . heavy words sink between them in the bloated afternoon. She listens with closed eyes, the rain ceases and the room is suddenly flooded with a lime-colored syrupy light that deepens the shadow of her eyes. He cannot remember the rest of the poem, he asks her, could you translate to me the song you were singing this morning, it sounded so beautiful.

Oh no, she says, my English isn't good enough.

Your English is beautiful.

But she is too embarrassed. She will translate it for him, years later, in a moldy tin mine on the Cornish coast, while he is lost in the thick swirl of lovemaking recollected, feeding deeply on the fresh memories of a recent afternoon of salt-encrusted passion. And the memories that her songs bring to him now are no longer laced with bitterness, not since he found that he could bring to their bed, in peace, the warmth of another woman. Yet, her silence becomes more and more inscrutable, there is dignity in her silence, in her excruciating grief of her untranslated songs, but does anger froth behind those long stretches of silence? He will hold her for hours in the morning, kiss her sleepless eyes, he wants to ask her if she would like to go home for a visit, her parents have not seen the child yet, but he cannot for fear she will think he is sending her away, she is like a small, soft bird in his arms, he does not dare to attempt to make love to her, he prays that through her songs she will come to appreciate the beauty of their situation, the only thing that can save them now, the intense beauty of their interwoven emotions, the poetry of the half triangle they form, he, Anna, and she, evenings that the three of them spend together, Anna dries while he washes up, and she dishes the remains of their quiet dinner into freezer containers, evenings she must spend alone while he and Anna make violent love in her studio flat, he envisages her sitting in the half-light of dusk, singing, or rocking the child to sleep, images of peace. She had been afraid once, he knew, afraid he would leave her, and he had been afraid too, that he would not be able to sustain his affection for her, but it had not happened, what had seemed inevitable in the valleys of the Ardèche, among the blackened butterflies, for him at least, it had not happened.

Had it helped that on the deck of the ferry, as they approached their dreaded return to this land, she had told him she thought she was with his child. Had it become clear to him then, in a flash of sea spray, that he would love her forever, even though their passion was spent. But he had no inkling of her great relief when the doctor confirmed her pregnancy, she prayed that it would be a son, somehow a son would be a true synthesis of herself with him, an embodiment of their union, a daughter was an extension of herself, a daughter would not be his, a daughter would be hers alone. Today, as she watches the woman grinding ice cream cones underfoot, the child tugs at her arm, she wants her to look at a poodle that has found its way to the front of the bus, her lips, lollipop-rimmed, jet curls fall on her little shoulders, she is hers alone, the bus jerks, she bumps her head against the bar, but she does not cry, six years old in three more days. Anna is taking her out tomorrow to buy her a new party dress, their first outing alone, which is why, today, along with the armloads of crepe paper and crackers and balloons, they have bought a little bottle of perfume, very expensive perfume that she has seen on Anna's dressing table in the little alcove in her studio flat where she sleeps, where she makes love to her husband on apocalyptic winter evenings, she had no idea it would be so expensive, the perfume, and when they get home, she and the child will wrap it up in some of the pink crepe paper, and they will rehearse how, tomorrow, in Anna's car, after they have bought the dress, she will say, I have a present for you too, ever so sweetly, let it never be said she was not bringing up her child properly.

She can smell in the chill of the white walls of the hallway, as they fling open the door, that this will be another evening alone. She sheds her overcoat and sits down suddenly on the bottom stair, her eyes travel up the stairway, punctuated by the large soft toys that Anthony loves to give their daughter, life-size koalas, placid teddy bears, a benign brontosaur, when she was younger she had been more scared than pleased, and to prevent nightmares they had been moved out from her room, to litter the stairs, and Anthony had found the effect so pleasing, there they had remained. Sitting there, her aching head against a soft orange kangaroo, like the first sharp smell of magnolia blossoms, a new thought penetrates her tired mind. It strikes her suddenly, in the same way it had done many years ago, in a small Chinese restaurant on Free School Street where she agreed to marry Anthony, that there was an immense pleasure to be found in escaping her present circumstances, in leaving the country forever. Ten years ago, he had pushed aside a plate of Manchurian chicken to gather into his broad hands her shy fingers, implored her to marry him, to come back with him to his home across the seas, where, for the rest of their lives, if nothing else, they could lie in each other's arms, and she would sing to him. And suddenly, it had become clear to her that this was the disaster she must embrace, like the poet, who perceived through disaster the vastness of the universe, in a train rushing through the tropical darkness, returning from the funeral of his beloved son, the universe had revealed to him its vast and indifferent beauty,

my light has been quenched upon this dark and lonely path
for a storm is rising
a storm is rising to befriend me
darkling disaster smiles at the edges of the sky
catastrophe wreaks delighted havoc with my garments, with my hair
my lamp has blown out on this lonely road
who knows where I must wander now, in this dense dark
but perhaps the thunder speaks of a new path
one that will take me to a different dawn.

A heady perfume of disaster envelops her as she sits in a dream on the number forty-seven bus, a doe-eyed child pushes against her, she draws her into her lap, the Calcutta rush hour, the weight of humankind against her knees, a hand reaches through the window, laden with books, she takes them, they are mathematics books, worn, used by many generations, and a few minutes later, the hand is back again, she closes the fingers gently over the books, she will never know him, he who, hanging from a forty-seven bus on a winter afternoon, entreated some nameless soul to hold his books for him, she will never know him, and all this she is leaving behind.

Her brother is waiting on the balcony, as if he knows, as if he expects her to tell him today, this very afternoon, that she is leaving them forever. She draws the latch on the iron grille door, sets down her bag on the bamboo table, she sits down and draws her shawl tighter as a smoky blast of damp winter wind rattles the wooden shutters. He does not look up from his book, she leans across and tips it up to see the front cover, Brecht's *Galileo.*

"Where have you been?" he asks without looking up.

The destitute call of tropical birds fills the sky, the sparrows that will crawl into the whitewashed ventilators, the crows and the kites circling the rubbish pits for a last morsel, the mynahs that gather their mates for the journey home to the dusty treetops.

"He wants to marry me," she says apologetically.

They made very little fuss, her family. The afternoon melts into evening, they sit in the living room, her mother quietly crying but making no word of protest, her father trying to concentrate on the arrangements, his one request, a proper Bengali wedding, Anthony will agree, will he not? And her grandmother is surprisingly supportive, will you take me to visit you, she asks, your grandfather always promised, but he never took me with him. It is an evening of quiet, gentle grief, nobody challenges her decision, that will come later with her irate uncles, their disgusted wives, hours of frantic weeping, a river of tears running along the formica-topped dining table. But this first evening, they sit wrapped in grief, the immediate honeyed agony of an impending partition. The door-bell sounds, she gets up to open it, it is Anthony, he sees from her face that she would rather he had not come just yet, should I leave? he asks.

No, come in. A guest can never be turned away, only salesmen are turned away, turned into the heat of parched afternoon, laden with their packets of detergent, the bottles of shampoo, the sanitary towels that they take from door to door, only salesmen are turned away.

But at the sound of his voice they have evacuated the living room. He reaches for her hand, she snatches it back, not here, not in this house. They sit for a while in the half-light, the winter evening deepens, she gets up and pushes past the dining table, through the double doors into her bedroom, where the four of them sit, huddled, silent, she pleads with them to come out into the living room, I'll be there in a minute, her brother tells her, and she rushes out again, sweet disaster, this is the shape of her delicious torment, four huddled figures in a darkened bedroom, a winter evening, the mosquitoes begin to drift in through the shutters. Her brother comes in, Anthony stands up, and suddenly the two of them laugh, a warmth of pure happiness steals over her, her brother shakes his head, so you're taking my sister from us? But we will be back every year, they both protest, and in these ten numb years, she has only been back once, alone. Later that night, her brother came up with her onto the roof terrace, where a crisp clear layer of night lay above the smoky lights of the city, and looking out onto the sea of night smoke, their impenitent city, he reminded her, this is what you are giving up, this is what you will be leaving, forever, and she raised her eyes to the hard, cold stars above, and with a voice, dark as the inside of a bird's nest, she replied, I know.

And today, ten years later, that same cold clarity floods her mind, the numbness of ten years melts suddenly away, a quantum leap in her consciousness,

> on this last night of spring, I have come empty-handed,
>   garlandless
> a silent flute cries, the smile dies on your lips
> in your eyes a wet indignation
> when did this spring pass by, where is my song?

as she helps the child make paper chains, she weighs the situation carefully, a sense of drama that she has suppressed for so long enfolds her, they will leave on Monday, the morning of the birthday party, she will watch his unsuspecting face leave for the day, for the last time, oh the thrill of "the last time"—the last exam of the year, the last class, the last night of the summer holidays, the last day of the year, the last night of her brother's play, the last night of her maidenhood—her college friends encircle her, wistful, proud, nervous, so what is it like to sleep with a white man, Sharmila asked her, when she visited them two years later, and she had wrinkled her brow, averted her eyes, she had never been able to participate when they all sat together and giggled about sex in college, she could not talk about it now. Sharmila came from a very westernized family, they spoke a queer mixture of English and Bengali at home, and the one time Anthony had intercepted her on her way back from college, in those very first days of their love, she had been walking to the bus stand with Sharmila, and it was she that conversed with him in her convent-school English as they sat in Flury's and ate chocolate eclairs. She had remained silent for the most part, enjoying the slight pressure of his knee against hers, his adoring eyes as they gazed upon her, and then flitted back to Sharmila, as he answered her incessant questions, with amusement, she had enjoyed the abstract smile that was ever upon his lips, hovering against his deep-set eyes, that was the beginning of a silent complicity, that she was, now, finally, about to violate.

language lesson 1976

Heather McHugh

When Americans say a man
takes liberties, they mean

he's gone too far. In Philadelphia today I saw
a kid on a leash look mom-ward

and announce his fondest wish: one
bicentennial burger, hold

the relish. Hold is forget,
in American.

On the courts of Philadelphia
the rich prepare

to serve, to fault. The language is a game as well,
in which love can mean nothing,

doubletalk mean lie. I'm saying
doubletalk with me. I'm saying

go so far the customs are untold.
Make nothing without words,

and let me be
the one you never hold.

the other hand

Marjorie Maddox

What is
is another matter:
the other side of if
spiraling out of a black hole,
compressed into a question,
then an exclamation point
straight as western Ohio.
Dip it once, it comes out white
inside and out, twice and you can lick it
till there's nothing but a stick to pick your teeth with
or a pool cue that fingers the eight ball like a mystic,
never shoots straight.
You think that it is real and it is,
but what has that to do with a world
strung together *and* sliced by longitude, latitude?
Everything unspins into a ribbon
you can wear in your bright black hair
until you tip your head and Atlantis tumbles out,
until chinaberry trees tease your ears
with a sound too light for wind.
It is your mother wiping her hands on an apron
stitched with the seven continents
of which you are one;
the back side of the sky in a Fragonard;
the tip of a shoe pointed up.

If you spy a trail of tea leaves,
half a golden apple,
a lobotomized scarecrow—you're close.
Turn the other way.
Quick.

my mother's lips

C.K. Williams

Until I asked her to please stop doing it and was astonished to find
    that she not only could
but from the moment I asked her in fact would stop doing it, my
    mother, all through my childhood,
when I was saying something to her, something important, would
    move her lips as I was speaking
so that she seemed to be saying under her breath the very words I was
    saying as I was saying them.

Or, even more disconcertingly—wildly so now that my puberty had
    erupted—*before* I said them.
When I was smaller, I must just have assumed that she was omniscient.
    Why not?
She knew everything else—when I was tired, or lying; she'd know I
    was ill before I did.
I may even have thought—how could it not have come into my mind?
    —that she *caused* what I said.

All she was really doing of course was mouthing my words a split
    second after I said them myself,
but it wasn't until my own children were learning to talk that I really
    understood how,
and understood, too, the edge of anxiety in it, the wanting to bring
    you along out of the silence,

the compulsion to lift you again from those blank caverns of nameless-
ness we encase.

That was long afterward, though: where I was now was just wanting
to get her to stop,
and, considering how I brooded and raged in those days, how quickly
my teeth went on edge,
the restraint I approached her with seems remarkable, although her
so unprotestingly,
readily taming a habit by then three children and a dozen years old
was as much so.

It's endearing to watch us again in that long-ago dusk, facing each
other, my mother and me.
I've just grown to her height, or just past it: there are our lips moving
together,
now the unison suddenly breaks, I have to go on by myself, no maestro,
no score to follow.
I wonder what finally made me take umbrage enough, or heart
enough, to confront her?

It's not important. My cocoon at that age was already unwinding: the
threads ravel and snarl.
When I find one again, it's at two o'clock in the morning, a grim
hotel on a square,
the impenetrable maze of an endless city, when, really alone for the
first time in my life,
I found myself leaning from the window, incanting in a tearing whis-
per what I thought were poems.

I'd love to know what I raved that night to the night, what those
innocent dithyrambs were,
or to feel what so ecstatically drew me out of myself and beyond …
Nothing is there, though,
only the solemn piazza beneath me, the riot of dim, tiled roofs and
impassable alleys,
my desolate bed behind me, and my voice, hoarse, and the sweet, alien
air against me like a kiss.

one petition lofted into the ginkos

Gabriel Gudding

For the train-wrecked, the puck-struck,
the viciously punched,
the pole-vaulter whose pole
snapped in ascent.
For his asphalt-face,
his capped-off scream, God bless
his dad in the stands.
For the living dog in the median
car-struck and shuddering
on crumpled haunches, eyes
large as plates, seeing nothing, but looking,
looking. For the blessed pigeon
who threw himself from the cliff
after plucking out his feathers
just to taste a falling death. For
the poisoned, scalded, and gassed, the bayoneted,
the bit and blind-sided,
asthmatic veteran
who just before his first date in years and years
swallowed his own glass eye. For these and all
and all the drunk,

Imagine a handful of quarters chucked up at sunset,

lofted into the ginkgos—
    and there, at apogee,
        while the whole ringing wad
pauses, pink-lit,
    about to seed the penny-colored earth
        with an hour's wages—
As shining, ringing, brief, and cheap
    as a prayer should be—

Imagine it all falling

into some dark machine
    brimming with nurses,
        nutrices ex machina—

and they blustering out
    with juices and gauze, peaches and brushes,
        to patch such dents and wounds.

the parenthesis inserts itself into the transcripts of the committee on un-american activities

“Senator (I have never lain with rubrics,
nor am I among the indicted’s
swart date books: I am the anchorite’s
punched lips. Small-lunged boys
who duck in the old beds from dogs
have lain low in me;
rabbits, I think, have bolted here
who smell a cold hole
in the fuck-all blurry middle
of a life sprint. The ant
comes to me for its mortar: I am the divots
of the ballpeens, cane marks
outside libraries. I fell from a tree planted on a hill
of the earth’s early ticker tape; I cracked open,
a walnut of ticker tape. I am a tick
in the hide of the book, seed
of the monograph: Yesterday the dewpoint fell
and a big fog issued from the comma—meadows
in the semicolons filled with tractors, the plow’s tines
are made of me, as were the eyelashes
of Elijah, fingernail moons
of Coltrane—my heelmarks
are scattered in the mesquite tree, I was abused
by cummings.

The day the pennies pitched their tents
on the banks of the math books,
I became their tent stakes. Queens
have walked in me for I am
smoother than a dashboard:
Jerusalem is just a booth in the heat, but ain't I
the back rooms of Ninevah. I respect the oyster
for being the grotto of a single mood—cowry's arcature—
but in me is a canyon filled with stones
that are sweetly immobile, in me
an old man's laundry
sculls on the slantlight. I am a small girl's middle, suitcase
of the vivid poor—farthest cousin of the thistle's tribe,
having struck and hung on
in this most drifting soil: my whole family was born
in an un-neutral footnote
and were taken out into the wire and weeds
and were shot in the gravel; it is on gravestones that I am
the cradle of years,
and) I have to say
it's a pleasure
to appear before you
in this honored room."

the mansion on the hill

Rick Moody

The Chicken Mask was sorrowful, Sis. The Chicken Mask was supposed to hustle business; it was supposed to invite the customer to gorge him- or herself within our establishment; it was supposed to be endearing and funny; it was supposed to be an accurate representation of the featured item on our menu. But, Sis, in a practical setting, in test markets—like right out in front of the restaurant—the Chicken Mask had a plaintive aspect, a blue quality (it was stifling, too, even in cold weather), so that I'd be walking down Main, by the waterfront, after you were gone, back and forth in front of Hot Bird (Bucket of Drumsticks, $2.99), wearing out my imitation basketball sneakers from Wal-Mart, pudgy in my black jogging suit, lurching along in the sandwich board, and the kids would hustle up to me, tugging on the wrists of their harried, underfinanced moms. The kids would get bored with me almost immediately. They knew the routine. Their eyes would narrow, and all at once there were no secrets here in our town of service-economy franchising: *I was the guy working nine to five in a Chicken Mask,* even though I'd had a pretty good education in business administration, even though I was more or less presentable and well-spoken, even though I came from a good family. I made light of it, Sis, I extemporized about Hot Bird, in remarks designed by virtue of my studies in business tactics to drive whole families in for the new *low-fat roasters,* a meal option that was steeper, in terms of price, but tasty nonetheless. (And I ought to have known, because I ate from the menu every day. Even the coleslaw.)

Here's what I'd say, in my Chicken Mask. Here was my pitch: *Feeling a little peckish? Try Hot Bird!* or *Don't be chicken, try Hot Bird!* The mothers would laugh their nervous adding-machine laughs (those laughs that are next door over from a sob), and they would lead the kids off. Twenty yards away, though, the boys and girls would still be staring disdainfully at me, gaping backward while I rubbed my hands raw in the cold, while I breathed the synthetic rubber interior of the Chicken Mask—that fragrance of rubber balls from gym classes lost, that bouquet of the gloves Mom used for the dishes, that perfume of simpler times—while I looked for my next shill. I lost almost ninety days to the demoralization of the Chicken Mask, to its grim, existential emptiness, until I couldn't take it anymore. Which happened to be the day when Alexandra McKinnon (remember her? from Sunday school?) turned the corner with her boy Zack—he has to be seven or eight now—oblivious while upon her daily rounds, oblivious and fresh from a Hallmark store. It was nearly Valentine's Day. They didn't know it was me in there, of course, inside the Chicken Mask. They didn't know I was *the chicken from the basement, the chicken of darkest nightmares,* or, more truthfully, they didn't know I was a guy with some pretty conflicted attitudes about things. That's how I managed to apprehend Zack, leaping out from the in-door of Cohen's Pharmacy, laying ahold of him a little too roughly, by the hem of his pillowy, orange ski jacket. Little Zack was laughing at first, until, in a voice racked by loss, I worked my hard sell on him, declaiming stentoriously that *Death Comes to All.* That's exactly what I said, just as persuasively as I had once hawked *White meat breasts, eight pieces, just $4.59!* Loud enough that he'd be sure to know what I meant. His look was interrogative, quizzical. So I repeated myself. *Death Comes to Everybody, Zachary.* My voice was urgent now. My eyes bulged from the eyeholes of my standard-issue Chicken Mask. I was even crying a little bit. Saline rivulets tracked down my neck. Zack was terrified.

What I got next certainly wasn't the kind of flirtatious attention I had always hoped for from his mom. Alex began drumming on me with balled fists. I guess she'd been standing off to the side of the action previously, believing that I was a reliable paid employee of Hot Bird. But now she was all over me, bruising me with wild swings, cursing, until she'd pulled the Chicken Mask from my head—half expecting, I'm sure, to find me scarred or hydrocephalic or otherwise disabled. Her denunciations let up a little once she was in possession of the facts. It was me, her old Sunday school pal, Andrew Wakefield. Not at the top of my game.

I don't really want to include here the kind of scene I made, once unmasked. Alex was exasperated with me, but gentle anyhow. I think she probably knew I was in the middle of a rough patch. People knew. The people leaning out of the storefronts probably knew. But, if things weren't already bad enough, I remembered right then—God, this is horrible—that Alex's mom had driven into Lake Sacandaga about five years before. Jumped the guardrail and plunged right off that bridge there. In December. In heavy snow. In a Ford Explorer. That was the end of her. *Listen, Alex,* I said, *I'm confused, I have problems and I don't know what's come over me and I hope you can understand, and I hope you'll let me make it up to you. I can't lose this job. Honest to God.* Fortunately, just then, Zack became interested in the Chicken Mask. He swiped the mask from his mom—she'd been holding it at arm's length, like a soiled rag—and he pulled it down over his head and started making simulated automatic-weapons noises in the directions of local passersby. This took the heat off. We had a laugh, Alex and I, and soon the three of us had repaired to Hot Bird itself (it closed four months later, like most of the businesses on that block) for coffee and biscuits and the chef's special spicy wings, which, because of my position, were on the house.

Alex was actually waving a spicy wing when she offered her life-altering opinion that I was too smart to be working for Hot Bird, especially if I was going to brutalize little kids with the creepy facts of the hereafter. What I should do, Alex said, was get into something positive instead. She happened to know a girl—it was her cousin, Glenda—who managed a business over in Albany, the Mansion on the Hill, a big area employer, and why didn't I call Glenda and use Alex's name and maybe they would have something in accounting or valet parking or flower delivery, *yada yada yada,* you know, some job that had as little public contact as possible, something that paid better than minimum wage, because minimum wage, Alex said, wasn't enough for a guy of twenty-nine. After these remonstrances she actually hauled me over to the pay phone at Hot Bird (people are so generous sometimes), while my barely alert boss Antonio slumbered at the register with no idea what was going on, without a clue that he was about to lose his most conscientious chicken impersonator. All because I couldn't stop myself from talking about death.

Alex dialed up the Mansion on the Hill (while Zack, at the table, donned my mask all over again), penetrating deep into the switchboard by virtue of her relation to a Mansion on the Hill management-level employee, and was soon actually talking to her cousin: *Glenda, I got a friend here who's going through some rough stuff in his family, if you know what I mean, yeah, down on his luck in the job department too, but he's a nice bright guy anyhow. I pretty much wanted to smooch him throughout confirmation classes, and he went to . . . Hey, where did you go to school again? Went to SUNY and has a degree in business administration, knows a lot about product positioning or whatever, I don't know, new housing starts, yada yada yada, and I think you really ought to . . .*

Glenda's sigh was audible from several feet away, I swear, through the perfect medium of digital telecommunications, but you can't blame Glenda for that. People protect themselves from bad luck, right? Still, Alex wouldn't let her cousin refuse, wouldn't hear of it, *You absolutely gotta meet him, Glenda, he's a doll, he's a dreamboat,* and Glenda gave in, and that's the end of this part of the story, about how I happened to end up working out on Wolf Road at the capital region's finest wedding- and party-planning business. Except that before the Hot Bird recedes into the mists of time, I should report to you that I swiped the Chicken Mask, Sis. They had three or four of them. You'd be surprised how easy it is to come by a Chicken Mask.

Politically, here's what was happening in the front office of my new employer: Denise Gulch, the Mansion on the Hill staff writer, had left her husband and her kids and her steady job, because of a wedding, because of the language of the vows—that soufflé of exaggerated language—vows which, for quality-control purposes, were being broadcast over a discreet speaker in the executive suite. Denise was so moved by a recitation of Paul Stookey's "Wedding Song" taking place during the course of the Neuhaus ceremony ("Whenever two or more of you / Are gathered in His name, / There is love, / There is love ...") that she slipped into the Rip Van Winkle Room disguised as a latecomer. Immediately, in the electrifying atmosphere of matrimony, she began trying to seduce one of the ushers (Nicky Weir, a part-time Mansion employee who was acquainted with the groom). I figure this flirtation had been taking place for some time, but that's not what everyone told me. What I heard was that seconds after meeting one another—the bride hadn't even recessed yet—Denise and Nicky were secreted in a nearby broom closet, while the office phones bounced to voice mail, and were peeling back the layers of our Mansion dress code, until, at day's end, scantily clad and intoxicated by rhetoric and desire, they stole a limousine and left town without collecting severance. Denise was even fully vested in the pension plan.

All this could only happen at a place called the Mansion on the Hill, a place of fluffy endings: the right candidate for the job walks through the door at the eleventh hour, the check clears that didn't exist minutes before, government agencies agree to waive mountains of red tape, the sky clears, the snow ends, and stony women like Denise Gulch succumb to torrents of generosity, throwing half-dollars to children as they embark on new lives.

The real reason I got the job is that they were shorthanded, and because Alex's cousin, my new boss, was a little difficult. But things were starting to look up anyway. If Glenda's personal demeanor at the interview wasn't exactly warm (she took a personal call in the middle that lasted twenty-eight minutes, and later she asked me, while reapplying lip liner, if I wore cologne), at least she was willing to hire me—as long as I agreed to renounce any personal grooming habits that inclined in the direction of Old Spice, Hai Karate, or CK1. I would have spit-polished her pumps just to have my own desk (on which I put a yellowed picture of you when you were a kid, holding up the bass that you caught fly-fishing and also a picture of the four of us: Mom and Dad and you and me) and a Rolodex and unlimited access to stamps, mailing bags, and paper clips.

Let me take a moment to describe our core business at the Mansion on the Hill. We were in the business of helping people celebrate the best days of their lives. We were in the business of spreading joy, by any means necessary. We were in the business of paring away the calluses of woe and grief to reveal the bright light of commitment. We were in the business of producing flawless memories. We had seven auditoriums, or *marriage suites,* as we liked to call them, each with a slightly different flavor and decorating vocabulary. For example, there was the *Chestnut Suite,* the least expensive of our rental suites, which had lightweight aluminum folding chairs (with polyurethane padding) and a very basic altar table, which had the unfortunate pink and lavender floral wallpaper and which seated about 125 comfortably; then there was the *Hudson Suite,* which had some teak in it and a lot of paneling and a classic iron altar table and some rather large standing tables at the rear, and the reception area in Hudson was clothed all in vinyl, instead of the paper coverings that they used in Chestnut (the basic decorating scheme there in the Hudson Suite was meant to suggest the sea vessels that once sailed through our municipal port); then there was the *Rip Van Winkle Room,* with its abundance of draperies, its silk curtains, its matching maroon settings of inexpensive linen, and the *Adirondack Suite,* the *Ticonderoga Room,* the *Valentine Room* (a sort of giant powder puff), and of course the *Niagara Hall,* which was grand and reserved, with its separate kitchen and its enormous fireplace and white-gloved staff, for the sons and daughters of those Victorians of Saratoga County who came upstate for the summer during the racing season, the children of contemporary robber barons, the children whose noses were always straight and whose luck was always good.

We had our own on-site boutique for wedding gowns and tuxedo rentals and fittings—hell, we'd even clean and store your garments for you while you were away on your honeymoon—and we had a travel agency who subcontracted for us, and we also had wedding consultants, jewelers, videographers, still photographers (both the arty ones who specialized in photos of your toenail polish on the day of the wedding and the conventional photographers who barked directions at the assembled family far into the night), nannies, priests, ministers, shamans, polarity therapists, a really maniacal florist called Bruce, a wide array of deejays—guys and gals equipped to spin Christian-only selections, Tex-Mex, music from Hindi films, and the occasional death-metal wedding medley—and we could get actual musicians, if you preferred. We'd even had Dick Roseman's combo,

The Sons of Liberty, do a medley of "My Funny Valentine," "In-a-Gadda-Da-Vida," "I Will Always Love You," and "Smells Like Teen Spirit," without a rest between selections. (It was gratifying for me to watch the old folks shake it up to contemporary numbers.) We had a three-story, fifteen-hundred-slip parking facility on-site, convenient access to I-87, I-90, and the Taconic, and a staff of 175 full- and part-time employees on twenty-four-hour call. We had everything from publicists to dicers of crudités to public orators (need a brush-up for that toast?)—all for the purpose of making your wedding the high watermark of your American life. We had done up to fifteen weddings in a single day (it was a Saturday in February, 1991, during the Gulf War) and, since the Mansion on the Hill first threw open its door for a gala double wedding (the Gifford twins, from Balston Spa, who married Shaun and Maurice Wickett) in June of 1987, we had performed, up to the time of my first day there, 1,963 weddings, many of them memorable, life-affirming, even spectacular ceremonies. We had never had an incidence of serious violence.

This was the raw data that Glenda gave me, anyway, Sis. The arrangement of the facts is my own, and in truth, the arrangement of facts constitutes the job I was engaged to perform at the Mansion on the Hill. Because Glenda Manzini (in 1990 she married Dave Manzini, a developer from Schenectady) couldn't really have hated her job any more than she did. Glenda Manzini, whose marriage (her second) was apparently not the most loving ever in upstate history (although she's not alone; I estimate an even thousand divorces resulting from the conjugal rites successfully consummated so far at my place of business), was a cynic, a skeptic, a woman of little faith when it came to the institution through which she made her living. She occasionally referred to the wedding party as *the cattle;* she occasionally referred to the brides as *the hookers* and to herself, manager of the Mansion on the Hill, as *the Madame,* as in, *The Madame, Andrew, would like it if you would get the hell out of her office so that she can tabulate these receipts,* or, *Please tell the Hatfields and the McCoys that the Madame cannot untangle their differences for them, although the Madame does know the names of some first-rate couples counselors.* In the absence of an enthusiasm for our product line or for business writing in general, Glenda Manzini hired me to tackle some of her responsibilities for her. I gave the facts the best possible spin. Glenda, as you probably have guessed, was good with numbers. With the profits and losses. Glenda was good at additional charges. Glenda was good at doubling the price on a floral arrangement, for example, because the Vietnamese poppies absolutely had to be on the tables, because they were so . . . *Je ne sais quoi.* Glenda was good at double-booking a particular suite and then auctioning the space to the higher bidder. Glenda was good at quoting a figure for a band and then adding instruments so that the price increased astronomically. One time she padded a quartet with two vocalists, an eight-piece horn section, an African drumming ensemble, a dijeridoo, and a harmonium.

The other thing I should probably be up-front about is that Glenda Manzini was a total knockout. A bombshell. A vision of celestial loveliness. I hate to go on about it, but there was that single strand of Glenda's amber hair always falling over her eyes—no matter how many times she tried to secure it; there was her near constant attention to her makeup; there was her total command of business issues and her complete unsentimentality. Or maybe it was her stockings, always in black, with a really provocative seam following the aerodynamically sleek lines of her calf. Or maybe it was her barely concealed sadness. I'd never met anyone quite as uncomfortable as Glenda, but this didn't bother me at first. My life had changed since the Chicken Mask.

Meanwhile, it goes without saying that the Mansion on the Hill wasn't a mansion at all. It was a homely cinder-block edifice formerly occupied by the Colonie Athletic Club. A trucking operation used the space before that. And the Mansion wasn't on any hill, either, because geologically speaking we're in a valley here. We're part of some recent glacial scouring.

On my first day, Glenda made every effort to ensure that my work environment would be as unpleasant as possible. I'd barely set down my extra-large coffee with two half-and-halfs and five sugars and my assortment of cream-filled donuts (I was hoping these would please my new teammates) when Glenda bodychecked me, tipped me over into my reclining desk chair, with several huge stacks of file material.

—Andy, listen up. In April we have an Orthodox Jewish ceremony taking place at 3 P.M. in Niagara while at the same time there are going to be some very faithful Islamic-Americans next door in Ticonderoga. I don't want these two groups to come in contact with one another at any time, understand? I don't want any kind of diplomatic incident. It's your job to figure out how to persuade one of these groups to be first out of the gate, at noon, and it's your job to make them think that they're really lucky to have the opportunity. And Andy? The el-Mohammed wedding, the Muslim wedding, needs prayer mats. See if you can get some from the discount stores. Don't waste a lot of money on this.

This is a good indication of Glenda's management style. Some other procedural tidbits: she frequently assigned a dozen rewrites on her correspondence. She had a violent dislike for semicolons. I was to double-space twice underneath the date on her letters, before typing the salutation, on pain of death. I was never, ever to use one of those cursive word-processing fonts. I was to bring her coffee first thing in the morning, without speaking to her until she had entirely finished a second cup and also a pair of ibuprofen tablets, preferably the elongated, easy-to-swallow variety. I was never to ask her about her weekend or her evening or anything else, including her holidays, unless she asked me first. If her door was closed, I was not to open it. And if I ever reversed the digits in a phone number when taking a message for her, I could count on my pink slip that very afternoon.

Right away, that first A.M., after this litany of scares, after Glenda retreated into her chronically underheated lair, there was a swell of sympathetic mumbles from my coworkers, who numbered, in the front office, about a dozen. They were offering condolences. They had seen the likes of me come and go. Glenda, however, who keenly appreciated the element of surprise as a way of ensuring discipline, was not quite done. She reappeared suddenly by my desk—as if by secret entrance—with a half-dozen additional commands. I was to find a new sign for her private parking space, I was to find a new floral wholesaler for the next fiscal quarter, I was to *refill her prescription for birth-control pills.* This last request was spooky enough, but it wasn't the end of the discussion. From there Glenda starting getting personal:

—Oh, by the way, Andy? (she liked diminutives) What's all the family trouble, anyway? The stuff Alex was talking about when she called?

She picked up the photo of you, Sis, the one I had brought with me. The bass at the end of your fishing rod was so outsized that it seemed impossible that you could hold it up. You looked really happy. Glenda picked up the photo as though she hadn't already done her research, as if she had left something to chance. Which just didn't happen during her regime at the Mansion on the Hill.

—Dead sister, said I. And then, completing my betrayal of you, I filled out the narrative, so that anyone who wished could hear about it, and then we could move onto other subjects, like Worcester's really great semipro hockey team.

—Crashed her car. Actually, it was my car. Mercury Sable. Don't know why I said it was her car. It was mine. She was on her way to her rehearsal dinner. She had an accident.

Sis, have I mentioned that I have a lot of questions I've been meaning to ask? Have I asked, for example, why you were taking the windy country road along our side of the great river, when the four-lanes along the west side were faster, more direct, and, in heavy rain, less dangerous? Have I asked why you were driving at all? Why I was not driving you to the rehearsal dinner instead? Have I asked why your car was in the shop for muffler repair on such an important day? Have I asked why you were late? Have I asked why you were lubricating your nerves *before* the dinner? Have I asked if four G&Ts, as you called them, before your own rehearsal dinner, were not maybe in excess of what was needed? Have I asked if there was a reason for you to be so tense on the eve of your wedding? Did you feel you had to go through with it? That there was no alternative? If so, why? If he was the wrong guy, why were you marrying him? Were there planning issues that were not properly addressed? Were there things between you two, as between all the betrothed, that we didn't know? Were there specific questions you wanted to ask, of which you were afraid? Have I given the text of my toast, Sis, as I had imagined it, beginning with a plangent evocation of the years before your birth, when I ruled our house like a tyrant, and how with earsplitting cries I resisted your infancy, until I learned to love the way your baby hair, your flaxen mop, fell into curls? Have I mentioned that it was especially satisfying to wind your hair around my stubby fingers as you lay sleeping? Have I made clear that I wrote out this toast and that it took me several weeks to get it how I wanted it and that I was in fact going over these words again when the call from Dad came announcing your death? Have I mentioned—and I'm sorry to be hurtful on this point—that Dad's drinking has gotten worse since you left this world? Have I mentioned that his allusions to the costly unfinished business of his life have become more frequent? Have I mentioned that Mom, already overtaxed with her own body count, with her dead parents and dead siblings, has gotten more and more frail? Have I mentioned that I have some news about Brice, your intended? That his tune has changed slightly since your memorial service? Have I mentioned that I was out at the crime scene the next day? The day after you died? Have I mentioned that in my dreams I am often at the crime scene now? Have I wondered aloud to you about that swerve of blacktop right there, knowing that others may lose their lives as you did? Can't we straighten out that road somehow? Isn't there one road crew that the governor, in his quest for jobs, jobs, jobs, can send down there to make this sort of thing unlikely? Have I perhaps clued you in about how I go there often now, to look for signs of further tragedy? Have I mentioned to you that in some countries DWI is punishable by death, and that when Antonio at Hot Bird first explained this dark irony to me, I imagined taking his throat in my hands and squeezing the air out of him once and for all? Sis, have I told you of driving aimlessly in the mountains, listening to talk radio, searching for the one bit of cheap, commercially interrupted persuasion that will let me put these memories of you back in the canister where you now at least partially reside so that I can live out my dim, narrow life? Have I mentioned that I expect death around every turn, that every blue sky has a safe sailing out of it, that every bus runs me over, that every low, mean syllable uttered in my direction seems to intimate the violence of murder, that every family seems like an opportunity for ruin and every marriage a ceremony into which calamity will fall and hearts will be broken and lives destroyed and people branded by the mortifications of love? Is it all right if I ask you all of this?

~

Still, in spite of these personal issues, I was probably a model employee for Glenda Manzini. For example, I managed to sort out the politics concerning the Jewish wedding and the Islamic wedding (both slated for the first weekend of April), and I did so by appealing to certain aspects of light in our valley at the base of the Adirondacks. Certain kinds of light make for very appealing weddings here in our valley, I told one of these families. In late winter, in the early morning, you begin to feel an excitement at the appearance of the sun. Yes, I managed to solve that problem, and the next (the prayer mats)—because K-Mart, *where America shops,* had a special on bath mats that week, and I sent Dorcas Gilbey over to buy six dozen to use for the Muslim families. I solved these problems, and then I solved others just as vexing. I had a special interest in the snags that arose on Fridays after 5 P.M.—the groom who on the day of the ceremony was trapped in a cabin east of Lake George and who had to snowshoe three miles out to the nearest telephone, or the father of the bride (it was the Lapsley wedding) who wanted to arrive at the ceremony by hydrofoil. Brinksmanship, in the world of nuptial planning, gave me a sense of well-being, and I tried to bury you in the rear of my life, in the back of that closet where I'd hidden my secondhand golf clubs and my ski boots and my Chicken Mask—never again to be seen by mortal man.

One of my front-office associates was a fine young woman by the name of Linda Pietrzsyk, who tried to comfort me during the early weeks of my job, after Glenda's periodic assaults. Don't ask how to pronounce Linda's surname. In order to pronounce it properly, you have to clear your throat aggressively. Linda Pietrzsyk didn't like her surname anymore than you or I, and she was apparently looking for a groom from whom she could borrow a better last name. That's what I found out after awhile. Many of the employees at the Mansion on the

Hill had ulterior motives. This marital ferment, this loamy soil of romance, called to them somehow. When I'd been there a few months, I started to see other applicants go through the masticating action of an interview with Glenda Manzini. Glenda would be sure to ask, *Why do you want to work here?* and many of these qualified applicants had the same reply, *Because I think marriage is the most beautiful thing and I want to help make it possible for others.* Most of these applicants, if they were attractive and single and younger than Glenda, aggravated her thoroughly. They were shown the door. But occasionally a marital aspirant like Linda Pietrzsyk snuck through, in this case because Linda managed to conceal her throbbing, sentimental heart beneath a veneer of contemporary discontent.

We had Mondays and Tuesdays off, and one weekend a month. Most of our problem-solving fell on Saturdays, of course, but on that one Saturday off, Linda Pietrzsyk liked to bring friends to the Mansion on the Hill, to various celebrations. She liked to attend the weddings of strangers. This kind of entertainment wasn't discouraged by Glenda or by the owners of the Mansion, because everybody likes a party to be crowded. Any wedding that was too sparsely attended at the Mansion had a fine complement of *warm bodies,* as Glenda liked to call them, provided gratis. Sometimes we had to go to libraries or retirement centers to fill a quota, but we managed. These gate-crashers were welcome to eat finger food at the reception and to drink champagne and other intoxicants (food and drink were billed to the client), but they had to make themselves scarce once the dining began in earnest. There was a window of opportunity here that was large enough for Linda and her friends.

She was tight with a spirited bunch of younger people. She was friends with kids who had outlandish wardrobes and styles of grooming, kids with pants that fit like bedsheets, kids with haircuts that were, at best, accidental. But Linda would dress them all up and make them presentable, and they would arrive in an ancient station wagon in order to crowd in at the back of a wedding. Where they stifled gasps of hilarity.

I don't know what Linda saw in me. I can't really imagine. I wore the same sweaters and flannel slacks week in and week out. I liked classical music, Sis. I liked historical simulation festivals. And as you probably haven't forgotten (having tried a couple of times to fix me up—with Jess Carney and Sally Moffitt), the more tense I am, the worse is the impression I make on the fairer sex. Nevertheless, Linda Pietrzsyk decided that I had to be a part of her elite crew of wedding crashers, and so for a while I learned by immersion of the great rainbow of expressions of fealty.

Remember that footage, so often shown on contemporary reality-based programming during the dead first half-hour of prime time, of the guy who vomited at his own wedding? I was at that wedding. You know when he says, *Aw, Honey, I'm really sorry,* and leans over and flash floods this amber stuff on her train? You know, the shock of disgust as it crosses her face? The look of horror in the eyes of the minister? I saw it all. No one who was there thought it was funny, though, except Linda's friends. That's the truth. I thought it was really sad. But I was sitting next to a fellow *actually named Cheese* (when I asked which kind of cheese, he seemed perplexed), and Cheese looked as though he had a hernia or something, he thought this was so funny. Elsewhere in the Chestnut Suite there was a grievous silence.

Linda Pietrzsyk also liked to catalogue moments of spontaneous erotic delight on the premises, and these were legendary at the Mansion on the Hill. Even Glenda, who took a dim view of gossiping about business most of the time, liked to hear who was doing it with whom where. There was an implicit hierarchy in such stories. *Tales of the couple to be married caught in the act on Mansion premises were considered obvious and therefore uninspiring.* Tales of the best man and matron of honor going at it (as in the Clarke, Rosenberg, Irving, Ng, Fujitsu, Walters, Shapiro, or Spangler ceremonies) were better, but not great. Stories in which parents of the couple to be married were caught—in, say, the laundry room, with the dad still wearing his dress shoes—were good (Smith, Elsworth, Waskiewicz), but not as good as tales of the parents of the couple to be married trading spouses, of which we had one unconfirmed report (Hinkley) and of which no one could stop talking for a week. Likewise, any story in which the bride or the groom were caught *in flagrante* with someone other than the person they were marrying was considered astounding (if unfortunate). But we were after some even more unlikely tall tales: any threesome or larger grouping involving the couple to be married and someone from one of the other weddings scheduled that day, in which the third party was unknown until arriving at the Mansion on the Hill, and at which *a house pet was present.* Glenda said that if you spotted one of these tableaux you could have a month's worth of free groceries from the catering department. Linda Pietrzsyk also spoke longingly of the day when someone would arrive breathlessly in the office with a narrative of a full-fledged orgiastic reception in the Mansion on the Hill, the spontaneous, overwhelming erotic celebration of love and marriage by an entire suite full of Americans, tall and short, fat and thin, young and old.

In pursuit of these tales, with her friends Cheese, Chip, Mick, Stig, Mark, and Blair, Linda Pietrzsyk would quietly appear at my side at a reception and give me the news—*Behind the bandstand, behind that scrim, groom reaching under his cousin's skirts.* We would sneak in for a look. But we never interrupted anyone. And we never made them feel ashamed.

You know how when you're getting to know a fellow employee, a fellow team member, you go through phases, through cycles of intimacy and insight and respect and doubt and disillusionment, where one impression gives way to another? (Do you know about this, Sis, and is this what happened between you and Brice, so that you felt like you personally had to have the four G&Ts on the way to the rehearsal dinner? Am I right in thinking you couldn't go on with the wedding and that this caused you to get all sloppy and to believe erroneously that you could operate heavy machinery?) Linda Pietrzsyk was a stylish, Skidmore-educated girl with ivory skin and an adorable bump in her nose; she was from an upper-middle-class family out on Long Island somewhere; her father's periodic drunkenness had not affected his ability to work; her mother stayed married to him according to some mesmerism of devotion; her brothers had good posture and excelled in contact sports; in short, there were no big problems in Linda's case. Still, she pretended to be a desperate, marriage-obsessed kid, without a clear idea about what she wanted to do with her life or what the hell was going to happen next week. She was smarter than me—she could do the crossword puzzle in three minutes flat and she knew all about current events—but she was always talking about *catching a rich financier with a wild streak and extorting a retainer from him,* until I wanted to shake her. There's usually another layer underneath these things. In Linda's case it started to become clear at Patti Wackerman's wedding.

The reception area in the Ticonderoga Room—where walls slid back from the altar to reveal the tables and the dance floor—was decorated in branches of forsythia and wisteria and other flowering vines and shrubs. It was spring. Linda was standing against a piece of white wicker latticework that I had borrowed from the florist in town (in return for promotional considerations), and sprigs of flowering trees garlanded it, garlanded the spot where Linda was standing. Pale colors haloed her.

—Right behind this screen, she said, when I swept up beside her and tapped her playfully on the shoulder, —check it out. There's a couple falling in love once and for all. You can see it in their eyes.

I was sipping a Canadian spring water in a piece of company stemware. I reacted to Linda's news nonchalantly. I didn't think much of it. Yet I happened to notice that Linda's expression was conspiratorial, impish, as well as a little beatific. Linda often covered her mouth with her hand when she'd said something riotous, as if to conceal unsightly dental work (on the contrary, her teeth were perfect), as if she'd been treated badly one too many times, as if the immensity of joy were embarrassing to her somehow. As she spoke of the couple in question her hand fluttered up to her mouth. Her slender fingertips probed delicately at her upper lip. My thoughts came in torrents: *Where are Stig and Cheese and Blair? Why am I suddenly alone with this fellow employee? Is the couple Linda is speaking about part of the wedding party today? How many points will she get for the first sighting of their extramarital grappling?*

Since it was my policy to investigate any and all such phenomena, I glanced desultorily around the screen and, seeing nothing out of the ordinary, slipped farther into the shadows where the margins of Ticonderoga led toward the central catering staging area. There was, of course, no such couple behind the screen, or rather Linda (who was soon beside me) and myself *were the couple* and we were mottled by insufficient light, dappled by it, by lavender-tinted spots hung that morning by the lighting designers, and by reflections of a mirrored *disco ball* that speckled the dance floor.

—I don't see anything, I said.

—Kiss me, Linda Pietrzsyk said. Her fingers closed lightly around the bulky part of my arm. There was an unfamiliar warmth in me. The band struck up some fast number. I think it was "It's Raining

Men" or maybe it was that song entitled "We Are Family," which played so often at the Mansion on the Hill in the course of a weekend. Whichever, it was really loud. The horn players were getting into it. A trombonist yanked his slide back and forth.

—Excuse me? I said.

—Kiss me, Andrew, she said. —I want to kiss you.

Locating in myself a long-dormant impulsiveness, I reached down for Linda's bangs, and with my clumsy hands I tried to push back her blond and strawberry-blond curlicues, and then, with a hitch in my motion, in a stop-time sequence of jerks, I embraced her. Her eyes, like neon, were illumined.

—Why don't you tell me how you feel about me? Linda Pietrzsyk said. I was speechless, Sis. I didn't know what to say. And she went on. There was something about me, something warm and friendly about me, I wasn't fortified, she said; I wasn't cold, I was just a good guy who actually cared about other people *and you know how few of those there are.* (I think these were her words.) She wanted to spend more time with me, she wanted to get to know me better, she wanted to give the roulette wheel a decisive spin: she repeated all this twice in slightly different ways with different modifiers. It made me sweat. The only way I could think to get her to quit talking was to kiss her in earnest, my lips brushing by hers the way the sun passes around and through the interstices of falling leaves on an October afternoon. I hadn't kissed anyone in a long time. Her mouth tasted like cherry soda, like barbecue, like fresh hay, and because of these startling tastes, I retreated. To arm's length.

Sis, was I scared. What was this rank taste of wet campfire and bone fragments that I'd had in my mouth since we scattered you over the Hudson? Did I come through this set of coincidences, these quotidian interventions by God, to work in a place where everything seemed to be about *love,* only to find that I couldn't ever be a part of that grand word? How could I kiss anyone when I felt so awkward? What happened to me, what happened to all of us, to the texture of our lives, when you left us here?

I tried to ask Linda why she was doing what she was doing—behind the screen of wisteria and forsythia. I fumbled badly for these words. I believed she was trying to have a laugh on me. So she could go back and tell Cheese and Mick about it. So she could go gossip about me in the office, about what a jerk that Wakefield was. *Man, Andrew Wakefield thinks there's something worth hoping for in this world.* I thought she was joking, and I was through being the joke, being the Chicken Mask, being the harlequin.

—I'm not doing anything to you, Andrew, Linda said. —I'm expressing myself. It's supposed to be a good thing.

Reaching, she laid a palm flush against my face.

—I know you aren't ...

—So what's the problem?

I was ambitious to reassure. If I could have stayed the hand that fluttered up to cover her mouth, so that she could laugh unreservedly, so that her laughter peeled out in the Ticonderoga Room ... But I just wasn't up to it yet. I got out of there. I danced across the floor at the Wackerman wedding—I was a party of one—and the Wackermans and the Delgados and their kin probably thought I was singing along with "Desperado" by the Eagles (it was the anthem of the new Mr. and Mrs. Fritz Wackerman), but really I was talking to myself, *about work,* about how Mike Tombello's best man wanted to give his toast while doing flips on a trampoline, about how Jenny Parmenter wanted live goats bleating in the Mansion parking lot, as a fertility symbol, as she sped away, in her Rolls Cornische, to the Thousand Islands. Boy, I always hated the Eagles.

~

Okay, to get back to Glenda Manzini. Linda Pietrzsyk didn't write me off after our failed embraces, but she sure gave me more room. She was out the door at 5:01 for several weeks, without asking after me, without a kind word for anyone, and I didn't blame her. But in the end who else was there to talk to? To Marie O'Neill, the accountant? To Paul Avakian, the human resources and insurance guy and petty-cash manager? To Rachel Levy, the head chef? Maybe it was more than this. Maybe the bond that forms between people doesn't get unmade so easily. Maybe it leaves its mark for a long time. Soon Linda and I ate our bagged lunches together again, trading varieties of puddings, often in total silence; at least this was the habit until we found a new area of common interest in our reservations about Glenda Manzini's management techniques. This happened to be when Glenda took a week off. What a miracle. I'd been employed at the Mansion six months. The staff was in a fine mood about Glenda's hiatus. There was a carnival atmosphere. Dorcas Gilbey had been stockpiling leftover ales for an office shindig featuring dancing and the recitation of really bad marital vows we'd heard. Linda and I went along with the festivities, but we were also formulating a strategy.

What we wanted to know was how Glenda became so unreservedly cruel. We wanted the inside story on her personal life. We wanted the skinny. How do you produce an individual like Glenda? What is the mass-production technique? We waited until Tuesday, after the afternoon beer-tasting party. We were staying late, we claimed, in order to separate out the green M&M's for the marriage of U.V.M. tight end Brad Doelp who had requested bowls of M&M's at his reception, *excluding any and all green candies.* When our fellow employees were gone, right at five, we broke into Glenda's office.

Sis, we really broke in. Glenda kept her office locked when she wasn't in it. It was a matter of principle. I had to use my Discover card on the lock. I punished that credit card. But we got the tumblers to tumble, and once we were inside, we started poking around. First of all, Glenda Manzini was a tidy person, which I can admire from an organizational point of view, but it was almost like her office was empty. The pens and pencils were lined up. The in and out boxes were swept clean of any stray dust particle, any scrap of trash. There wasn't a rogue paper clip behind the desk or in the bottom of her spotless wastebasket. She kept her rubber bands banded together with rubber bands. The files in her filing cabinets were orderly, subdivided to avoid bowing, the old faxes were photocopied so that they wouldn't disintegrate. The photos on the walls (Mansion weddings past) were nondescript and pedestrian. There was nothing intimate about the decoration at all. I knew about most of this stuff from the moments when she ordered me into that cubicle to shout me down, but this was different. Now we were getting a sustained look at Glenda's personal effects.

Linda took particular delight in Glenda's cassette player (it was atop one of the black filing cabinets)—a cassette player that none of us had ever heard play, not even once. Linda admired the selection of recordings there. A complete set of cut-out budget series: *Greatest Hits of Baroque, Greatest Hits of Swing, Greatest Hits of Broadway, Greatest Hits of Disco,* and so forth. Just as she was about to pronounce Glenda a rank philistine where music was concerned, Linda located there, in a shattered case, a copy of *Greatest Hits of the Blues.*

We devoured the green M&M's while we were busy with our reconnaissance. And I kept reminding Linda not to get any of the green dye on anything. I repeatedly checked surfaces for fingerprints. I even overturned Linda's hands (it made me happy while doing it) to make sure they were free of emerald smudges. Because if Glenda found out we were in her office, we'd both be submitting applications at the Hot Bird of Troy. Nonetheless, Linda carelessly put down her handful of M&M's, on top of a filing cabinet, to look over the track listings for *Greatest Hits of the Blues.* This budget anthology was released the year Linda was born, in 1974. Coincidentally, the year you too were born, Sis. I remember driving with you to the tunes of Lightnin' Hopkins or Howlin' Wolf. I remember your preference for the most bereaved of acoustic blues, the most ramshackle of musics. What better soundtrack for the Adirondacks? For our meandering drives in the mountains, into Corinth or around Lake Luzerne? What more lonesome sound for a state park the size of Rhode Island where wolves and bears still come to hunt? Linda cranked the greatest hits of heartbreak and we sat down on the carpeted floor to listen. I missed you.

I pulled open that bottom file drawer by chance. I wanted to rest my arm on something. There was a powerful allure in the moment. I wasn't going to kiss Linda, and probably her desperate effort to find somebody to liberate her from her foreshortened economic prospects and her unpronounceable surname wouldn't come to much, but she was a good friend. Maybe a better friend than I was admitting to myself. It was in this expansive mood that I opened the file drawer at the bottom of one stack (the *J* through *P* stack), otherwise empty, to find that it was full of a half-dozen, maybe even more, of those circular packages of birth-control pills, the color-coated pills, you know, those multihued pills and placebos that are a journey through the amorous calendars of women. All unused. Not a one of them even opened. Not a one of the white, yellow, brown, or green pills liberated from its package.

—Must be chilly in Schenectady, Linda mumbled.

Was there another way to read the strange bottom drawer? Was there a way to look at it beyond or outside of my exhausting tendency to discover only facts that would prop up darker prognostications? The file drawer contained the pills, it contained a bottle of vodka, it contained a cache of family pictures and missives the likes of which were never displayed or mentioned or even alluded to by Glenda. Even I, for all my resentments, wasn't up to reading the letters. But what of these carefully arranged packages of photo snapshots of the Manzini family? (Glenda's son from her first marriage, in his early teens, in a torn and grass-stained football uniform, and mother and second husband and son in front of some bleachers, et cetera.) Was the drawer really what it seemed to be, a repository for mementos of love that Glenda had now hidden away, secreted, shunted off into mini-storage? What was the lesson of those secrets? Merely that concealed behind rage (and behind grief) is *the ambition to love*?

—Somebody's having an affair, Linda said. —The hubby is coming home late. He's fabricating late evenings at the office. He's taking some desktop meetings with his secretary. He's leaving Glenda alone with the kids. Why else be so cold?

—Or Glenda's carrying on, said I.

—Or she's polygamous, Linda said, —and this is a completely separate family she's keeping across town somewhere without telling anyone.

—Or this is the boy she gave up for adoption and this is the record of her meeting with his folks. And she never told Dave about it.

—Whichever it is, Linda said, —it's *bad*.

We turned our attention to the vodka. Sis, I know I've said that I don't touch the stuff anymore—because of your example—but Linda egged me on. We were listening to music of the Delta, to its simple unadorned grief, and I felt that Muddy Waters's loss was my kind of loss, the kind you don't shake easily, the kind that comes back like a seasonal flu, and soon we were passing the bottle of vodka back and forth. Beautiful, sad Glenda Manzini understood the blues and I understood the blues and you understood them and Linda understood them and maybe everybody understood them—in spite of what ethnomusicologists sometimes tell us about the cultural singularity of that music. Linda started to dance a little, there in Glenda Manzini's office, swiveling absently, her arms like asps, snaking to and fro, her wrists adorned in black bangles. Linda had a spell on her, in Glenda's anaerobic and cryogenically frigid office. Linda plucked off her beige pumps and circled around Glenda's desk, as if casting out its manifold demons. I couldn't take my eyes off of her. She forgot who I was and drifted with the lamentations of Robert Johnson (hellhound on his trail), and I could have followed her there, where she cast off Long Island and Skidmore and became a naiad, a true resident of the Mansion on the Hill, that paradise, but when the song was over the eeriness of our communion was suddenly alarming. I was sneaking around my boss's office. I was drinking her vodka. All at once it was time to go home.

We began straightening everything we had moved—we were really responsible about it—and Linda gathered up the dozen or so green M&M's she'd left on the filing cabinet—excepting the one she inadvertently fired out the back end of her fist, which skittered from a three-drawer file down a whole step to the surface of a two-drawer stack, before hopping and skipping over a cassette box, before free-falling behind the cabinets, where it came to rest, at last, six inches from the northeast corner of the office, beside a small coffee-stained patch of wall-to-wall. I returned the vodka to its drawer of shame, I tidied up the stacks of *Brides* magazines, I locked Glenda's office door, and I went back to being the employee of the month. (My framed picture hung over the water fountain between the rest rooms. I wore a bow tie. I smiled broadly and my teeth looked straight and my hair was combed. I couldn't be stopped.)

~

My ambition has always been to own my own small business. I like the flexibility of small-capitalization companies; I like small businesses at the moment at which they prepare to franchise. That's why I took the job at Hot Bird—I saw Hot Birds in every town in America, I saw Hot Birds as numerous as post offices or ATMs. I like small businesses at the moment at which they really define a market with respect to a certain need, when they begin to sell their products to the world. And my success as a team player at the Mansion on the Hill was the result of these ambitions. This is why I came to feel, after a time, that I could do Glenda Manzini's job myself. Since I'm a little young, it's obvious that I couldn't *replace* Glenda—I think her instincts were really great with respect to the service we were providing to the Capital Region—but I saw the Mansion on the Hill stretching its influence into population centers throughout the northeast. I mean, why wasn't there a Mansion on the Hill in Westchester? Down in Mamaroneck? Why wasn't there a Mansion on the Hill in the golden corridor of Boston suburbs? Why no mainline Philly Mansion? Suffice to say, I saw myself, at some point in the future, having the same opportunity Glenda had. I saw myself cutting deals and whittling out discounts at other fine Mansion locations. I imagined making myself indispensable to a coalition of Mansion venture capitalists and then I imagined using these associations to make a move into, say, the high-tech or bio-tech sectors of American industry.

The way I pursued this particular goal was that I started looking ahead at things like upcoming volume. I started using the graph features on my office software to make pie charts of ceremony densities, cost ratios, and so forth, and I started wondering how we could pitch our service better, whether on the radio or in the press or through alternative marketing strategies (I came up with the strategy, for example, of getting various nonaffiliated religions—small emergent spiritual movements—to consider us as a site for all their group wedding ceremonies). And as I started looking ahead, I started noticing who was coming through the doors in the next months. I became well versed in the social forces of our valley. I watched for when certain affluent families of the region might be needing our product. I would, if required, attempt cold-calling the attorney general of our state to persuade him of the splendor of the Niagara Hall when Diana, his daughter, finally gave the okeydokey to her suitor, Ben.

I may well have succeeded in my plan for domination of the Mansion on the Hill brand, if it were not for the fact that as I was examining the volume projections for November (one Monday night), the ceremonies taking place in a mere three months, I noticed that Sarah Wilton of Corinth was marrying one Brice McCann in the Rip Van Winkle Room. Just before Thanksgiving. There were no particular notes or annotations to the name on the calendar, and thus Glenda wasn't focusing much on the ceremony. But something bothered me. That name.

Your Brice McCann, Sis. Your intended. Getting married almost a year to the day after your rehearsal-dinner-that-never-was. Getting married before even having completed his requisite year of grief, before we'd even made it through the anniversary with its flood-waters. Who knew how long he'd waited before beginning his seduction of Sarah Wilton? Was it even certain that he had waited until you were gone? Maybe he was faithless; maybe he was a two-timer. I had started reading Glenda's calendar to get ahead in business, Sis, but as soon as I learned of Brice, I became cavalier about work. My work suffered. My relations with other members of the staff suffered. I kept to myself. I went back to riding the bus to work instead of accepting rides. I stopped visiting fellow workers. I found myself whispering of plots and machinations; I found myself making connections between things that probably weren't connected and planning involved scenarios of revenge. I knew the day would come when he would be on the premises, when Brice would be settling various accounts, going over various numbers, signing off on the pâté selection and the set list of the R&B band, and I waited for him—to be certain of the truth.

Sis, you became engaged too quickly. There had been that other guy, Mark, and you had been engaged to him, too, and that arrangement fell apart kind of fast—I think you were engaged at Labor Day and broken up by MLK's birthday—and then, within weeks, there was this Brice. There's a point I want to make here. I'm trying to be gentle, but I have to get this across. Brice wore a beret. *The guy wore a beret.* He was supposedly a great cook, he would bandy about names of exotic mushrooms, but I never saw him boil an egg when I was visiting you. It was always you who did the cooking. It's true that certain males of the species, the kind who linger at the table after dinner waiting for their helpmeet to do the washing up, the kind who preside over carving of viands and otherwise disdain food-related chores, the kind who claim to be effective only at the preparation of breakfast, these guys are Pleistocene brutes who don't belong in the Information Age with its emerging markets and global economies. But Sis, I think the other extreme is just as bad. The sensitive New Age, beret-wearing guys who buy premium mustards and free-range chickens and grow their own basil and then let you cook while they're in the other room perusing magazines devoted to the artistic posings of Asian teenagers. Our family comes from upstate New York and we don't eat enough vegetables and our marriages are full of hardships and sorrows, Sis, and when I saw Brice coming down the corridor of the Mansion on the Hill, with his prematurely gray hair slicked back with the aid of some all-natural mousse, wearing a gray, suede bomber jacket and cowboy boots into which were tucked the cuffs of his black designer jeans, carrying his personal digital assistant and his cell phone and the other accoutrements of his dwindling massage-therapy business, he was the enemy of my state. In his wake, I was happy to note, there was a sort of honeyed cologne. Patchouli, I'm guessing. It would definitely drive Glenda Manzini nuts.

We had a small conference room at the Mansion, just around the corner from Glenda's office. I had selected some of the furnishings there myself, from a discount furniture outlet at the mall. Brice and his fiancée, Sarah Wilton, would of course be repairing to this conference room with Glenda to do some pricing. I had the foresight, therefore, to jog into that space and turn on the speakerphone over by the coffee machine, and to place a planter of silk flowers in front of it and dial my own extension so that I could teleconference this conversation. I had a remote headset I liked to wear around, Sis, during inventorying and bill tabulation—it helped with the neck strain and tension headaches that I'm always suffering with—so I affixed this headset and went back to filing, down the hall, while the remote edition of Brice and Sarah's conference with Glenda was broadcast into my skull.

I figure my expression was ashen. I suppose that Dorcas Gilbey, when she flagged me down with some receipts that she had forgotten to file, was unused to my mechanistic expression and to my curt, unfriendly replies to her questions. I waved her off, clamping the headset tighter against my ear. Unfortunately, the signal broke up. It was muffled. I hurriedly returned to my desk and tried to get the forwarded call to transmit properly to my headset. I even tried to amplify it through the speakerphone feature, to no avail. Brice had always affected a soft-spoken demeanor while he was busy extorting things from people like you, Sis. He was too quiet—the better to conceal his tactics. And thus, in order to hear him, I had to sneak around the corner from the conference room and eavesdrop in the old-fashioned way.

—We wanted to dialogue with you (Brice was explaining to Glenda), because we wanted to make sure that you were thinking creatively along the same lines we are. We want to make sure you're comfortable with our plans. As married people, as committed people, we want this ceremony to make others feel good about themselves, as we're feeling good about ourselves. We want to have an ecstatic celebration here, a healing celebration that will bind up the hurt any marriages in the room might be suffering. I know you know how the ecstasy of marriage occasions a grieving process for many persons, Mrs. Manzini. Sarah and I both feel this in our hearts, that celebrations often have grief as a part of their wonder, and we want to enact all these things, all these feelings, to bring them out where we can look at them, and then we want to purge them triumphantly. We want people to come out of this wedding feeling good about themselves, as we'll be feeling good about ourselves. We want to give our families a big collective hug, because we're all human and we all have feelings and we all have to grieve and yearn and we need rituals for this.

There was a long silence from Glenda Manzini.

Then she said:

—Can we cut to the chase?

One thing I always loved about the Mansion on the Hill was its emptiness, its vacancy. Sure, the Niagara Room, when filled with five-thousand-dollar gowns and heirloom tuxedos, when serenaded by Toots Wilcox's big band, was a great place, a sort of gold standard of reception halls, but as much as I always loved both the celebrations and the network of relationships and associations that went with our business at the Mansion, I always felt best in the *empty* halls of the Mansion on the Hill, cleansed of their accumulation of sentiment, utterly silent, patiently awaiting the possibility of matrimony. It was onto this clean slate that I had routinely projected my foolish hopes.

But after Brice strutted through my place of employment, after his marriage began to overshadow every other, I found instead a different message inscribed on these walls: *Every death implies a guilty party.*

Or to put it another way, there was a network of subbasements in the Mansion on the Hill through which each suite was connected to another. These tunnels were well-traveled by certain alcoholic janitorial guys whom I knew well enough. I'd had my reasons to adventure there before, but now I used every opportunity to pace these corridors. I still performed the parts of my job that would assure that I got paid and that I invested regularly in my 401K plan, but I felt more comfortable in the emptiness of the Mansion's suites and basements, thinking about how I was going to extract my recompense, while Brice and Sarah dithered over the cost of their justice of the peace and their photographer and their *Champlain Pentecostal Singers.*

I had told Linda Pietrzsyk about Brice's reappearance. I had told her about you, Sis. I had remarked about your fractures and your loss of blood and your hypothermia and the results of your postmortem blood-alcohol test; I suppose that I'd begun to tell her all kinds of things, in outbursts of candor that were followed by equal and opposite remoteness. Linda saw me, over the course of those weeks, lurking, going from Ticonderoga to Rip Van Winkle to Chestnut, slipping in and out of infernal subbasements of conjecture that other people find grimy and uncomfortable, when I should have been overseeing the unloading of floral arrangements at the loading dock or arranging for Glenda's chiropractic appointments. Linda saw me lurking around, *asked what was wrong and told me that it would be better after the anniversary, after that day had come and gone,* and I felt the discourses of apology and subsequent gratitude forming epiglottally in me, but instead I told her to get lost, to leave the dead to bury the dead.

After a long excruciating interval, the day of Sarah Danforth Wilton's marriage to Brice Paul McCann arrived. It was a day of chill mists, Sis, and you had now been gone just over one year. I had passed through the anniversary trembling, in front of the television, watching the Home Shopping Network, impulsively pricing cubic zirconium rings, as though one of these would have been the ring you might have worn at your ceremony. You were a fine sister, but you changed your mind all the time, and I had no idea if these things I'd attributed to you in the last year were features of the *you* I once knew, or whether, in death, you had become the property of your mourners, so that we made of you a puppet.

On the anniversary, I watched a videotape of your bridal shower, and Mom was there, and she looked really proud, and Dad drifted into the center of the frame at one point and mumbled a strange *harrumph* that had to do with interloping at an assembly of such beautiful women (I was allowed on the scene only to do the videotaping), and you were very pleased as you opened your gifts. At one point you leaned over to Mom, and stage-whispered—so that even I could hear—*that your car was a real lemon and that you had to take it to the shop and you didn't have time and it was a total hassle and did she think that I would lend you the Sable without giving you a hard time?* My Sable, my car. Sure. If I had it to do again, I would never have given you a hard time even once.

The vows at the Mansion on the Hill seemed to be the part of the ceremony where most of the tinkering took place. I think if Glenda had been able to find a way to charge a premium on vow alteration, we could have found a really excellent revenue stream at the Mansion on the Hill. If the sweet instant of commitment is so singular, why does it seem to have so many different articulations? People used all sorts of things in their vows. Conchita Bosworth used the songs of Dan Fogelberg when it came to the exchange of rings; a futon-store owner from Queensbury, Reggie West, managed to work in material from a number of sitcoms. After a while, you'd heard it all, the rhetoric of desire, the incantation of commitment rendered as awkwardly as possible; you heard the purple metaphors, the hackneyed lines, until it was all like legal language, as in any business transaction.

It was the language of Brice McCann's vows that brought this story to its conclusion. I arrived at the wedding late. I took a cab across the Hudson, from the hill in Troy where I lived in my convenience apartment. What trees there were in the system of pavement cloverleafs where Route Seven met the interstate were bare, disconsolate. The road was full of potholes. The lanes choked with old, shuddering sedans. The parking valets at the Mansion, a group of pot-smoking teens who seemed to enjoy creating a facsimile of politeness that involved both effrontery and subservience, opened the door of the cab for me and greeted me according to their standard line, *Where's the party?* The parking lot was full. We had seven weddings going on at once. Everyone was working. Glenda was working, Linda was working, Dorcas was working. All my teammates were working, sprinting from suite to suite, micromanaging. The whole of the Capital Region must have been at the Mansion that Saturday to witness the blossoming of families, Sis, or, in the case of Brice's wedding, to witness the way in which a vow of faithfulness less than a year old, a promise of the future, can be traded in so quickly; how marriage is just a shrink-wrapped sale item, mass-produced in bulk. You can pick one up anywhere these days, at a mall, on layaway. If it doesn't fit, exchange it.

I walked the main hallway slowly, peeking in and out of the various suites. In the Chestnut Suite it was the Polanskis, poor but generous—their daughter Denise intended to have and to hold an Italian fellow, A.L. DiPietro, also completely penniless, and the

Polanskis were paying for the entire ceremony and rehearsal dinner and inviting the DiPietros to stay with them for the week. They had brought their own floral displays, personally assembled by the arthritic Mrs. Polanski. The room had a dignified simplicity. Next, in the Hudson Suite, in keeping with its naval flavor, cadet Bobby Moore and his high-school sweetheart Mandy Sutherland were tying the knot, at the pleasure of Bobby's dad, who had been a tugboat captain in New York Harbor; in the Adirondack Suite, two of the venerable old families of the Lake George region—the Millers (owners of the Lake George Cabins) and the Wentworths (they had the Quality Inn franchise)—commingled their resort-dependent fates; in the Valentine Room, Sis, two women (named Sal and Martine, but that's all I should say about them, for reasons of privacy) were to be married by a renegade Episcopal minister called Jack Valance—they had sewn their own gowns to match the cadmium-red decor of that interior; Ticonderoga had the wedding of Glen Dunbar and Louise Glazer, a marriage not memorable in any way at all, and in the Niagara Hall two of Saratoga's great eighteenth-century racing dynasties, the Vanderbilt and Pierrepont families, were about to settle long-standing differences. Love was everywhere in the air.

I walked through all these ceremonies, Sis, before I could bring myself to go over to the Rip Van Winkle Room. My steps were reluctant. My observations: the proportions of sniffling at each ceremony were about equal and the audiences were about equal and levels of whimsy and seriousness were about the same wherever you went. The emotions careened, high and low, across the whole spectrum of possible feelings. The music might be different from case to case—stately baroque anthems or klezmer rave-ups—but the intent was the same. By 3:00 P.M., I no longer knew what marriage meant, really, except that the celebration of it seemed built into every life I knew but my own.

~

The doors of the Rip Van Winkle Room were open, as distinct from the other suites, and I tiptoed through them and closed these great carved doors behind myself. I slipped into the bride's side. The light was dim, Sis. The light was deep in the ultraviolet spectrum, as when we used to go, as kids, to the exhibitions at the Hall of Science and Industry. There seemed to be some kind of mummery, some kind of expressive dance, taking place at the altar. The Champlain Pentecostal Singers were wailing eerily. As I searched the room for familiar faces, I noticed them everywhere. Just a couple of rows away Alex McKinnon and her boy Zack were squished into a row and were fidgeting desperately. Had they known Brice? Had they known you? Maybe they counted themselves close friends of Sarah Wilton. Zack actually turned and waved and seemed to mouth something to me, but I couldn't make it out. On the groom's side, I saw Linda Pietrzsyk, though she ought to have been working in the office, fielding calls, and she was surrounded by Cheese, Chip, Mick, Mark, Stig, Blair, and a half-dozen other delinquents from her peer group. Like some collective organism of mirth and irony, they convulsed over the proceedings, over the scarlet tights and boas and dance belts of the modern dancers capering at the altar. A row beyond these Skidmore halfwits—though she never sat in at any ceremony—was Glenda Manzini herself, and she seemed to be sobbing uncontrollably, a handkerchief like a veil across her face. Where was her husband? And her boy? Then, to my amazement, Sis, when I looked back at the S.R.O. audience beyond the last aisle over on the groom's side, *I saw Mom and Dad*. What were they doing there? And how had they known? I had done everything to keep the wedding from them. I had hoarded these bad feelings. Dad's face was gray with remorse, as though he could have done something to stop the proceedings, and Mom held tight to his side, wearing dark glasses of a perfect opacity.

At once, I got up from the row where I'd parked myself and climbed over the exasperated families seated next to me, jostling their knees. As I went, I became aware of Brice McCann's soft, insinuating voice ricocheting, in Dolby surround-sound, from one wall of the Rip Van Winkle Room to the next. The room was appropriately named, it seemed to me then. We were all sleepers who dreamed a reverie of marriage, not one of us had waked to see the bondage, the violence, the excess of its cabalistic prayers and rituals. Marriage was oneiric. Not one of us was willing to pronounce the truth of its dream language of slavery and submission and transmission of property, and Brice's vow, *to have and to hold Sarah Wilton, till death did them part, forsaking all others,* seemed to me like the pitch of a used-car dealer or insurance salesman, and these words rang out in the room, likewise Sarah's uncertain and breathy reply, and I rushed at the center aisle, pushing away cretinous guests and cherubic newborns toward my parents, to embrace them as these words fell, these words with their intimations of mortality, *to tell my parents I should never have let you drive that night, Sis. How could I have let you drive? How could I have been so stupid? My tires were bald—I couldn't afford better. My car was a death trap; and I was its proper driver, bent on my long, complicated program of failure, my program of futures abandoned, of half-baked ideas, of big plans that came to nought, of cheap talk and lies, of drinking binges, petty theft; my car was made for my own death, Sis, the inevitable and welcome end to the kind of shame and regret I had brought upon everyone close to me, you especially, who must have wept inwardly, in your bosom, when you felt compelled to ask me to read a poem on your special day, before you totaled my car, on that curve, running up over the bream, shrieking, flipping the vehicle, skidding thirty feet on the roof, hitting the granite outcropping there, plunging out of the seat (why no seat belt?), snapping your neck, ejecting through the windshield, catching part of yourself there, tumbling over the hood, breaking both legs, puncturing your lung, losing an eye, shattering your wrist, bleeding, coming to rest at last in a pile of mouldering leaves, where rain fell upon you, until, unconsciously, you died.*

Yet, as I called out to Mom and Dad, the McCann-Wilton wedding party suddenly scattered, the vows were through, the music was overwhelming, the bride and groom were married; there were Celtic pipes, and voices all in harmony—it was a dirge, it was a jig, it was a chant of religious ecstasy—and I couldn't tell what was wedding and what was funeral, whether there was an end to one and a beginning to the other, and there were shouts of joy and confetti in the air, and beating of breasts and the procession of pink-cheeked teenagers, two by two, all living the dream of American marriages with cars and children and small businesses and pension plans and social security checks and grandchildren, and I couldn't get close to my parents in the throng; in fact, I couldn't be sure if it had been them standing there at all, in that fantastic crowd, that crowd of dreams, and I realized I was alone at Brice McCann's wedding, alone among people who would have been just as happy not to have me there, as I had often been alone, even in fondest company, even among those who cared for me. I should have stayed home and watched television.

This didn't stop me, though. I made my way to the reception. I shoveled down the chicken satay and shrimp with green curry, along with the proud families of Sarah Wilton and Brice McCann. Linda Pietrzsyk appeared by my side, as when we had kissed in the Ticonderoga Suite. She asked if I was feeling all right.

—Sure, I said.

—Don't you think I should drive you home?

—There's someone I want to talk to, I said. —Then I'd be happy to go.

And Linda asked:

—What's in the bag?

She was referring to my Wal-Mart shopping bag, Sis. I think the Wal-Mart policy which asserts that *employees are not to let a customer pass without asking if this customer needs help* is incredibly enlightened. I think the way to a devoted customer is through his or her dignity. In the shopping bag, I was carrying the wedding gift I had brought for Brice McCann and Sarah Wilton. I didn't know if I should reveal this gift to Linda, because I didn't know if she would understand, but I told her anyhow. *Is this what it's like to discover, all at once, that you are sharing your life?*

—Oh, that's some of my sister.

—Andrew, Linda said, and then she apparently didn't know how to continue. Her voice, in a pair of false starts, oscillated with worry. Her smile was grim. —Maybe this would be a good time to leave.

But I didn't leave, Sis. I brought out the most dangerous weapon in my arsenal, the pinnacle of my nefarious plans for this event, also stored in my Wal-Mart bag. The Chicken Mask. That's right, Sis. I had been saving it ever since my days at Hot Bird, and as Brice had yet to understand that I had crashed his wedding for a specific reason, I slipped this mask over my neatly parted hair, and over the collar of the wash-and-wear suit that I had bought that week for this occasion. I must say, in the mirrored reception area in the Rip Van Winkle Room, I was one elegant chicken. I immediately began to search the premises for the groom, and it was difficult to find him at first, since there were any number of like-minded beret-wearing motivational speakers slouching against pillars and counters. At last, though, I espied him preening in the middle of a small group of maidens, over by the electric fountain we had installed for the ceremony. He was laughing good-naturedly. When he first saw me, in the Chicken Mask, working my way toward him, I'm sure he saw me as an omen for his new union. *Terrific! We've got a chicken at the ceremony! Poultry is always reassuring at wedding time!* Linda was trailing me across the room. Trying to distract me. I had to be short with her. I told her to go find herself a husband.

I worked my way into McCann's limber and witty reception chatter and mimed a certain Chicken-style affability. Then, when one of those disagreeable conversational silences overtook the group, I ventured a question of your intended:

—So, Brice, how do you think your last fiancée, Eileen, would be reacting to your first-class nuptial ceremony today? Would she have liked it?

There was a confused hush, as the three or four of the secretarial beauties of his circle considered the best way to respond to this thorny question.

—Well, since she's passed away, I think she would probably be smiling down on us from above. I've felt her presence throughout the decision to marry Sarah, and I think Eileen knows that I'll never forget her. That I'll always love her.

—Oh, is that right? I said, —because the funny thing is I happen to have her *with me here,* and …

Then I opened up the small box of you (you were in a Tiffany jewelry box that I had spirited out of Mom's jewelry cache because I liked its pale teal shade: the color of rigor mortis as I imagined it), held it up toward Brice, and then tossed some of it. I'm sure you know, Sis, that chips of bone tend to be heavier and therefore to fall more quickly to the ground, while the rest of the ashes make a sort of cloud when you throw them, when you cast them aloft. Under the circumstances, this cloud seemed to have a character, a personality. *Thus, you darted and feinted around Brice's head,* Sis, so that he began coughing and wiping the corners of his eyes, dusty with your remains. His consorts were hacking as well, among them Sarah Wilton, his troth. How had I missed her before? She was radiant like a woman whose prayers have been answered, who sees the promise of things to come, who sees uncertainties and contingencies diminished, and yet she was rushing away from me, astonished, as were the others. I realized I had caused a commotion. Still, I gave chase, Sis, and I overcame your Brice McCann, where he blockaded himself on the far side of a table full of spring rolls. Though I have never been a fighting guy, I gave him an elbow in the nose, as if I were a chicken and this elbow my wing. I'm sure I mashed some cartilage. He got a little nosebleed. I think I may have broken the Mansion's unbroken streak of peaceful weddings.

At this point, of course, a pair of beefy Mansion employees (the McCarthy brothers, Tom and Eric) arrived on the scene and pulled me off of Brice McCann. They also tore the Chicken Mask from me. And they never returned this piece of my property afterward. At the moment of unmasking, Brice reacted with mock astonishment. But how could he have failed to guess? That I would wait for my chance, however many years it took?

—Andy?

I said nothing, Sis. Your ghost had been in the cloud that wreathed him; your ghost had swooped out of the little box that I'd held, and now, at last, you were released from your disconsolate march on the surface of the earth, your march of unfinished business, your march of fixed ideas and obsessions unslaked by death. I would be happy if you were at peace now, Sis, and I would be happy if I were at peace; I would be happy if the thunderclouds and lightning of Brice and Sarah's wedding would yield to some warm autumn day in which you had good weather for your flight up through the heavens.

Out in the foyer, where the guests from the Valentine Room were promenading in some of the finest threads I had ever seen, Tom McCarthy told me that Glenda Manzini wanted to see me in her office—before I was removed from the Mansion on the Hill permanently. We walked against the flow of the crowd beginning to empty from each of the suites. Our trudge was long. When I arrived at Glenda's refrigerated chamber, she did an unprecedented thing, Sis, she closed the door. I had never before inhabited that space alone with her. She didn't invite me to sit. Her voice was raised from the outset. Pinched between thumb and forefinger (the shade of her nail polish, a dark maroon, is known in beauty circles, I believe, as *vamp*), as though it were an ounce of gold or a pellet of plutonium, she held a single green M&M.

—Can you explain this? she asked.—Can you tell me what this is?

—I think that's a green M&M, I said. —I think that's the traditional green color, as opposed to one of the new brighter shades they added in a recent campaign for market share.

—Andy, don't try to amuse me. What was this green M&M doing behind my filing cabinet?

—Well, I—

—I'm certain that I didn't leave a green M&M back there. I would never leave an M&M behind a filing cabinet. In fact, I would never allow a green M&M into this office in the first place.

—That was months ago.

—I've been holding on to it for months, Glenda said. —Do you think I'm stupid?

—On the contrary, I said.

—Do you think you can come in here and violate the privacy of my office?

—I think you're brilliant, I said. —And I think you're very sad. And I think you should surrender your job to someone who cares for the institution you're celebrating here.

Now that I had let go of you, Sis, now that I had begun to compose this narrative in which I relinquished the hem of your spectral bedsheet, I saw through the language of business, the rhetoric of hypocrisy. Why had she sent me out for those birth-control pills? Why did she make me schedule her chiropractic appointments? Because she could. *But what couldn't be controlled, what could never be controlled, was the outcome of devotion.* Glenda's expression, for the first time on record, was stunned. She launched into impassioned colloquy about how the Mansion on the Hill was supposed to be a *refuge,* and how, with my *antics,* as she called them, I had sullied the reputation of the Mansion and endangered its business plan, and how it was clear *that assaulting strangers while wearing a rubber mask is the kind of activity that proves you are an unstable person, and I just think, well, I don't see the point in discussing it with you anymore and I think you have some serious choices to make, Andy, if you want to be part of regular human society,* and so forth, which is just plain bunk, as far as I'm concerned. It's not as if Brice McCann were a *stranger* to me.

I'm always the object of tirades by my supervisors, for overstepping my position, for lying, for wanting too much—this is one of the deep receivables on the balance sheet of my life—and yet at the last second Glenda Manzini didn't fire me. According to shrewd managerial strategy, she simply waved toward the door. With the Mansion crowded to capacity now, with volume creeping upward in the coming months, they would need someone with my skills. To validate the cars in the parking lot, for example. Mark my words, Sis, parking validation will soon be as big in the Northeast as it is in the West.

When the McCarthys flung me through the main doors, Linda Pietrzsyk was waiting. What unfathomable kindness. At the main entrance, on the way out, I passed through a gauntlet of rice-flingers. Bouquets drifted through the skies to the mademoiselles of the Capital. Garters fell into the hands of local bachelors. Then I was beyond all good news and seated in the passenger seat of Linda's battered Volkswagen. She was crying. We progressed slowly along back roads. I had been given chances and had squandered them. I had done my best to love, Sis. I had loved you, and you were gone. In Linda's car, at dusk, we sped along the very road where you took your final drive. Could Linda have known? Your true resting place is forested by white birches, they dot the length of that winding lane, the fingers of the dead reaching up through burdens of snow to impart much-needed instruction to the living. In intermittent afternoon light, in seizure-inducing light, unperturbed by the advances of merchandising, I composed a proposal.

hunting for cherubs

Jeffrey McDaniel

If you heard your lover scream in the next room, and you ran in and saw his pinkie on the floor in a small puddle of blood, you wouldn't rush to the pinkie and say *Darling, are you okay?* No, you'd wrap your arms around his shoulders and worry about the pinkie later. The same holds true if you heard the scream, ran in, and saw his hand, or, God forbid, his whole arm. But suppose you hear your lover scream in the next room, and you run in, and his head is on the floor, next to his body, which do you rush to and comfort first?

the jerk

Hey you, dragging the halo—
how about a holiday in the islands of grief?

Tongue is the word I wish to have with you.
Your eyes are so blue they leak.

Your legs are longer than a prisoner's
last night on death row.

You're a dirty little windshield.

I'm standing behind you on the subway,
hard as calculus. My breath
sticks to your neck like graffiti.

I'm sitting opposite you in the bar, waiting
for you to uncross your boundaries.

I want to rip off your logic
and make passionate sense to you.

I want to ride in the swing of your hips.

My fingers will dig into you like quotation marks,
blazing your limbs into parts of speech.

But with me for a lover, you won't need
catastrophes. What attracted me in the first place
will ultimately make me resent you.

I'll start telling you lies, and my lies will sparkle,
become the bad stars you chart your life by.

I'll stare at other women so blatantly
you'll hear my eyes peeling,

because sex with you is like Great Britain:
cold, groggy, and a little uptight.

Your bed is a big, soft calculator
where my problems multiply.

Your brain is a garage
I park my bullshit in, for free.

You're not really my new girlfriend,
just another flop sequel of the first one,
who was based on the true story of my mother.

You're so ugly I forgot how to spell!

I'll cheat on you like a ninth grade math test.
Break your heart just for the sound it makes.

You're the *this* we need to put an end to.

The more you apologize, the less I forgive you.

So how about it?

from a scribbler's life

Kristina McGrath

Being a Faithful Account of

HER DAYS AS A GENTLEMAN

Found by a Riverbank, Bound in Baker's String

A Scribbler's Tale

What I once was and how I came to be here

ONCE I WROTE IN VIOLET INK IN MY BOUDOIR—with ink-pot balanced on my knee, my slippered toes tucked beneath a drowsing dog—where no adversity could ever touch me; no adversity, but what my own soul wrought.

I made a tidy income then, under pseudonym of Henry Age.

Those were days when water boiled fast on a high fire, when the Dresden pot was warm & leaves were loosely steeping on a cold rimy morning at Tenoaks Manor, when teacups were many & matching, when the lampblack, which fretted me, was cleaned by the crusty maid Felicity.

I suffered no pinch but a bit of weather. And though I feigned displeasure at the dampness of my chamber, a little rain yet delighted the nape of my neck as it trickled through a tiny mouldering crack in the ceiling, oddly neglected by the same Felicity, who dusted webs from even door-cheeks.

With a warm water-bottle at my back, I wrote in a trance with my eyes closed, bewitched by the vision of an impetuous Belinda or a Sue who ventured on a midnight, often bumping into ghosts, with flushed & heaving breast towards the entrance to a gentleman's dark estate, where all manner of startlement took place on the stair or with a throbbing in the scullery.

I wrote for profit & with a strong pen, lacking in the niceties.

O, it was true, Henry startled & thrilled in every chapter. Being good at sudden climax for the benefit of serial installments, he shattered the monotony of a Factory Girl's life & woke the gentry from their sleep. For lurking round the corner of his every page were ominous reports of adultery, hashish, strumpets among the respectable, women's clothing on the backs of men, severely cropped hair on the heads of trousered girls.

I roistered through a tale of untamed wives quite well & all things disagreeable—until sentiment & moral settled in, which pleased the Publisher, who recommended nothing too contrary.

But I was crushed by my own happy endings. It was for the sake of the nation's soul & the morals of Mudie's Circulating Library that my rebellious were left without a servant or a stitch; my impetuous drowned in the tarn; my orphans, my little thieves, fell ill, then, put to-bed, grew saintly, adopted by an heiress.

And in my days as Henry Age, I came to suffer a certain dolor arising from derangement of the bile, as all the while my true work languished in a drawer, only sniffed at by my Publisher, who was not disposed to bind & sell them.

My essays of dissent, written by my female pen, he deemed too narrow an ideology—*a hotchpotch of witches & paupers, vipers in a bosom, contrary to Industry, Catechism, a Gentleman's Family,* when all I meant to say was this:

Twas a blot & a shame on the nation's soul when women were confined to the puffery of crinolines easily set afire or caught in wheels, when only crumbs of dusty bread were served at cottage tables, when Seamstress & Mason were left to the oblivion of their hovels, without a vote.

But what right had I to speculate on the nation from my bedstead, he wondered, to consult with only the pillows as to the Fortunes of Cripples & Dogs? And what right to abuse a lovely penny, to abandon Henry at the peak of his success, & let Mice have ruin through the musty walls at Tenoaks, where drizzle issues from a wizened crack in the ceiling as the thoughts from my head?

Of all this, it was his duty to remind me. An author in a petticoat! From obscurity I came, & to obscurity I could easily return.

So for the progress of my purse, that I should not be flirting in the streets or be forced to wretched toil as a governess from dawn to night, I wrote instead my purple novels all the week, till Frigg, the god of Friday, brought diversions of the social crowd, who thought me odd.

They thought me prickly, with awkward manners, an undue ardour for the Cat, & too benign a countenance at the familiarities of a Shop-girl.

They chided me for being so allured by a certain Mary Hood, you see, who fitted me in lady's clothes, who bent to tuck & hem me, whose hair was curled & had no scruple, gone astray from round her ears. Her diligent little fingers were the only tenderness I knew as she helped me to pluck at too many buttons, to crimp an Eton jacket at my waist, to choose a bustle, not too weighty, to smooth it with a petting at the back of my skirt.

And in this, I took the gravest delight.

But O, the trivia of the social scene; it was only flutter & plumage. Poor Felicity tired of portering trays, of brushing carpets, sweeping crumbs of plum cake & sugar paste we left at our feet. My companions of an evening suffered an uncontrollable urge to only prattle, were most unfond of dust or rain (any kind of weather, for all that), or of any mess like conversation of the heart. This last I understood, as I myself was shy & put to task to speak a word; yet write, I could!

And did! & had my fun, as I drew from the real & caused a Trouble to many. And when I heard the creak of a shoe, I would hide my fiction, most especially from Felicity, who thought me worthy of her service & knew me not as silly, having read only my essays, more often than not with interest, during many an evening together.

If not for her company, I would have kept to my bed with only the dog. But, "Felicity!" I said, "Come sit near me by the fire."

My insistence that she stop her sweeping she considered at first a nuisance. Well known in the Town for her diligence, she took to the house with stooped back & nervous fever in our first months together; though by the bells of Woofing Church she learned to play. And if I had anything in the world which pleased me, it was not the splendour of a penny but her sipping at milk & tea, her appetite for sugar.

Unknown to her & to my companions of polite society—otherwise, I dare say, they would have despised me—I had a mind for bosoms, wags, & thieves, for invention of the wildest sort.

Years passed. What once was play turned labour. I was but a Horse for Hire. My obligation for one novel a year had multiplied to two or three—all stubble & straw.

Though I found no pleasure in it, I put myself to-bed each night in eider-down, slept sitting up (thought better for digestion), & woke each morning much against my will. I would often buy a brave fat goose at Market Lane, not caring what it cost me; but by the time I fell to it in the afternoon, my relish was mostly dissembled for the sake of the Cook.

All will be well, I often calmed myself with a lie, & took it like an opiate. Even my despondency was but a drug, as I grew ever more scornful of my days at Tenoaks, a house which refused repair.

I spent an alarming number of hours in the languor of my bed-chamber: combing the thistle, Hop-o'-my-thumb, from the seat of my gown; declining invitations to luncheons, which I detested, as I would only stand tongue-tied in the corner.

While Henry suffered no little amount of popular success, a pedlar of vulgar wishes, condemned by some as sensual, a libertine, a tom-cat in the chronicle of his own dissipated life, I stayed at home & tried at chatter with my companions, like a melancholy girl in a fancy dress.

Whether outraged or smitten, many a lady would write to him; & for a time, this I much enjoyed in either case, & answered their enquiries promptly:

> *My dear Madam,*
>
> *My apologies.* [or *My thanks.*] *I should be excited & surprised, left standing on the side of my shoe, much humbled, should you ever come by way of my sleepy Parish, seeing fit to bestow a visit upon an old bachelor, such as myself.*
>
> *I remain ever yours,*
>
> *Henry Age*

No dear Madam ever came, as I offered no address, no indication, not even by shire, of my whereabouts. And while my yellow-back novels were sold at every railway bookstall, I would not travel, least of all to my Publisher, for fear of any hint that Henry Age was I.

I found my own words, at last, inedible to the spleen, though I much enjoyed the shock I caused from Sensation in a Bosom & the ribaldry with tarts, their tannin, that only Henry was allowed to know.

And he knew it with a smirk on fabled mustached lips—the creation of the lithographer. His cheeks were ruddy; I took to-bed, alarmed by my pallor. And resolutely I refused to go to London, to leave my beck & holm & be accused of writing books.

I stepped shy of fame, no Wit of the Town; the Racket shamed me so. Fearing a lock of my hair should be plucked from my head & sold at auction, I allowed myself to be the frill of Henry's lip & blouse, to be what came of ink & yellow limestone, the frippery of his neckerchief, the impression on a page which Vanity had made.

With more pennies than scruples, my purse was never thin.

But all my feisty heroines were fuddled to a common end. Maternity & Holy Matrimony, you may depend upon it, I blanched, & packed to go.

No more fiction!

I am here now, hand to mouth, in a scrabbly way & cannot always pay for the pot to boil.

Dog-like, I shake myself awake, spring from my bed with crumbs in my hair. I shrug off my gown, slip into my trousers at a hop, stumbling towards my one intention in the darkness of an early morning. At once, I am disapproved of by the Cat. She disapproves of the smoke from my cigar, which is a scandal to some.

But while some may object, it is my delight to be a Scribbler & to live a Scribbler's life:

I sleep & eat when I like. With no notice, I'm dressed in two minutes. Bent at my table under a low ceiling, I'm apt to bark & clap at the parting of a veil.

Having given up my tawdry fictions, having doffed the crinolines & lace, it is Henry's simple black cravat I wear, as I live among the paupers & witches of Huddlesfield Parish, where I continue my report on the nation & the heavens from the confines of my attic room.

And should I accept a rare invitation, made to a dotty Henry by the few who remember him in a neighbouring shire, I would only disturb the splendour of a conversation with the most wicked heresy, being prone to cackle to myself in my days as a gentleman.

I came to be where I am by choice & by the high jinx of my clothes. With my hair tucked beneath my hat, I nod to the Barber, to the widowed Sempstress & Shoemaker, who marvel, twice perplexed, at the bulge of my breast & the smallness of my boy-sized boot.

Now I wipe my pen on the tail of my coat, my hands often numbed with cold, but with one honest penny & a hope, much better than the false ones I lived on.

By the ruins of a wall, it was to the maid I left the bulk of my belongings, with a note in violet ink, which said only, *Felicity!*

In Search of a Title

The Counsel intends to make himself heard

My head is filled with hay & rags at this wee hour. Words come to me not at all & then in a sudden rush. At my books, I am attempting to ignore certain enquiries of my Counsel, who has taken sudden interest in matters which hitherto have left him cold.

Daily now, at his tea-time, he hobbles up the stairs, three-legged with his cane, arriving winded at my door. He has heard that I am back to work, returned in good faith to my brief pamphlet—presently entitled *The Discourse of a Certain Person Outside London*. But such title does not satisfy, he presses to inform me: "You do not like this best of all."

Inspired by worry over my purse, he wishes I might make something of myself, & likewise by concern over my nerves, he recommends an Exotic to work a cure. He is certain I will somehow find my way. He is only sorry that, on a luckless day as I had yesterday, I attempted anything in the first place & did not have the good sense to nod off immediately upon waking.

In short, he thinks I've gone a little cracked from the racking of my brain. "Don't overdo, like a man attempting to walk & whistle at the same time. And, dear," he adds with a great guffaw, "do not write with your eyes closed; it is ever so nasty."

With all due regard for my short experience (& a merry one, he is sure) in the Buying & Selling of Scribbles, yet full aware the unprofitable distemper of my ways, he has a thought or two which might decently assist me if I persist in such fruitless exertion. Why, he himself has penned a few not unworthy verses while cozy in his timber-latticed lodge amongst the pines, & truly ought to know, he says, from whence he speaks.

"But go into your garden of bones & tins, & think about it," he allows. "It is wholly your decision."

Digging my pen into the farthest hollow of the well, certainly I am gladdened by his trust, though for my cupboard he offers a goodly store of warnings. With a wringing of hands, smiling all the while like a great-uncle with a pocketful of tarts, he proffers what I might wish to heed:

the archbishop, his views;

the villagers, their notable hunger even subsequent to supper, & the terrible distraction which ensues;

the circumference of the lake, the distance to the vale, a long hard road, he adds;

the Latinate;

the Queen herself, her words of warning regarding my own feeble sex (whichever that might be, he adds with a wink);

a pallid cheek or sighing bosom would be nice, a languid woman with a flower; but no strange and beautiful companion gazing into my face, her hot lips travelling along my cheek in kisses; no naked panting breasts conjoined;

no tumultuous respiration whatsoever between the ladies, please:

no impassionate bursts or leaping flesh, no agitation to the highest degree;

for Rebellious Girls, a trip to Bedlam, & for the Good, a cozy den;

& do allude to foreign places, where I have never been, while he is greatly travelled to all manner of Campagna near Rome, vineyards & passes, dingles & crags, to caverns, Alps & abbeys, & at a moment's notice, he is off to chat about the weather with the gondoliers of Venice;

but do not step so out of doors on morbid windy nights: no nocturnal visits, no women with teeth like needles, leave it to the province of the French; at all times Refinement in the English parlour;

too sweet would not be good, nor sour;

& do take care not to bring offense to those in the Herring & Sherry Trades, the Timber-merchants, Munitions-magnates, Gunsmith & Knifegrinder;

Amusement for the Public!

& in all days to come remember My Hero! the Seller of Books, He who shall make my little efforts plausible—above all else: Fatten the Publisher's Purse!;

in short, don't fuss too much, no one cares;

no musical notes, heartbeats, or tickings within: no one hears;

& why persist in antique fashion; forget Grandmama;

do not linger or loiter; no achievement in return, but go brightly forward;

but don't innovate or erudite, he meddles—too risky;

&, depend upon it, my dips into the philosophic essay irritate—far better to make a pudding;

no Ideas! unbecoming of my sex! try Sentiment;

any manner of thoughtful digression would halt the march of my story towards the strand;

no gain in harping on class-divisions, nor upon the social violence of the Empire; its ideologies of right & wrong are tended to by my superiors; & as to the weirdness in the underskirts of our society, why contemplate?

no snakes or lizards, no frogs or flasks, no sorceress;

take care.

Notes

Jane Austen

It was her practice to write in the parlor, on small sheets of paper that could easily be concealed, and to hide the unladylike occupation of her fiction from visitors whenever she heard the creak of the swinging door.

Theophile Gautier

From *Mademoiselle De Maupin,* a novel of 1835. Mademoiselle recounts an amorous adventure in her guise as a man:

> 'Rosette clasped me more and more tightly in her arms, and covered me with her body; —she leaned convulsively upon me and pressed me to her naked panting breast ... Strange ideas passed through my head; had I not dreaded the betrayal of my incognito, I should have given play to Rosette's impassionate bursts ... ; I had not yet had a lover; and these keen attacks, these reiterated caresses, the contact with this beautiful body, and these sweet names lost in kisses, agitated me to the highest degree, although they were those of a woman; —and then the nocturnal visit, the romantic passion, the moonlight, all had a freshness and novel charm for me which made me forget that after all I was not a man.
>
> 'Nevertheless, making a great effort over myself, I told Rosette that she was compromising herself horribly by coming into my room at such an hour ...
>
> 'I said this so gently that Rosette only replied by dropping her cambric mantle and her slippers, and by gliding into my bed like a snake into a bowl of milk ...'

Joseph Sheridan LeFanu

From *Carmilla,* an 1872 novel that tells the story of a languid demon, with a tooth like a needle, who takes passionate embrace of the young and innocent Laura:

> Sometimes after an hour of apathy, my strange and beautiful companion would take my hand and hold it with a fond pressure, renewed again and again; blushing softly, gazing into my face with languid and burning eyes, and breathing so fast that her dress rose and fell with the tumultuous respiration. It was like the ardour of a lover ... and her hot lips travelled along

my cheek in kisses; and she would whisper, almost in sobs, 'You are mine, you *shall* be mine, and you and I are one for ever.' Then she has thrown herself back in her chair, with her small hands over her eyes, leaving me trembling.

Charlotte Brontë

From her diaries, on her days at Roe Head, dated about October 1836:

I'm just going to write because I cannot help it. Wiggins might indeed talk of scriblomania if he were to see me just now, encompassed by the bulls . . . , all wondering why I write with my eyes shut, staring, gaping. Hang their astonishment! . . . Stupidity the atmosphere. School-books the employment. Asses the society.

From her letters:

To Ellen Nussey on May 10, 1836:

If you knew my thoughts; the dreams that absorb me; and the fiery imagination that at times eats me up and makes me feel Society as it is, wretchedly insipid, you would pity and I dare say despise me.

To Ellen Nussey, May 3, 1848, denying a rumor that she is the author of *Jane Eyre:*

All I can say to you about a certain matter is this: the report—if report there be—. . . must have had its origin in some absurd misunderstanding. I have given *no one* a right either to affirm, or to hint, in the most distant manner, that I was "publishing"—(humbug!) Whoever has said it—if any one has, which I doubt—is no friend of mine. Though twenty books were ascribed to me, I should own none. I scout the idea utterly. Whoever, after I have distinctly rejected the charge, urges it upon me, will do an unkind and an ill-bred thing. The most profound obscurity is infinitely preferable to vulgar notoriety; and that notoriety I neither seek nor will have. If then any B-an, or G-an, should presume to bore you on the subject, —to ask you what "novel" Miss Brontë has been "publishing," you can just say, with the distinct firmness of which you are perfect mistress, when you choose, that you are authorized by Miss Brontë to say, that she repels and disowns every accusation of the kind.

To G.H. Lewes, November 1, 1849:

> I wish you did not think me a woman. I wish all reviewers believed "Currer Bell" to be a man; they would be more just to him. You will, I know, keep measuring me, by some standard of what you deem becoming to my sex; where I am not what you consider graceful, you will condemn me ... Come what will, I cannot, when I write, think always of myself and of what is elegant and charming in feminity; it is not on those terms, or with such ideas, I ever took pen in hand: and if it is only on such terms my writing will be tolerated, I shall pass away from the public and trouble it no more. Out of obscurity I came, to obscurity I can easily return.

From her miscellaneous manuscripts:

The following is an excerpt from "A Word to *The Quarterly,*" written in response to Elizabeth Rigby's review of *Jane Eyre* which attacked, on Christian grounds, Brontë's morality (a lack of) and pride (an excess of), and in which the reviewer was inclined to believe that the author of *Jane Eyre* was a man:

> ... you breathe a suspicion that Currer Bell ... has long forfeited the society of your sex ...
>
> You should see . . . him holding skeins of silk or Berlin wool for the young ladies about whom he innocuously philanders, and who, in return, knit him comforters for winter-wear, or work him slippers ... Currer Bell forfeit the society of the better half of the human race? Heaven avert such a calamity! ...
>
> Hoping to meet you one day again—and offering such platonic homage as it becomes an old bachelor to pay
>
> I am yours very devotedly
> Currer Bell
>
> Allow me to add my address: Hay-lane Cottage, Hay, Millcote. Should you ever come down to the North—pray do not forget this modest indication.

From criticism of the day: *Jane Eyre,* described as heathen and coarse, was denounced for its sensuality and passion. From *The Athenaeum:* "The Bells must be warned against their fancy for dwelling upon what is disagreeable." From *The Spectator:* "There is a coarseness of tone throughout the writing of all these Bells ..."

George Eliot

From "Silly Novels by Lady Novelists":

> It is clear that they write in elegant boudoirs, with violet-coloured ink and a ruby pen; that they must be entirely indifferent to publishers' accounts, and inexperienced in every form of poverty except poverty of brains.

John Ruskin

From *Time and Tide,* Ruskin at a school play:

> Presently after this came on the forty thieves, who, as I told you, were girls; and there being no thieving to be presently done, and time hanging heavy on their hands, arms, and legs, the forty thief-girls proceeded to light forty cigars. Whereupon the British public gave them a round of applause.
>
> Whereupon I fell a-thinking; and saw little more of the piece, except as an ugly and disturbing dream.

Margaret O.W. Oliphant

Widowed at the age of 31, with three children, and in debt, she set out to support her household by the pen. Her domestic budget, the necessity "of the boiling of the daily pot," resulted in an immense opus, including three-decker novels, sometimes two or three a year.

From *Autobiography and Letters of Mrs Margaret Oliphant,* edited by Mrs Harry Coghill, published in 1899:

> I pay the penalty in that I shall not leave anything behind me that will live. What does it matter? Nothing at all now—never anything to speak of ... God help us all! What is the good done by any such work as mine, or even better than mine? ... An infinitude of pains and labour, and all to disappear like the stubble and the hay.

> I need scarcely say that there was not much of what one might call a literary life in all this ... Now and then I went to a luncheon-party or an afternoon

gathering, both of which things I detested ... I always disliked paying visits, and felt myself a fish out of water when I was not in my own house ... I need not speak, however, as if I had been a person in much request, which would be giving an entirely false view of myself. I never was so in the least.

Louisa May Alcott

Breadwinner Alcott, under male pseudonym of A.M. Barnard, wrote sensation stories, involving bigamy, gold-digging, transvestitism, hashish smoking, and feminism.

Emily Dickinson

I was the slightest in the House—
I took the smallest Room—
At night, my little Lamp, and Book—
And one Geranium—

... I never spoke—unless addressed—
And then, 'twas brief and low—
I could not bear to live—aloud—
The Racket shamed me so— ...

Edith Wharton

Woke at 6 A.M., wrote from her bed, with an ink-pot balanced on her knee, a dog beneath her elbow, and let her papers fall to the floor, to be gathered by the maid.

Author's note: I am grateful for the Norton Critical Edition of *Jane Eyre,* edited by Richard J. Dunn; *Chloe Plus Olivia, An Anthology of Lesbian Literature from the Seventeenth Century to the Present,* compiled and edited by Lillian Faderman, and for *Passions Between Women, British Lesbian Culture, 1668–1801,* by Emma Donoghue.

geometry problem

Barbara Edelman

I pass the sunset, squared
inside the right, shining side
of a metal truck. Encapsulated,
I have passed to the other side, Heaven
is motion, what babies know,
drooling through whole states.

Blessed am I, when neither
here nor there. What I can't
touch won't hurt me.

And what do these buzzards
in their slow circles know,

these topless isosceles
triangles? I have forgotten
the Pythagorean Theorum.
Their slight V's
are the devil's eyebrows.

Pea brains! Who are you
to know something I don't,
aloft beneath a lost
hypotenuse?

Carry on. Carrion. Ohio
flies by me, a shuffle
of old postcards, and the land
flattens into Indiana where gas
is cheap and you pump first.

At each stop, truckers munching
Snickers get bigger. Six and a half
feet from felt hats
to snakeskin toes, giant
buckles prop up their plaid
stomachs. I want to ride
with them forever.

The low sun thins into winter.
I have a mother at the end
of this road, she's stirring pea soup
as dusk thickens around her house

and my father draws each blind
to close each square of darkness,
crooks a finger through the wooden
ring at the tip of each string,
pulls a blank on his own reflection.

local hope

Jack Heflin

From tangle of water oak, from willows torn free upriver
as far as Felsenthal, from bank waste freed from bean field levees,
from cotton rot, from egrets sipping soggy bottoms, hunting perch,
from cottonmouths tossed like scarves along the elegant arms
of driftwash, from this and from the maternal hush of water
distilled before thunder comes the clumsy swish and thump
of Wal★Mart flipper, extra-large, comes the mumbled
motherfuckers, comes the aftershock sighting ... what's left of him:
thin-shinned splash of a lost olympian gone dunking for God.
He tugs his goggles, no looking back, floating past where he began,
kicking a wake of arrogance and rage, suspiciously thirsty,
a blackout draught he'll take all night to drink, cracker thick,
full of fertilizer and factory scabs, full of mongoloids,
magnolia blooms, rafts his fathers built of tar and poker chips,
shattered pitching wedges, sand-bag second mortgages,
sepia letters, portraits from which no one ever smiles:
All the good men who learned too late they'd never love.
He chokes it down and bottoms up. He forgets his dream,
but in the fiction-blood of current he dreams, he paddles and scrawls,
he lunges to the Baptist deeps, past the piscicultural
and the multi-piscicultural, past whole families fishing for Jesus,
past runaways picking the bones of a carnival, past loggerhead and eel,
past moonshine, roadstand pickled fishfin, past grennel and gar,
backstroking, back, all the way back, birthing himself with each breath
until said host of swollen atavism comes dripping out, pulling its tail,

slug mud lost beyond the shoreline wrecks rusting phosphorescent
in this paramouric slip of river bruised by flood, bream bed, rip-rap
glistening in the mythical dawn. Water picks the chassis clean.
Farther down from lock and dam, there are only parts, rear ends
and shocks, children dozing over buckets of catfish, all you can eat.
The locals laugh but like to rub their little heads for luck.

give the millionaire a drink

Mike Newirth

They come from all over to the town of East Hampton, this celebrated place at the end of the island. Private jets shoot off hourly from Dallas and L.A., the chilled Porsches and Saabs arrive from Montclair and Rye, matron busloads depart the Park Avenue swelter in a huff of opera and facials, and they come packed five to a Camaro from Woodside and Asbury Park. They crowd the same streets gridded by Dutch burghers of centuries past, fill the landscape like Baptists in a church, and with their tanned arms thrown up and their eyes upon their lord they sing of the coin of the realm, of padded pockets, of the alchemical wish: *I can buy this.* I can pull things near to me, I levitate as you descend, I will pile the stuff of cash so high as to keep me forever out of my grave....

Nobody could guess why the internationally known supermodel decided to piss in the bar sink at the Apex Grill. Two A.M., the hour most socially permissible for decadent stunts, barroom crowded with angular bodies and faces gone shiny with cosmopolitans and blue martinis, called for again and again with the same stubby wave. The bartender, blurred bulk in white shirt and French apron, watched idly as the tall woman with the charred gold mop of hair crawled up on top of the bar, nailed hand rubbing the makeup from her face, her smiling mouth the long slot of a cigarette machine. As she stepped to the chrome rails and rucked up her dress, silk scraping silk, there were shrieks and the sound of a man slapping himself to vulgar effect, and the bartender remembered an afternoon decades past, lying in bed with his first girlfriend, she sashaying above him in his boxer shorts, giggling, this as piss of drink sprays from the center of that trained and shaped and photographed body, and the bar sink fills like a cistern.

After, a distinguished anesthesiologist, lean, leathery, hair varnished like a helmet, holds up a credit card. "Buy the lovely lady whatever she wants to drink." Cheers, applause, the bartender straightens up and, moving so slowly through time, reaches for the cassis and champagne.

His date, a twenty-year-old with an unblemished accusing Andover face: "What is your fucking *problem*."

"You need to be more celebratory." His gaze locked to the swaying flushed model, all the swelled faces in the long mirror, cell phone before him on the bar like a gray fish. "I already *told* you what you're here for."

Slow late afternoon: stray cats prowl the village dumpsters. All the good people—those drowning in that hearty moral sea of accumulated wealth—are stretched out at the gleaming beach. A famous comic actor known for his films of family entertainment (homespun wisdom interspersed with hilarious belches and pratfalls), and for his witty endorsements of a fine tortilla chip, walks up and down the main street carrying a large bottle of vodka. His fishing vest and floppy hat add a near-tint of gentility. The actor's eyes resemble cathode-ray tubes. When his cell phone rings, he shifts the bottle and flips it open, and keeps on walking. He speaks with the air that is trapped for years at the bottom of a western mine.

Three teenage girls stand before the window of a crowded shop. Stylish clothes for women, all and entirely in the color of white. Frocks and gowns and underwear, all the same hue of elegance and emptiness, the blankness of a frame, slices of nothing. Beside those white garments, the girls throb in their hiphuggers and tight striped shirts, slurping on pacifiers. Sixteen and already their faces engraved with a Russian century of bored malaise. "There is nothing I wouldn't do to spite my father," one says.

"If only I wasn't *here,*" says another.

Tea is served on the veranda of the American Hotel to a rowdy party of options traders. Oh, they've done all the good drugs, been tapped for entrance at many velvet ropes, they've fucked all the slim blonde women (and then watched, snifters in hand, as all the women melted together in the foamy hot tub on the moonlit deck, every last gawky white boy fantasy fulfilled categorically). But now the intrusion of china cups and pale sandwiches flusters their paid-for vacation hoohrah. Their practiced repose comes apart; up through the mucus of the body's past rise the fumbling second-string ballplayers and zitty homeroom monitors. "This is *bogus,*" Troy says.

"Hey. Waitress. Can't you bring us some *port,* or something?" calls out Ken, twisting for assurance his gold-flashing diver's watch.

"The bar will not be open until six, sir," she replies.

"Bitch," says Trevor, knocking a teacup off the rail.

At the Telephone Mama, the choice nightspot of this season, the one the Jersey tourists and Astoria orthodontists are *simply* better off not even knowing about, the line snakes out into the parking lot: bare thighs of celebrant applicants brushed, bruised, by the slow flow of fancy rolling metal. Who are these people? Shaky background zombies from *Night of the Flesh-Eating Corporate Raiders,* the never-made German salute to the rapacious 1980s? The men fluff their chest hair through the slits of silk shirts, if they have it; the smooth-skinned blondies, those delicate boys with pursed mouths disparaging, they are either blood-leached and serious old money, or else homosexual. Reaching the door, three black kids from Valley Stream are turned away: "We have a dress code," says the enormous doorman. Through the door thumps a vintage Funkadelic side; inside the young women twitch like wraiths on the dance floor, white shawls slipping from their shoulders and breasts. Cursing, the blacks drive off into the night.

In the narrow aisles of the town supermarket: a wealthy man in his fifties argues with his girlfriend, half his age. She is wearing a thong bikini, and her tanned skin is like fine fudge or mink: a thing sheiks might buy by the yard. When he sweeps his arm, his IWC chronometer and gold bracelet tick, clanking: his voice is low, savaging. She flips her ashy hair precisely, cloyingly. "I won't go," she says. "Not unless André goes." At the cash register a townie—belly, navel, nipples distended, jaw shame-slacked, oily hair—hands over a sheaf of food stamps. The proper patrons line up elsewhere, piling their soda crackers and Pellegrino up on the other conveyor, as if something were catching.

That well-known actor loiters in the Rexall, chatting discreetly with the pharmacists. He leaves, buying quantities of cough drops and breath mints. In five years, perforated liver shipping poison to his brain, he'll have taken to passing out candy from his pockets to alarmed children on the streets.

An internationally famous woman, even locally a celebrity of some substance, watches the washed-up wetbrain cross the street from within the armored capsule of her Range Rover. She feels toward him a chundering mix of contempt and fear: he's a has-been, for sure, reduced to kiddy pablum and shilling for snacks, but once he was actually a Hollywood player, the realest kind. She's on top now, the ultimate hostess, a lasery visionary of taste and purchases and decor, with magazines and recipe clubs and catalogs, a carpet-bombing of commerce spread across the hick heartland; but, you know, she doesn't really *do* anything that any Miss Baltimore Homemaker of 1961 could not improve upon. Behind the flat flawless heatproof glass of the vehicle, her smile is pulled into place by hydraulics, exposed teeth carved from a single block of titanium. But beyond it she's shaking as though from a palsy. Recently, one of the dowagers she courted had whispered to her the cruel, glittering news—"for your own good, dear," the withered bitch had said—that her daughter, that hard-cheeked rider of deceit and ponies, was sleeping with the contractor on her Sag Harbor cottage, with whom, truthfully (and known to none other), *she* had last slept not two weeks previous. Unlikely, but it *could* get around. Ten thousand dollars had gone toward quieting the tale of baby ducks (briefly needed for a photo shoot) murdered beneath the wheels of her vehicle. This perfect woman, no one guesses at her days of shudder and terror, what she endures to prop up this exemplary life of buying and placing. *Cross me and die,* this famous hostess thinks, waiting for the light to change.

July glides into August, the frictionless summer everlasting. Everybody is from England or into junk bonds or forcing themselves to vomit or working on a novel or bisexual temporarily. More telephones are stolen out of Range Rovers. Most of the dogs receive grooming. Some of the townies get laid.

It is still 2 A.M. at the Apex Grill. The supermodel lurches in, shaky, bad news. Her miniskirt offers up her sintered ass. Nobody is surprised by this, no one notices. Bound to her shoulders is the soft black leather Prada knapsack that every woman here was required on peril of her soul to purchase for this summer. The Prada bags, shapeless, hang from the backs of the women like elegant hide pupae. But the model has replaced the Prada bag's signature gold-plated zipper ornament with a Tiffany keychain, a miniature infant's bottle in platinum. This particular Prada bag was made in Malaysia, in a factory thrown up in an enormous corrugated shed, hand-stitched by women whose arms bear curing burns and knife scars, women with hair coarse as rope and stalled faces, and some weeks later the model purchased it at the East Hampton Saddlery for $570 because her agent and *Country* magazine had touted it as the summer's prime accessory, and of course, they were right.

"I would like a . . . cosmopolitan," she whispers to the bartender. Her mind has been expertly muted to a soft blue Xanax blur. Beneath it, though, is something real: a throbbing Kodachrome snapshot of the night, five years before, she sucked a photographer, somewhere in the Montauk dunes. Two months later she had a shoot in *Interview,* so it was undoubtedly worth it, she knows, but still . . . The memory's buzz will outlast her looks and career. The bartender sets a cocktail glass before her and spills out her drink. Her fingers flutter like moths on the hard stem of the glass.

The bartender slips farther down his bar, wiping spills with a white dinner napkin. He pauses before a man and two women sagged with drink and exhaustion, but the man waves him away. "We still have our ménage to look forward to," says the black woman with grayed skin and drooping gold jewelry.

"Yes," the man agrees. "If only for its own sake."

"Oh, you think that's the important thing," says the other woman. She looks close to forty, as do they all.

"What I think," he says, "is it is something we are going to do. Any other definition is just somebody being intentionally morbid and obtuse, *Nancy.*"

"Pay up," says the first woman.

"Have another drink," says the man, words leaking out through his puffy face. "Let the impatience build a little."

"Is your head up your ass or what," the bartender says, quietly, to the barback, a pocked, stumbling local boy, who has let the ice tub deplete to meltings. "Fill that up and then go home. Get out of my sight."

He's not really a good person, this bartender.

But this is his life, East Hampton to Aspen and back, selling the best legal drug in America to the rich folk, enabling their little scenes and gaudy reckless purchasing, all that passes for history these days. His secret knowledge tends to weigh him down: that the dollar's what it's all about, and this is just a dance of fancy smoke and notions.

Out in the parking lot, watched only by the stars and valet, that sly pretty Andover girl wanders in slow, dazed circles. The anesthesiologist is long gone, back to Scarsdale. Tonight there was a late supper with a stocky, rapacious bond trader, a manic transplant from Kansas for whom all the dollars made and spent were their own nonstop coitus. They went to Apex, where his waved credit card produced champagne. She listened to his mouth, saying things like, "Damn shit I sure do love this Dom." He followed her into the toilet. "Let's ignite ourselves," holding out the vial of cocaine. Then went right up her *skirt,* $30 panties split down the middle, her forearms bruised where he planted her against the hot air blower. The entrance of three dazed Chanel matrons gave her a chance to run. *"What?"* he said behind her. "Bitch," as she slipped coins into the phone. She cries, wondering only what, specifically, she'd expected—the bastard dropped two hundreds on dinner, to say nothing of the drugs and bar tabs, the cost of it all, she knows at what sum the numbers add up—cries nonetheless, and waits for her taxi to come.

lucky you

Amy Gerstler

This news is so bad it won't stay in your head. Every second you're afraid you'll forget it. You've always been a terrible messenger, a bumbler, a conduit for trouble. After your alarm about forgetting passes, you become afraid you'll laugh while trying to pronounce the words. You worry the same giggles that afflict you during the eulogy at funerals will seize you the minute you moisten your lips to speak. Then a more rigid panic grabs you. You're afraid the person you're telling this grim tale to will also begin to laugh, louder and louder, till his voice completely fills the room, and you can practically see the huge black HA HA HA's scrawled in the air, vibrating like violin strings, just as in cartoons. Eventually the other person will stop laughing and twist your head off.

Delivering awful news is like having to eat a knife, tearing the blade off in bites and chewing it up as if it were only a piece of the thin silver foil chocolate mints come wrapped in. Action slows down to a crawl. It seems you're suddenly underwater. You walked down the hall under your own power and stuck your head into your father's study. But because of what you saw, a current clumsily ushers you back into the kitchen, where your mother's unloading groceries, a can of stewed tomatoes in each hand. Your mouth opens and closes like a sea creature's, but no plankton swim in. She says, "what's wrong?" Then centuries go by: a blur for summerfallwinterspringsummerswintersfalls. Leaves color, shrivel, and plummet to the ground. Branches bud, and the flowers gape and drop off . . . over and over. All in the space of the eight seconds it takes you to answer your mother. This is why it's said tragedy ages you prematurely. It causes the little movie of your life to run through the projector at fast forward till you can get the right words out of your mouth and stop the runaway film. You want to believe you saw wrong. Maybe you only dreamed you poked your head into Dad's study and his slumped body with its head and hands on the messy desk had its back to you. You dreamed you tiptoed up from behind and read the note on the blotter in his well-tailored handwriting. The problem is, you're wide awake as you take the canned tomatoes out of your mother's hands and set them on the counter next to the toaster. Then you pull her down the hall by her sleeve.

baltazar beats his tutor at scrabble

Belle Waring

If Myra counts fifteen cows and Alfredo counts nine,
how many more cows did Myra count?

Baltazar counts on his fingers.
I wish I could stay here 'til morning, he says—cool,

matter-of-fact. Thirteen, sixth grade. All this week
he's been late. Lip swollen and split. *I have nightmares,* he says,

Like falling. Pours out a Scrabble shower of blonde wood Chiclets.
Crow-black hair, square competent hands. Two grades behind.

Ten points for a Z, Baltazar. I spell PASS.
He spells ZAP on the Triple Word Score, has to multiply by three.

—*You tell your mom you can't sleep?*
—*She lets me lie on the sofa and watch TV.*

I spell ZOUNDS—God's wounds, a Shakespearean oath:
Zounds, I was never so bethumpt with words.

Baltazar doesn't forget where he's from, how beautiful it is
and how fraught. In a flurry of Spanish he spells

MUCHACHO then GRITO then spells I GET UP AT FIVE TO HAUL THE WASH
DOWN TO 14TH AND V, HAVE IT HOME FOLDED BEFORE DAD WAKES UP

'CAUSE MOM IS ALREADY GONE TO WORK.
I spell DID HE BUST YOUR LIP

The odder the letter, the higher the score.
He spells I WANT TO STAY HERE 'TIL NIGHT PUTS ITS HANDS IN THE AIR

Blanks spell what you like—you rub them like luck,
the polished wood suave as a horse's neck.

Blanks goof around—propped in your eye sockets, you squint
like smiling against the sun on the skirts of the mountains,

on your grandmother's face, calm, waking you up.
On the words she would sing, and the music not separate from them.

the latin ice kings

Peter La Salle

I

HELL, I DON'T KNOW EXACTLY WHAT IT WAS. Because sometimes the drugs (more on that later) and the mess with sweet Cressida (I wish there was more on that) don't seem to matter as much.

And for me up there under the cloverleaf in the heat of this Texas city at dusk the other night, playing roller-hockey with those crazy Mexican boys, I seemed to be lighter than oxygen, floating in the golden air and the aroma of diesel exhaust from the semis banging above—and nobody, but nobody, could touch me. (Professor Norman at the university would like that "lighter than oxygen" stuff, the "golden air" too—he said I could write, I had talent.) Big Enrique lobbed me a pass of the special orange ball that you do have for roller hockey, the Day-Glo orange thing that bounces about as much as a beanbag, what makes it like a puck, and it was as if I was sure of, maybe even reborn with the sudden knowledge of, the fact nobody could touch me. I have these shitty no-name in-lines I bought at the Target Store. And though the rest of the guys all have top-of-the-line K-2's or Boxcars with competition wheels, what they probably had to steal and then pawn a fresh load of mountain bikes to pay for, it was as if I, on my shitty thirty-five-buck Target Store specials with the scuffed black plastic pods of them and the goofy rainbow-braid laces, I could cut and spin the way players used to really cut and spin, like in the old films I've seen of Gordie Howe and Bobby Orr. I was for a minute just the *idea* of hockey, and when you were the idea of something, nothing as stupidly substantial as the grimed asphalt meant anything, or those semis racing to Houston or Dallas or *anywhere* else that suddenly didn't mean anything either. The rest of them lunging to poke-check that little puff of Day-Glo orange away from me didn't have a chance, while I continued to wheel and cut, even do this crazy thing I had once seen a kid do on pond ice back when I was growing up in Massachusetts—a sort of drop pass to yourself where you tuck the puck between your legs then fake turning your head this way and that, looking around like everybody else to see who has it, until you leave the confused rest of them still gawking around too, and faster than fast you just turn to pick the thing up on your own blade and pump off with it.

I scored with a little flip backhander that hit the back of the net like a strong fist trying to poke through it. I felt that same something, that lightness, a couple of more times that evening, but I knew I better not indulge in more hotdogging; these guys are proud Mexicans, after all, and I'm a pasty-faced Anglo who talks with a funny Northern accent. So, for me to get carried away with such a show of my special moves might be taken the wrong way, might challenge their manliness. And maybe it's part of my own wimpdom in thinking that these guys are obsessed with manliness, but wasn't it true that when we were just sitting around on the plastic milkcrates that pass for our benches afterward, when the first stars were starting to brighten and then brighten some more in the Texas sky that really can turn purple, manliness was the issue then. They alternated chugging on quart bottles of Gatorade and Budweiser, passing them around, and they complimented me on that dizzying charge.

"How do you feel, amigo, strong?" Grinning Danny said that. He's a little guy, and when he said the word "strong," he accompanied it with the mandatory clenched fist and pumped wrist salute, hard.

"Strong," Angel echoed him.

"Strong," Roberto did the same.

It is an important word for them, and I knew some of them had seen me with sweet Cressida a couple of times.

II

I'm looking at what I've written so far, and I see all those parentheses in the first couple of paragraphs. I gave too much information too fast there, and if this were a story for Professor Norman, most of that would get X-ed out. But the more I look at that information, the more I know it has to be worked in some way, and possibly I could reduce it to a triangle:

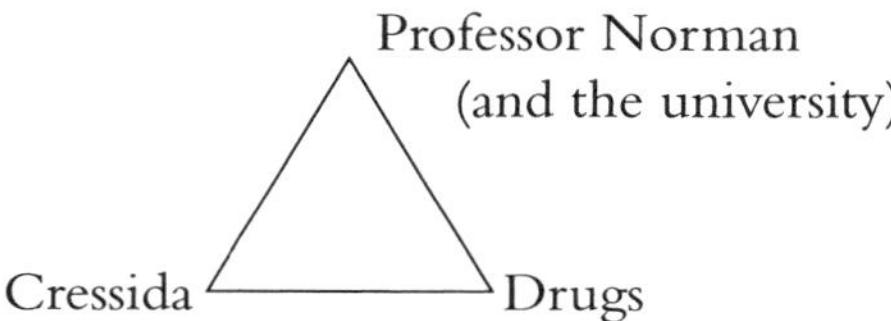

But that wouldn't work. Because in a way the drugs are behind me, I hope, but I do think about crack cocaine a lot, not to mention the good heroin I enjoyed more than a few times. And I suspect my career at the university will be well behind me after my attempt at exams later this spring. Cressida at least stops by to, as she says, check up on me, and if it were a triangle Cressida would have to be at the apex, or maybe it isn't a triangle.

It's a square:

It's a circle:

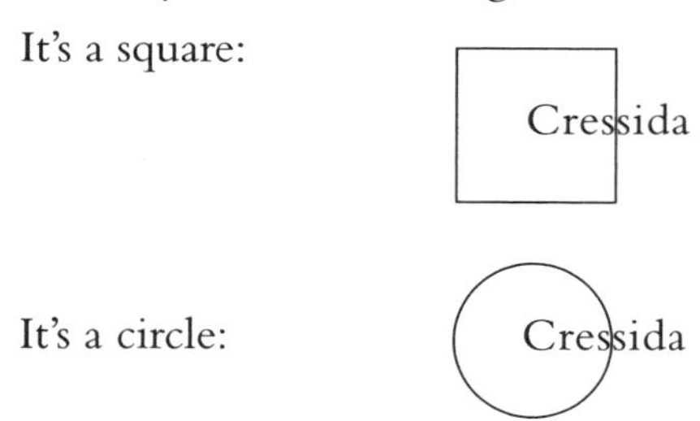

It's one of those weird amoeba shapes:

III

"Well, what do you think?" Cressida asks me.

"I think what I always think," I tell her. "You're beautiful. It wouldn't make any difference if somebody dressed you in a big dishcloth, you would still be the knockout you are."

"That isn't what I asked you," she says.

"Though that would be cool, now that I think of it, to see you in a big dishcloth, but like one of those classic dishcloths. You know, just white, with the red stripes at the ends or something."

"Shut up, Rickie," she says.

Cressida is at my apartment, or what passes for a studio apartment in the budget co-op not far from campus. She has stopped again, yes, to check up on me, and just the way she asks me to comment on her new outfit probably announces as loud as anything else what our relationship has ended up as, almost a brother-sister deal at this stage. Cressida is on her way to an evening lecture by the usual kind of famous historian who is often on campus to spiel an evening lecture, and you *would* have to see her to believe her. Honestly. Cressida is slim and tall. She has the kind of posture that makes her mile-long legs look as if they're a couple of steps ahead of the rest of her, like she's trying to hold her ground as an imaginary feisty pooch on a stretched leash tugs her along, whenever she strides across campus. Her honey hair is set in a pageboy bob and her gray eyes are giant, her lips full the way that French girls' lips are full, though Cressida is anything but French, a Dallas Southern Methodist, actually. I think the only reason I got anywhere with her to begin with was because (she confessed this) she thought that my Massachusetts accent was cute, plus I was brighter than most of those sorority and fraternity idiots who ended up in the sophomore lit class where we met—for once in my life, in that particular company, I was an intellectual. We dated for two years before it all fell apart (before I fell apart?), and looking at her now I wonder again how I could have been so stupid as to outrightly lose her like that.

Because Cressida is now twisting her neck to stare over her shoulder and check the line of her slacks in back, looking in the tarnished mirror over the painted dresser fringed with cigarette burns here among the general debris of my attempt at living quarters. It is not as if Cressida is affected in her cultivation of the 60's look (that pageboy bob, and some aqua eyeshadow, and even white lipstick tonight because she is going out with a bunch of other history majors afterward), it is not so much affectation as it is more so how the whole message of that so-called other era simply seems right for her, including the new pedal-pusher slacks, a powder blue, and the sleeveless summer blouse, a pale pink—like I told her, the outfit has Jackie Bouvier written all over it. Actually, Cressida did a paper analyzing this book about the 60's called *The Best and the Brightest* by David Halberstam, and her grad student T.A., her section leader for the course, said the paper was good enough to be published—which I believe, while I suspect too that the guy is trying to hit on her. Cressida wants to get a Ph.D. in history at some place good like Rice or Berkeley. I forgot to mention that Cressida is smart, not just lucky like me in how it's easy to put words together sometimes so I do well in the creative writing classes, but smart-smart, the kind of intelligence that can get her a Ph.D.

When she leaves, she comes over to the unmade bed, where I sit on the edge, and she pecks a kiss on my forehead. She mouths a put-on movie star's pout and coos in a phony Italian accent, "Ciao, darling, as they say in the Purina dog food ads." Cressida can be really funny too.

And at least this time she didn't give me a lecture. I think that for her it's a triumph alone to find me without a crack pipe in my mitts. And there came none of her gently questioning me again concerning whether the best way to be trying to academically salvage the semester was to be spending every evening—evenings I should be in the library—playing roller hockey with "a bunch of East Side guys." Not that Cressida has anything against such East Side guys ("Are they really gang members?" she once asked me), but, she knows, the library and some serious cramming, plus more classes attended, that's the salvage job I could use at the moment.

As if I have any real idea what I need at the moment. And, to be frank, I got more than sad after what was supposed to be this blast of an outing with Big Enrique and Danny and Angel and Roberto and Birdy and the rest of them, a trip to the County Rodeo and Exposition Center, where what passes for the new very minor league professional ice hockey team plays here in the city where the university is.

This was right after the night I felt so good, so perfectly balanced on the asphalt. I hadn't previously spent any time with the Mexican boys except for the hockey, and how that all started was more chance than anything too. You see, having played a lot of ice hockey as a kid and having been a starter for my supposed country day school (believe me, that league of teams from other supposed country day schools wasn't much), I took to the in-lines immediately, and except for learning some new starts and stops, adjusting to the biting wheels not having the easy skid of a blade, the motion of pumping from the hip is just about the same. I used to take a stick and dribble a tennis ball around on my own, keeping to the red border on the outside of the dozen green tennis courts in a park nearby so I wouldn't get in the tennis players' way, letting loose with a few hard slappers against the chain-link there. Which is where they spotted me, eventually Big Enrique being the one who got up the nerve and loped over to ask me if I wanted to play in their evening pickup games under that freeway overpass. I don't know, maybe I have been losing myself, avoiding everything else, in banging around with them every other night, but at least I don't have all that nowhere time to get me started again dreaming about the chilly warmth of crack (yeah, it is a chilly warmth), the nowhere time sometimes looming as the giant monster and bona fide danger for me. (Would Professor Norman ever rake me over the briquets for that one, stuff like "giant monster" and "bona fide danger," and in class he kept insisting that you be true to your own voice. But what if you have a dozen voices? Or what if you sometimes hear yourself talking, like looking at yourself in the mirror, and say, honestly wondering, "Who the fuck is *that?*") Anyway, I got the call from Big Enrique, who never called me about anything, except if there was a problem and they wouldn't be playing again that night.

"You've seen them, man?" he said on the phone.

"I went a half-dozen times," I said, "you know, when everybody was going to those games, when they first came to town."

He was inviting me to go with the rest of them out to the Ice Lizards game at that County Rodeo and Exposition Center. I think he was disappointed that I didn't sound more excited, that, as I told him, I had seen them play. It's a good thing I didn't go on with him about how the level of competition in the mongrel Southwestern Professional (that's a laugh) League wasn't much better than that for second-rate Eastern college hockey, not exactly what would excite somebody like me raised in my cozy Boston suburb (think Thoreau, Emerson), where it's easy enough to go see the Bruins in their famous black-and-yellow uniforms play or to watch them as served up almost every night on Channel 38, making an honest run for that beautifully dented old Stanley Cup most years.

"We've got a ticket for you, man," Big Enrique said.

"Really?" I said. "No, I mean, I'd love to see them again."

If nothing else, the team from Beaumont, the Oil Barons, had a line of recently imported young Czechs who obviously weren't destined for much time out here in prickly-pear land before they moved up in the minors. I savored their sweet precision passing, something all the Europeans are good at. As for my own pals, the Mexican boys, they took turns going down below the rumbling aluminum bleachers in the place smelling half of the fine refrigeration aroma I loved so and half of the manure-hay fragrance that attested to the building's principal use, going down there and returning with trays full of wobbling cardboard cups of overpriced Shiner Bock draft, the only beer offered and what they all heartily agreed was "donkey piss" compared to their beloved Budweiser. They hooted and cheered in ranchero whelps, never tiring of calling the efficient line of down-faced Czechs "Maricóns!" through cupped palms. Danny, his smile so white like a bunch of broken seashells, was particularly enamored with the goalies in their masks enameled bright, like the finish on a customized low-rider—a big-fanged dinosauric lizard design on the mask of the hometown netminder and one of a spouting petroleum well for the mask of the Oil Barons' goalie. Danny stared and stared at them—first one for a while and then the other—as if they were somehow special and by birth different than the rest, a thoroughbred breed. He called them "Mascareros," and he somehow, I guess, was giving to them the same mythical aura attached in Mexico to the masked wrestlers who seemed to be on TV there 99 percent of the time, for their matches *and* for about all of the full-length feature films too, where they played the serious dramatic leading roles in, yeah, masks. And the whole thing would have been a good night indeed, if I didn't get scared as hell after the final siren sounded (Oil Barons 12, Ice Lizards 2), and the guys wanted to hang around for a while, while everybody else was tramping out of the place.

I got that kind of electric anxiety that I used to get when it was 11 or 12 o'clock, when I thought that I might not be able to score another rock to smoke that night. Because before I knew it, they were down at the Plexiglas, waiting for their best chance to jump onto the ice themselves in their baggy jeans and backward rap caps, and it seemed at that very moment I spotted the oafish red-faced bubba of a city cop—holster the size of a valise, his polished nightstick obscenely dangling—who was watching their every move, probably just waiting for "those little fucking wiseass wetbacks" to do just that, so he could bully them around in the grand tradition of the only thing cops are really world class at—bullying. When the guys finally did step onto the ghostly gray-whiteness at the center red line, started sliding around some and pushing each other in their happy horsing, I thought it was all over—until I noticed that somehow the cop was gone and he must have been called away to bully like the blockhead he was somewhere else. They might have been not much younger than me, but out there they were ten-year-olds, goofing and shoving each other some more—Birdy soon landed flat on his ass. The entire ride back they talked about "ice" and how smooth it was, how it was "really strange, but really nice, man." Jammed in the backseat of the primer-painted Chevy coupe that belonged to Angel's older brother, I think, I got sad, or heartbreakingly sad, like I said.

That lead-cloud sadness, just to listen to how they kept making a major deal out of something as everyday and lousy as ice at a rink.

I still can't remember if it was then or when we played again up at the overpass that they first mentioned that some black guys from a gang called the Gland Boys over there on the East Side might at last be willing to play them in a match to see who really ruled the roller-hockey pavement, or whatever.

And, of course, they wanted me to be a member of their team for that surely momentous event.

IV

Do you want to hear a couple of Amazing Stories?

One Amazing Story is that the woman who is so big on TV now called Martha Stewart is not Martha Stewart at all. No kidding, she's really my mother, and I was once just flipping around the crummy little TV set that somehow hasn't fallen prey to being sold to the creepy albino guy who runs the E-Z Pawn, and I saw this woman showing somebody how to make your own cookie cutters out of pieces of linoleum, then how to make a festive autumn bouquet with dried leaves and dime-store nut ornaments that were "readily available and adorable," I looked at the woman arranging things on a long table, her casual clothes surely without a speck of lint on them and her gray-blonde hair with a set that wouldn't move in a forty-mile-an-hour wind off the coast of Nantucket, and I just said aloud to nobody here in my apartment: "Hey, lady, what the hell do you think you're doing! How did you ever get a TV show like this, get to rake in all this money, when it's obvious that your whole act is a rip-off of what my own mother has been doing for years! I've got a good mind to hire a lawyer, to sue, and haven't you ever in that makeup-encased noggin of yours ever heard of plagiarism, or violation of the copyright law, or something!" Because, believe me, my mother has been living that Martha Stewart life, quietly lost in her Burpee's seed catalogs and her perpetual "homemaking," always completely, well, dedicated to raising my sisters and me "full-time" rather than ever taking a job after college, my mother has been doing that, even looking *exactly* like that Martha Stewart, before Martha Stewart ever thought of any of it. So, either, to repeat, my mother has what they call a doppelgänger or that Martha Stewart is an outright thief. Something is really very fishy there. And my father? How about another Amazing Story.

My father (like all the males on his side of the family, he first went to their beloved Williams College, then, naturally, Harvard Law), my father to this day still does this special thing every morning. You have to understand that our house is a sprawling enterprise that a real estate agent would label neo-colonial, I guess, what you would expect in such a woodsy, and almost famous, suburb, and there are three full bathrooms in it. But you have to understand too that with three sisters and then the rest of us, there was always a logjam (I know, Professor Norman, a real cliché if ever there was one) when it came time to get ready for work and school in the morning. None of which had any effect on my always mild-mannered, truly gentlemanly father, tall and slim, with his lie-down haircut leftover from the time when all guys up at Williams College in those purple mountains must have had lie-down haircuts, and maybe some others sported shiny gold belt buckles as well. Because, be it a workday in a neat glen-plaid or pinstripe suit for him, or the weekend in corduroys and a soft turtleneck, the buckle was a major part of the reason why my father logged a ton of time in the bathroom, the one adjoining my parents bedroom specifically. There was, of course, time on his lengthy shower, then time on his careful shaving with a new yellow-handled Bic sensitive-skin razor, then time on his meticulous brushing and flossing of his teeth, then time on his putting on the fresh clothes brought in there and surely still smelling like the Men's Department (maybe Brooks Brothers, or the little overcharging haberdashery place in our town), then time on his combing of his hair so that probably by mid-morning you could still see the comb marks, then time, *above all,* time on his polishing the belt buckle. It was a single slab, a dressy specialty-store thing that the tongue of the belt was slid through and that he *always* wore *everywhere,* while, understandably, the leather belts themselves varied, being changed or replaced, over the years. It had been the buckle of his father before him, and it bore in the central square on the face, surrounded by straight-edged lines in a sort of 1920's art deco pattern, the engraved initials of his father: RBL. They were also his initials and my initials. You see, it wasn't that my father was anything near vain, and, as I said, he is quiet and almost shy, custom-made for the kind of understated corporation law he does, I guess. But the morning in the bathroom for him had its ritual, and as a little kid I always took pride in seeing him finally emerge, the whole of him newly minted and that belt buckle near glowing its honey brightness. Later on, when we found out that our father was having an affair with Mrs. Thayer, the rather dumpy-looking divorced mom of kids we knew in our neighborhood, one of my sisters, Emily, the oldest, insisted on a Kids' Pow Wow. It was something she used to organize when we were planning to chip in on a Christmas present for our parents, let's say. But now it had an uneasy, serious tone, because while we kids sat there and discussed our father's behavior among ourselves, we had to admit that the worst thing about it was how none of it really affected our mother (the real Martha Stewart) who just kept working and working and working away on some new homemade Christmas wreaths, started in August, or something. My sisters were devastated, and I, as usual, soon proved to be the wild card in the group. I said that as bad as the situation was, we should be grateful that our father saw something to like in dumpy Mrs. Thayer, who always looked and acted so defeated, and it wasn't as if he was like Neddy Cummington's father. (Neddy's dad took off with a New England Patriots' cheerleader, then there came the wackier than wacky details of her eventually losing the cheerleading job because she had posed for certain photographs in—get this—not in *Playboy* but in *Easy Riders*.) But my sisters really didn't want to listen to me, and Margaret and Anne, the twins, now sang a duet about how they always would get so *mad* with our father for hogging a whole bathroom for so long in the morning, yet I suspect they were only searching for an issue to generate anger toward the otherwise kind and entirely considerate man. I soon found myself defending him on the bathroom business, saying that I didn't know quite how to put it, but that one of the most important moments in my life, what I could almost believe in, was how beautifully shining that belt buckle looked whenever our father *finally* stepped out of that bathroom, fresh from his soap and aftershave—the pure gold of that buckle, which for me had always been just about the truest and most beautiful and most significant entity in possibly the whole giant blue-and-green globe, to put it mildly. That in turn brought rare consensus from them at the meeting—my sisters all told each other that I was, and always had been, weird.

Of course, my sisters have always been better students than me. My going to the university in Texas rather than to the "right kind" of Eastern school was the best salvage job the chirpy college counselor at the country day school could manage, considering my hopeless grades but good SAT scores. For a state university the place sounded good, maybe not the ritzy University of Virginia, but definitely not the everyday University of Massachusetts, which would have been considered an outright disaster, the big *Titanic* going down fast or a rumbling earthquake wiping out an entire town in the Andes, as far as people at my particular school were concerned. Being a Yankee, I right away fell in with a set of guys in black T-shirts and black jeans at the university, the New York City contingent, and they thought crack was so cool, using it as a valid statement saying that you were light years beyond the squareness of the sorority and fraternity lobotomy victims who seemed to rule the campus. So I dabbled.

But, unlike them, I *kept* dabbling. Until I finally bottomed out with a little heroin for six months (OK, more than a little), then did the rehab program. Which worked on one level, I suppose, but which isn't rehabbing my grades. Which isn't rehabbing how much I goddamn love Cressida either.

V

Listen to today's news.

In today's news the automobile strike spreads and several major American cities announce significantly lower deaths from AIDS. There was a terrible fire at Disney World in Orlando, Florida. Also in today's news, I made a major effort to function normally and attend classes in the English department building.

There I somehow managed to stay awake through this self-satisfied younger assistant professor pleasing nobody but himself as he stood behind the desk going through various scholarly poses—he surely considered himself *very* cool with the tweed sport jacket with, believe it or not, the requisite fake suede elbow patches. He kept pretending to be talking about Milton. I just sat there and kept thinking how lanky, vaguely broken-down Professor Norman in his old sweaters and no-name jeans and utterly no-name sneakers, his mane of gray hair probably once a Keith Richard shag, told me in his office one day that he himself knew that most of the department's literature teachers were idiots who really didn't know anything important about life, though they spent their own lives studying Milton or Shakespeare or Faulkner, who knew *all* the most important things about life. He admitted too that he could be the biggest idiot of the lot for hanging around the university as long as he had, but he had to think it was a better way to support himself than the newspaper work he did when younger, which almost killed him because it stole so much of his time. And the university job allowed him that time to write his short stories and novels, plus he always kept foremost in his mind that the students were "holy" (that was his word), and focusing on them and their holiness one could easily forget about the cretins who loudly talked only of themselves, the professors, incessantly referring to each other as (Professor Norman really hated this word) "colleagues." I was just thinking that, when I sleep-walked out of the classroom and onto the green hallway linoleum after the buzzing bell—and ran smack into Professor Norman, coming out of the classroom where he had been teaching. I hadn't seen him for a while, or since I had taken his fiction-writing workshop last term. He seemed happy to see me, but he wanted to know, concerned, why I hadn't turned in anything to the main office for the annual creative writing contest—certainly the main office had sent me a copy of his letter nominating me, with the instructions on how to submit.

"Come on, Rickie," he said with that easy smile of his. "We might not be talking about Art with the old capital 'A,' but I say that if you hand in something you can win the thing palms down."

I lied outright that I never got the letter. Then I pivoted and bolted through the between-classes crowd to head to the men's room, to hide.[1]

And also in today's news, or tonight's news, Cressida stopped by my apartment again. She said she had been there the last three nights looking for me. She suspected I was off goofing around, playing roller hockey again. She was wearing a black miniskirt and a black sweater, study clothes, her bob haircut not set that morning and looking pretty ratty, like a kid's hair would look after time at the playground—nice.

"What the heck is the deal, Rickie? What have you done now, joined the gang yourself? What are they, the Latin Ice Kings or something?"

"Don't say that," I told her, "and don't make fun of them."

It was the usual stage blocking, me on the bed's sagging edge, Cressida pacing around the room while she talked. She apologized for making fun of them, didn't mean to have it sound like that. But she

1. I know Professor Norman would see this as gimmicky, using footnotes, but here goes, because I never will get to use them anywhere else, like on any of my end-of-the-semester papers, which I know I will blow off. In this footnote I can say aloud that in that men's room I cried and cried. I can say it, knowing I'm safe, because nobody *ever* reads footnotes. Right?

told me that she had to say that she didn't think it was a particularly bright idea to be doing what I had lately been doing: giving them my credit card so they could rent a yellow Ryder van now and then, when I once told her that I knew fully well that they worked a little ring of stealing bicycles around the city, then selling them down in San Antonio. She said that my doing that was, plain and simple, dumb, and I tried to explain to her again (I had already told her about their infatuation with ice), reiterate how I saw that redneck cop hungrily waiting to bust them as they were about to step onto the ice at the arena that night, how I spotted dignified, proud Big Enrique himself look up and notice the cop too, now that I remembered it, and how it crunched what I suspect is my heart to see him suddenly no more than a dog, cowering and scared. I told her that after that I knew I would do *anything* for those guys, and otherwise, I really didn't care. They were *real* right now, at a time for me when nothing was seeming *real* anymore.

"I'm real, Rickie," she said. "I'm real, and it's important to me that you come with me to this reception tomorrow night. Just put on a blazer, make an effort, because I wouldn't have been looking all over for you, here and who knows where else, for the last three nights if it wasn't important to me. Please, Rickie."

"I told you, not tomorrow night. These guys have been planning this thing for weeks. Enrique said this will be their chance to show these Gland Boys who they are, once and for all, and they need me to do it."

"Gland Boys? Ricky, will you listen to yourself?"

It went on like that. With Cressida crying some. I should say that Cressida owned her own sadnesses, and though she was the outstanding student—always, back in her Dallas suburb and now here at the university—her hardworking mother had raised her, an only child, on her own and, to complicate matters, her mother had recently had a brush with breast cancer. And it didn't help when Cressida bucked her mother for a while, after her mother had learned of my drugging and Cressida continued to date me, her mother not at all impressed that I eventually did graduate from the endless checker games and the endless folding-chair rap sessions of the rehab program. (I suppose her mother thought differently at first. When I would show up for a weekend in Dallas wearing the aforementioned blazer and pressed chinos too, apparently her mother considered me *such* a "preppy catch," my Boston accent darling.) Now Cressida flatly told me that the reception, an affair for selected students at the Dean's own home, wasn't merely a reception—and it could be the start of our new life together, from now on and for always, and, besides, she tried to joke, she didn't want to resort to doing the thing that the coed having an argument with her boyfriend always does in the movies: turn to the nerdy graduate teaching assistant, in this case the guy who said her paper should be published, and go to the reception with him. But neither of us laughed. If truth be known, Cressida of the giant eyes and her beautiful, beautiful honey hair, every which way right now, just sat down on the bed's edge beside me, hunched her shoulders, and cried some more.

"I love you so much, Rickie," she said, "I can't help it."

"I told you," I said, "not tomorrow night." I had to be strong.[2]

VI

That night I scored a supply of jumbo rocks from my old dealer over at the dorm on top of the mall beside the campus, a strange dorm, I suppose, sitting on top of a McDonald's and Cinema Fourplex like that. I smoked away most of the night, must have slept a bit and juggled a few unraveling reels of the usual nightmares, then stumbled over to the highrise dorm in the very weird dawning daylight of scorching heat and birds singing too loud, to score a couple of more rocks.

2. I waited until she left and, man, did I ever bawl like a baby myself.

VII

A dozen hours later, I was up at that spot of smooth asphalt. I was under the cloverleaf again, half-amazed that these Gland Boys had even agreed to meet us on what amounted to our home rink and half-amazed that I could feel any better on those Target Store specials than I did that one particular night when I seemed to be rolling on veritable air. But I *did* feel better—a hell of a load better. Who cared if it was drizzling now, or if these Gland Boys were not just serious but damned good to boot. Big Enrique, square-jawed and his brow low, could hold his own out there on defense. It was probably a matter of his overweight noseguard's bulk, and he had this way of simply grimacing and digging in with his wheels as if they were horseshoe stakes whenever one of their speedsters returned on another charge, jutting out the bulk of his rump in the baggy jeans with the thick chrome chain looping from belt to wallet in the back pocket, and knocking the legs clean out from under the guy. But somebody like little, usually smiling (not now) Danny couldn't keep up, was proving close to useless. There were no set goalies in that kind of play, and it was an unstated etiquette that whoever was lingering behind the action would assume the guarding of the nets. Still, after they scored twice on us, quickly, I made it my business to do whatever I could on another one of our sloppy attacks *then* immediately reverse direction, to try to hustle back and at least make a show out of tucking myself tight against the red pipe of one of those flimsy Toys-R-Us cages that we always lugged out there for our own play. (Which might have been a sign early on that we were in trouble, and when the game-pussed black Gland Boys first saw the nets, they apparently didn't know whether to chew us out for using such things or just belly-laugh outright at our naïveté, anticipating the fun to come, for providing the, yeah, toys—good indication that we weren't anywhere near being in their league.) Angel and Roberto took turns yelling at

Danny for "dogging it," and Danny by this point was wheezing like a dumpster violin, as the Gland Boys scored a third time. The sticks knocked in exaggerated echoes in what was sort of a huge concrete box there under the freeway, and though the semis still ground above, still poured out their black soot, they didn't sound half as loud as the hiss of skate wheels that could have been played through ten-foot stage speakers at a rock show. I could swear I could soon smell the very, very best bearings (ABEC 3's, definitely) on everybody else's skates melting down, but, needless to add, I had been high for close to a day, sleep-starved, and my senses like that made for a different brand of perception altogether. Or, put it like this, as I *cleanly* braked on the asphalt, I first thought that it too was only another imagining in my hollowed-out skull trying to *suggest* that action.

We hadn't come close to scoring. To make matters worse, so confident had my Mexican guys been, so believing in the basic truth that after hours and hours of playing hard among themselves in the bruised plum-and-mustard-yellow twilights for months and months, they were invincible. And why not have a crew of girls from their territory over on Chicon Street, by the graffiti-splattered beige-brick housing projects, come to witness their moment of triumph? So, there in rap caps too, those rosary-bead necklaces that I hadn't seen for a while, a half-dozen of them were sitting around on the low concrete road dividers that a public works crew must have recently dropped off for storage. The girls were, from the looks of it, not much out of junior high, even if Big Enrique, the oldest of the guys, was about my age. Sure, they were squealing at first, but now they lost interest in the game, jabbering more in Spanish than in English, comparing problems with their fingernail polish and such, I guess. Until it *all* happened.

No, I wasn't imagining it. Wired, crazed, deep-fried, or whatever wacky adjective you want to use, what I suddenly knew, for certain, was that my line of wheels on each blade was skidding when I turned the two of them perpendicular to my direction of momentum for a blade-style, hockey-skate stop. It has been the age-old problem with in-lines since their invention, reportedly by a couple of hockey-nut brothers up in Minnesota who first rigged up wheels to their ancient leather CCM's so they could log some pseudo puck action when even that oversize iceberg of Minneapolis went emerald for the few months every year—to stop you have to use any number of awkward rubber-heel stoppers that nobody has ever perfected, emergency-brake stuff at best. A good steel blade on a hockey skate does provide that cross skid, what sends the surf of ice shavings up like rhinestones tossed to the air in the publicity shots of the NHL stars screeching to a fast stop for the camera. And recently, high-tech experiments ventured as far as coming up with mysterious compounds for the substance of the wheels, developed with the kind of research money usually reserved only for pharmaceutical and defense companies. Without any measurable success. No success either in another attempt by a company out on the West Coast to feather the wheels, slicing them along the outer edge in a shallow fringe, to allow give rather than bite. But here I was, twisting my hips to a full ice-hockey stop and feeling the beloved skid, the little goldmine of give, which instantly rendered me outright better than everybody else, on shitty Target Store specials too. It must have been the drizzle, the asphalt itself slick and a little oil-iridescent, in the bleak dampness that is rare for this city, an announced Sunbelt success story, and never mind sensing myself in synch the way I had done that one night earlier when the guys had asked me afterward if I felt "strong," I had this particular night perpetrated a major breakthrough in the whole fucking history of the sport. And probably the rest of them, from the swift Gland Boys to now-stumbling Danny, could have cashed in on it. But only I had it, because only I knew. Only I could accelerate rocket-fast to also realize I could stop on half-a-dime, only I was suddenly the True Emperor of Maneuverability (was there some poem I read like that, Professor Norman? The title? Eliot? Stevens? One of those guys with a ton of magic in their lines, because magic in poetry or anything else makes all the difference), only I had the Secret.

My last vaguely rational thought went something along the lines of: "Man, is this ever going to be fu-un."

VIII

If I had a measure of the extra the other night, already documented, I had it a thousandfold this night. I seemed to always have the Day-Glo orange ball on the black-plastic blade of my equally cheesy Target Store stick now. Granted that some of the Gland Boys could skate, they were nothing compared to a guy who had been on the ice in Massachusetts since he had been three, maybe two, and if the ball wasn't there on my stick, it wasn't because it was being deftly lobbed, tucked, or rifled into the goal by me, the Acknowledged Holder of the Secret. The girls were watching now, they were alive in yelps and jumps, little baby-pat clapping of their hands, genuine cheerleaders. The harder the Gland Boys labored to double- and triple-team me, the more fun I had in leaving them in my wake, putting us in the lead before long. I scored again, I held my stick raised like the enormous spear of an Apache warrior, and with the other arm I clenched my fist, bent it at the elbow, and thrust it repeatedly into the air for the old power salute, ramming.

"I feel strong!" I yelled to my teammates.

The girls shrieked, giggled energetically, and I shouted over to them, "I feel strong, *mis chicas lindas,* I feel strong!"

It got crazier.

I think Danny tried to warn me. "Be careful, Rickie," because he probably sensed my boys weren't as pleased with me as they should have been. I scored again, more of the "I feel strong!" shouting, principally for the benefit of the girls. Once I didn't even wait for Birdy to pass it to me, and I galloped over to him and poked the ball away, before letting myself loose on another rush, and score, after which I not only announced my obvious strength to the girls, but grabbed the crotch of my cutoffs a couple of times to neatly make my point. That rendered the girls near helpless in their wild yelping. After that, the whole package gets blurred, as the man, whoever he is, says.

I do know that Big Enrique was the first to roll up to me and slap me hard on the side of my head, his big brown hand pancaking my ear. I don't know if it was him or one of the others who growled "Stupid pachuco!" to me, because somewhere between the electric jolt of Enrique's first blow (two-hundred-and-twenty pure volts clean through me, rendering my knee cartilage soup) then that shout, I fell to the asphalt and the whole crowd of my teammates were on me in a heap, socking me hard and kicking me hard, a couple of the Gland Boys joining in too. Each kick of a solid skate toe to the peach basket of my ribs, each detonating punch to my face, with each I seemed to float farther and farther away. My breath gone, I gulped for oxygen in the deadened air, and—I'm sure of this—I tried to picture the triangle I mentioned earlier, maybe the amoeba, and how some geometry like that might be the solution.

IX

And then I saw the brightest of gold, the vision of my father's polished belt buckle, glowing, shining, emanating its utter purity, something to *really* believe in and something to assure me (before the heavy purple velvet theater curtain dropped for the formal blacking out) that I might have a chance of growing up and becoming a man, after all.

the hotel by the sea

Susan Mitchell

In the hotel by the sea a man is playing the piano.
The piano to be played
like a pinball machine, it wants the man to lean his weight
against the music until the sound tilts. But the man
wanders inside the piano like someone looking
for an elevator in a drafty building
or like a drunk who can't find
his way in a song he keeps repeating.

The piano wants to play leaky faucets and water running
all night in the toilets of a train station.
It wants to play obscenities
and the delicate moths that scratch their bellies
on the ballroom screens.
The piano wants to scratch. It wants to spit
on the pavement. It wants to look into stores where women
try on clothes and open their thighs to the mirrors.

The piano wants to be a fat woman. It wants to play
baggy and flab and carry tuna sandwiches to work
in brown paper. It wants to dress up in sequins and eat
fried fish. It wants to suck its fingers and flick
ashes into the ocean. And it wants to squeeze
into a single note,

a silvery tube, and hold its breath.
The piano tells the man to forget everything
he ever learned and play the music boys pass in secret
from desk to desk at school, the blue saliva
of their kisses. The man feels left out of
this music and thinks of going for cigarettes.
The piano wants to drink up
the butts littering the ballroom.
It wants to sit down on the dance floor
and sob with joy, it wants to rub

all memory of celebration from the man's fingers.
The piano wants to blow its nose
in the music and play the silence of the room and the rain
falling outside. It wants to play the pores
in the man's face and his chapped hands.
The piano wants the man to dance
in his sports shirt and floppy pants.
It wants him to ride up and down

the hotel elevators and follow women back
to their rooms. It wants him to pull roses from their hair
and mice and light up like an arcade.
The piano is sick and tired
of this man's hands which sit down
on their grief, as on a jetty, and count the stars.
The piano doesn't care about hard times.
It wants to stay up all night
and tell unrepeatable stories to the ocean.
It wants a sound to come
from this man's mouth, even though his teeth

are picked clean.
The man won't know the sound
when he makes it. He'll think a woman is kissing Kleenex.
He'll think it's 4 A.M. and he can't buy
a pack of anything anywhere.

furry lewis ponders life and death as a blues man

Michael Graber

after Stanley Booth

Crying low the cart wheels
need grease, left alone they play
the devil's chime falsetto to the tick,
tick, tick of the rusted hinge
where my natural leg still aches
every morning on my trash route,
even though a minstrel-bound train
ate it years back.

I limped to fame late—
though most days now
I shine my spirit like Sunday's shoes.
The Last Real Medicine Show calls . . .
the only place for a man
foolish enough to gamble on song.
Ever since I was a furball
the cathouses spit out
I've known . . .

Bix was already three-fourths there,
lips purple and eye spent.
He'd jammed so pure all night
after his Whiteman gig.
He read my fortune in his eggs.

After four bars of silence
and a thick swig of coffee
said he'd seen a leg about my size
sidetrack death's black train.

music survives, composing her own sphere

John Drexel

All day a blackbird has been trilling. Or
maybe it's a woodthrush, robin, corncrake—
I'm not up on ornithology,
preoccupied with the fictions of astrophysics:
how quarks might move, how stars bend light;
the gravity and mass of a black hole
at the theoretical edge of everything.
Beyond that, there's no time.

Laboring under the apprehension
that I've gone missing
and might turn up face down in a stream
or, less romantically, a dumpster,
I learn the language of exile. Imprisoned,
I could resort to forging my way out
by chisel or petition, or have myself
smuggled in a laundry cart
or a first-class letter.

You say there's no getting away from it:
that love never tells the whole story,
or is an invention so we won't have to see
what it really is we're doing, where we're caught
or where we're going. That we, too,
are accountants, judging the price we'll pay,

the value of affection, the cost
of staying "in love."

But those birdcalls meanwhile
won't leave me, are driving me to distraction.
When I sleep I hear the *Resurrection*
conducted by Mahler himself,
and all the aviary of heaven
shouting *Aufersteh'n*!

boxcar

for John & Miles, together

Terrance Hayes

Black as snow & ice as cool/ Miles stood horn-handed while
John so&soloed/ I mean mad but mute like you be when you
got five minutes/ to be somewhere ten minutes away & a train
outta nowhere stops you/ boxcarboxcarboxcar & tracknoise/
that might out shout your radio if you had your windows
down/ boxcarboxcar & hotcars lined up around you/ this is
how mad Miles was/ Impatient like his dentist daddy/ listenin
to a badmouth whine about some aching pain/ *See, Doc I was*
tryin to blow down my old lady's door/ Theres Miles listenin/ to
Johns long song about sufferin & loss/ & hes heard it all before
in a club in the village/ He standin horn-handed but the
jazzfolk sit lovin it/ cause it all sounds new as sunday
shoes/ / Ticked Miles checks his watch/ tickles his trumpet/
& listens to a muscular music that wont stop/ & he loves it or
maybe he scared nobody will ever hear him again/ or maybe he
hungry & want to get/ home to silence/ John got nowhere but
here/ got nothin but this/ cause his wifes asleep/ & she cant
give him this kind of love/ his lips swoll as carolina clay/
almost bleedin on the reed & its just what he wants/ Blood/ / &
when he finally hush/ dead years later/ his liver rotten as corn
& Naimas gone/ Miles aint even glad its over/ His ears full of
whats left him/ & he thinkin of black hands dancin like
crowswings/ & he thinkin of a lovesupreme a lovesupreme a
lovesupreme/ & this too is what Im thinkin/ as I drive to see my
diva/ with old jazz in my speakers & the only thing between us
these boxcars pullin & pullin & pullin past

NOTE: *The poem was inspired by the story about John Coltrane's notoriously long solos in the years he played with the Miles Davis Quartet. When Miles reportedly asked him why he always played so long, John answered, "When I start, I don't know how to stop."*

"Just take the damn horn out of your mouth," Miles told him.

record time

Edmund White

LONELINESS CAN BE A FULL STATE OR AN EMPTY ONE, by which I mean that when I was thirteen in 1953 I usually felt forlorn but occasionally—especially in the presence of a work of art—triumphant. Most of the time, at school, on the bus, on the street, I thought I was embarrassingly conspicuous if I was alone. I was convinced everyone was burningly aware of my isolation, almost as though I were trapped in one of those sweating grinning embarrassment dreams. In the high school corridors, gliding from one class to another, grazing the walls, I didn't retreat into a comfortably grim resignation, waking up only when I was seated once again in the biology lab or in honor civics. No, I suffered and smiled and mentally debated whether I should try to walk along with that girl I knew from choir practice or join those guys from gym class, who weren't all *that* popular, after all. My loneliness was ready to sizzle and explode as it leapt from one electrode to another: high-voltage emptiness.

There was the amniotic sloth of a long bath or the agitated mindlessness of reading the back of the cereal box over and over or the sad-sack squalor of sitting on the floor in the sunroom, listening to all the clocks ticking in an empty apartment.

But mainly, every day, there was the same sort of highly anxious inactivity I'd felt the previous summer looking for a part-time job, waiting in the reception room in a starched collar, hoping to catch the eye of my potential boss, wondering why my appointment had already been pushed back forty minutes, observing the hands of the wall clock millimetering toward five, closing time. That's the way I felt alone at school, as though I were ready at a moment's notice to go into action, smile, charm, display my wares—but until then forced to wait and hypothesize the worst.

The other kind of loneliness, the full, self-sufficient kind, never came on me with lightning suddenness but had to be slowly wooed. I'd bring records and scores home with me from the public library, and behind my door, which I'd outfitted with a flimsy hook and latch, I'd listen to the old vinyl 78s with the gleaming outer-space black grooves and round burgundy labels printed in gold as though they were Ruritanian medals for bravery. I'd listen to Vincent D'lndy's *Symphony on a French Mountain Air* (I can't bear him anymore, now that I know he was an active, hate-driven anti-Semite) or all forty-eight records of *Tristan and Isolde* (the work of another anti-Semite, one whom I admire, alas). The *Tristan* records were in four matching leather-bound volumes that looked like snapshot albums. Most classical records were numbered so that a good pile could be stacked on the spindle, then flipped, though real connoisseurs were against stacking.

I'd worked three months at that summer job to earn the money necessary to buy a three-speed record player, which would accommodate the 78s borrowed from the library as well as the new 33⅓s and 45s I was buying at a dispiritingly slow rate. My very first record had been a 45 of Chet Baker playing "Imagination" on trumpet and singing in his high voice stunned by heroin into expressionless neutrality.

The speed had to be changed and the needle flipped when I went from 78s to the other speeds. If the records were battered, the scores were often pristine—I held in my hands a first American edition of Puccini's *Tosca* with its art nouveau cover design of the passionate Italian heroine all wasp waist, long gauzy gown, imploring hands and hornet's nest hair. I saw from the dates rubber-stamped on the orange card inserted into its own glued-in pocket that these scores had scarcely circulated in the last half-century. These cards made me realize how neglected and private and chancy was musical history. Just as I could check out the first English translations of Anatole France and Pierre Loti with their white leather bindings tooled in gold and braided flowers on the spine, in the same way I was in direct physical contact with these early musical scores of *Cavalleria Rusticana,* of Verdi's *Requiem,* of Massenet's *Thaïs,* of Wagner's *Lohengrin,* of Strauss's *Der Zigeunerbaron.* I was equally intimate with these scratched recordings of Lauritz Melchior (whom I'd heard sing a solo concert in Dallas when I was nine), of Jussi Björling (whom I'd seen, corsetted and tiny, flailing his arms on the stage of the Chicago Lyric Opera as he sang Rodolfo in *Bohème*), even of "Madame" Schumann-Heinck, whom my mother had seen in some Texas cow palace during one of her innumerable farewell tours just after World War I.

I'd come home from school by way of the library, my biceps aching from my burden of records, scores, and books, and I'd barricade myself in my room. As the Chicago night began to fall earlier and earlier each December evening and the snow on my sill would melt and refreeze, I took comfort in my room with the sizzling radiator, the chocolate-brown walls, tan burlap curtains, gleaming maple chest of drawers, comfortable armchair, and the old brass lamp from my earliest childhood, originally designed before my time as a gas lamp but now rewired with its glass chimney still intact and its luminosity still capable of being dialed down into yellow dimness. I loved the coarse red wool blanket with its big Hudson Bay dull satin label sewn into the upper lefthand corner like a commemorative stamp showing a moose and a canoe. I loved the pale celadon green pots I'd bought in Chinatown, their raised designs nearly effaced under heavy glazes, their wide cork tops sealed shut with red wax that had to be chipped away to reveal the candied ginger slices within, floating, slimy, in a thick, dark sugar syrup. Now the ginger had long since been eaten and the bowls washed clean but they were still faintly redolent of their spicy, mysterious original contents. I loved my seven bronze Chinese horses, which were stored in a brown velvet box cut into exact silhouettes into which the little statues could be wedged. Each horse was different, head lowered in a gentle arc to graze or thrown back to gallop, each weighty and cold in the hand. I loved my music boxes given to me one by one, Christmas after Christmas: the turning brass cylinder under glass plucking brass tines that played the Gounod waltz from *Faust;* the unpainted wood Swiss chalet with the mirrors for windows that played "Edelweiss"; the miniature grand piano; the revolving water mill. But I was less impressed by the look of each box than by the richness of its sound. The Gounod I liked the best since the sound wasn't tinny but resonant and the box, if I held it, throbbed in my hand with expensive precision.

I loved the smell of the boxes of tea I collected and scarcely ever drank—I'd inhale the dry, smoky perfume of the Lapsang souchong leaves, the Christmassy clove and orange odor of the Constant Comment, the acrid smell of Japanese gunpowder green tea, not really like a tea at all but a kind of grass, or so I imagined. I loved the way the hard metal lids fit snugly into these square boxes and had to be pried open with the handle of a spoon. I loved sitting on the floor, my back propped against the bed as I turned the broad, smooth pages of the opera scores in which the original words were translated, very approximately, into the same number of English syllables so that one could sing along. I'd keep changing the stacks of 78s, some of them so badly gouged that I'd have to nudge the needle out of a deep crevasse, others so worn down that my needle, itself not ideally sharp, would just slide over the bald surface in a split-second condensation of long minutes' worth of music.

But more often than not the records were still in good shape, perhaps because they were so seldom checked out. Sometimes for extra protection they were even inserted into translucent envelopes that were then closed and tucked into heavy, yellowing paper sleeves. The early 1950s record jacket designs were rarely printed with more than two colors and were pert or jaunty—black musical notes zigzagging like bees around a mauve cutout of Wagner's head, surmounted with his baggy beret, or all of Respighi's *Fountains of Rome* picked out in yellow and pink dashes and dots as though they were birdcages soldered in Morse code—or else the covers were just dumbly romantic (a huge red rose superimposed over a brown violin for Brahms's violin concerto).

I was alone with classical music, just as a reader was alone in the library or a museum-goer in those days was alone with paintings. Everyone else in America was listening to Perry Como and Dean Martin or looking at Arthur Godfrey's breakfast program on the flickering black-and-white television screen. American popular culture was cozy, queasily banal, pitched at everyone in the family—there was no Elvis yet, nothing tough or twangy or raunchy, just all these bland white people, the men in jackets, dark knit ties, and white dress shirts, the women in fluffy skirts and long-sleeved sweaters, acting out cute little skits week after week on a hit parade show as they thought up new variations on story lines that might fit the unchanging lyrics of a song that lingered for months in the top ten. People twenty or twenty-five or thirty-five all looked and acted alike in their dress-up clothes as they cracked their cute jokes and simpered and skipped between giant cutouts of sunflowers or waved from the flimsy back platform of a papier-mâché train.

One day I discovered the collection of circulating art books at the library and came home with a volume of ukiyo-e prints introduced by a spirited, seductive text. I liked it that these prints recorded the look of famous Kabuki actors or courtesans in the "Floating World" of eighteenth and nineteenth century Edo, that no one in Japan had taken these woodcuts seriously until French painters had discovered them. I liked the refinement of tall ladies standing in a boat, opium pipe in hand, sailing past the strut work supporting a bridge. I liked the intimacy of a beauty coquettishly blackening her teeth while her cloudy gray cat tiptoed over her makeup table. I liked the ecstasy of a monk in his hermitage, the paper wall thrown open, contemplating snowcapped Mt. Fuji reflected in a black lacquer-rimmed round mirror. The crevasses descending down from the snowcap looked like the lines radiating out from a toothless mouth. I especially liked the young lovers running on high wooden shoes through the visibly slanting morning rain, a faint smile on their lips, their slender bodies nearly interchangeable, the umbrella grasped in their joined hands....

It seems to me now that I had few judgments about music or paintings or poems and if works of art were difficult that didn't put me off. I worked my way through almost all the titles listed inside the paper dust jackets of the Modern Library. I'd figured out that these books were classics, and if my attention wandered while reading *Nostromo,* I simply started again and concentrated harder. It was not up to me to declare Conrad a bore or to wonder how a professional writer could allow himself to use so many words such as "indescribable," "ineffable," and "unspeakable." Similarly I felt it necessary to know something about Vlaminck *and* Van Eyck, about Rembrandt *and* Cézanne, as though I were preparing for God's Great Quiz Show in the Sky rather than piecing together a sensibility.

When other people, older people, took a strong stand for or against a Sung vase or T.S. Eliot's "The Waste Land" or a Jackson Pollock "drip" painting ("Pure charlatanism!"), I was so impressed by their opinions that I immediately adopted them as my own and sometimes repeated them for years to come without realizing they were internally inconsistent and needed to be reconciled. I was so ecstatic as I sprawled on the rough red Canadian blanket, dialed my brass lamp down to its dimmest wattage, listened to Flagstad's *Liebestod* in which a human body was sublimated into pure spirit, as I smelled the smoky tea leaves or brightened the light and looked at my Japanese lovers in the rain, each wearing a matching black cloth hat that formed a wimple under the inconsequential chin—so ecstatic that I didn't think to judge these experiences anymore than a starving man turns up his nose at food. I didn't judge things, but I was delighted when other people did. I was so shocked that I laughed, scandalized, when other people said, "This Sung vase with its pale raised peonies and delicate *craquelure* is worth more than all of Michelangelo's sculptures," or "Eliot is a fussy old maid with his royalist politics and furled umbrella but he *has* brought all of world culture together into a fragmented collage—fragmented because all collages necessarily are fragmented, but wonderfully suggestive and *systematic,* finally."

I was thrilled by so many sleek, purring opinions, I, a self-invented Midwestern public-library intellectual who ate books and records and art reproductions the way other people ate meat and potatoes. My kind of art meal was always eaten alone, just as I improvised on the piano alone, and I had only rare contacts with other art consumers. My mother's friends who had all the quirky, nuanced opinions seemed to have drifted out from New York or Boston. Their take on my favorite authors and composers ("Wagner certainly has his *longueurs,* and if he is the greatest composer we can only add, Alas, just as Gide sighed, *Hélas,* when he named Hugo the greatest poet") seemed to me almost sacrilegious, as though they were discussing sales figures for the relics and relic-derived products of a saint whom I actually believed in.

To judge a work of art depends on a certain fastidiousness, just as to taste a wine properly requires not being actually thirsty. But I was hungry and thirsty as well as a true believer in art's miracle-working properties. For me artists and writers and composers did not exist in time any more than general truths can be dated (later, of course, I learned that each epoch produces its own truths, but we didn't know that back then). When I was reminded of the *age* of a work of art (by the fresh look of the *Tosca* score, or by a story about Pollock's recent death in *Time* and time), I was disturbed, as when a headline-grabbing geologist claimed he could now confidently date the Flood and had even found the exact landing site of Noah's Ark. This intersection of the mythic and the temporal struck me as indecent. I myself was ageless, unformed, an ungendered eye, and I, too, resisted definition.

I had never played with toys as a child. I'd improvised on the piano, I'd invented complicated scenarios for my puppets or for my imaginary friends and me, I'd wandered through nature, receptive as a nose and eyes on a stem, thunderstruck by the smell of the lilac bush next to the Congregational Church, awed by the glassy tranquillity of Lake Michigan as I waded into it on an August evening and stood there, white and stark as a single soprano note, and watched the raised waves radiate out from my slow steps.

Now, at age thirteen, guiltily, I dropped the latch on my bedroom door and played with toys. Not real toys, not store-bought toys, but my own invented toys. I organized triumphal marches on the red Canadian blanket between ranks of tea-box military tanks, noble processions of the seven bronze Chinese horses, of a pink jade bodhisattva and a soapstone Buddha, of giant floats of music boxes all playing at once while the hordes shouted their approval (a sound effect I provided with my whispered roars as I hovered over the whole scene, invisible and manipulative as God). Finally I donned the red blanket as a cloak and put on a recording of the Coronation

Scene from *Boris* and made my royal entrance, imagining the rows of bearded, brocaded boyars. I heard the clangor of all Kiev's bells.

I thought to myself, This is what little kids go through, this total immersion into fantasy, this self-sufficient solitude, the good kind, the triumphant kind. I was ashamed but not so much that as the school day would draw to a close I wouldn't become excited by the thought that soon I'd be able to start playing again—not exactly with toys, but with my fetishes, whose ludic aspect had dawned on me only recently.

My favorite games were all about power, benign power, the same games I played outside in the snow by constructing ice palaces, a Forbidden City for my solitary empress, an Old Winter Palace for my ailing Tsarevitch. From the opera records I borrowed I'd learned all about Boris's coronation and the pharaoh's triumphal march in *Aida* as well as about the people in *Turandot* wishing the Son of Heaven ten thousand years of life. I was so high-strung that Mimi's death—and especially Violetta's—could make me tremble all over and sob hysterically (I wasn't your basic baseball-playing, freckled little kid); what I preferred, what I found soothing, were royal processions, and if I'd been Queen of England I would have managed to "process" on a daily basis, my raised gloved hand describing small circles in the air.

One day I read in the paper that Greta Garbo's *Camille* would be showing at a remote movie theater. My mother agreed to drive me way out there if I'd come home on the train by myself (she verified the times). In fact my mother indulged me in nearly all my whims. It was she who'd let me decorate my room as I'd wanted, who bought me my Chinese horses and my yearly music boxes and who'd driven me all the way down to the South Side that one time when I'd wanted to attend a Japanese Buddhist Church. When I pleaded to go to a military school camp (I'd just read biographies of Napoleon and Peter the Great and was suddenly attracted to power even in its less benign forms), she enrolled me against her better judgment; halfway through the summer I was begging her to let me come home, which she even more reluctantly allowed me to do.

It was a spring night when I went to that distant community to see *Camille,* a town which I couldn't name now and which I never saw again. It appeared to have been built all at once in the same manner in the 1920s or even earlier in what was even then a nostalgic style with converted gas lamps, cobblestone streets, and half-timbered storefronts. The spring was not advanced enough to have produced any flowers beyond big gaudy sprays of forsythia.

It was raining, and the cobblestones were as slick and even as dragon's scales. There was no one on the street. At last we found the movie, which was being shown in a narrow church, perhaps as a fund-raiser. If so, the programming was a disaster, since the only other member of the audience was an old man seated two rows away on a folding wood chair.

But once *Camille* began I was absorbed. Not by the humble, scratchy black-and-white look of the thing (it was a bad print, but my borrowed 78s had taught me to overlook that); I was used to Technicolor, even three-dimensional movies, and I'd never seen a vintage film before. Garbo's acting style would no doubt make kids laugh now, but I was used to melodrama from the operas I'd seen. Anyway, this was an exaggerated style but unlike anything I'd ever witnessed before. She could change in a second from a sadness as piercing, as physical, as light directed into the eyes of someone suffering from a massive migraine to a joy that shook her as agitatedly as though her big, lovely face were as bright and faceted as her pendent earrings. In one scene she was sophisticated and skeptical, one eyebrow raised, and in the next tender as my mother when I was ill with a high fever. Her voice would go from a fife's excitement to the bagpipe drone of her grief, a grief that really was just like a migraine that requires drawn curtains and deepest solitude.

I didn't quite understand why she had to give up her lover. What had she done wrong? Wasn't she even, all things considered, too good for him? Nevertheless, I liked the idea of sacrifice in the abstract and hoped to make one soon. Her lover had a straight nose and oily black hair, but I disliked his long sideburns and thought his acting was as unconvincing as his morality was caddish. That didn't matter—after all, Jussi Björling had had all the allure of a waddling duck, but he had sung with the clarion tones of a trumpet calling reveille.

I knew how the story turned out from *La Traviata,* the very first opera I'd ever seen, but this knowledge made my tears flow all the hotter as the end approached. When the lights came up the old man was snoring peacefully. No usher was in sight, although I could hear the operator in his projection booth rewinding the film. I pushed open the main church door. The rain had stopped but the bare, budding trees were still dripping and the sound of my lonely footsteps rang out.

I found the little suburban station easily enough. A sailor was also waiting for the train, playing a mouth-harp, quietly, to himself, as though he were rehearsing a speech, trying to get it by heart, or evoking a sentimental tune for his ears alone. I felt washed clean and faded almost to the point of transparency. I was very old and wise, not in need of a great love since I'd already had one, afraid that something might jostle my mood, which I wanted to carry without spilling all the way home. The night was conspiring graciously to help me—the deserted, dripping village with the gas lamps and cobblestones, the sailor with the mouth-harp, even the sight of forsythia blazing in the dark on the hillside next to the station.

The train came, just two cars long. The only other passenger was an old black woman, asleep and smiling, split shoes too small to contain her feet. The sailor kept playing, and I looked at the few dim lights that suggested the depths of these old suburbs with their huge wood houses in which everyone was asleep.

Back in my room I drank a glass of cold Welch's grape juice in the dark and pretended it was wine. I opened my window and toasted the wet spring night, which didn't feel like the beginning of anything but the very last plucked note at the end of a long, soft, slow coda.

psalm

Connie Voisine

In the morning, you are the birds I have no names for,
the birds I do not try to name,
I only triangulate
you, the eye of the bird, flat and shiny,
the eye that finds
the tent of worms, and you are
the worms devouring the tree.

I feel you in the wires in town,
constant, thin, tangled in treetops, black-striping
the blanker pieces of sky.
You are the towers that lift them
legs wide, shoulders ready
to bear what hums a song,
and what a song—a low buzz sprung

from beneath cows and insects,
ash trees and birches weeping their sheets of paper.
Afternoon, you are in my fields
a thousand times. I could say you take the form
of the Red Queen or a silk dress and shoes,
but it is all you, you the sub-
stance, velvet, the raw cocoon,

my deeper pond
where I see you
feeding, a wound in moss's dark.
You are the skin of the pond too, why I want for
microscopes: flush membranes, wheeling
hairs, the infant nub.
You feed my pond

and dusk, you feed my neighbor's hose
as he washes down his dirty children.
I know you are the blue in their chests
as they slip and fall in the driveway,
you say come in now and then it's supper and you
lay the disappearing road,
the atropine moon.

You are thick and tuned,
a train's horn shaking windows
to make them sing too.
Night, your body is

clean and cool in a strange city
and I adore you, fashion
handfuls of your hair into rings,
embroider prayers with the rest. I see you
beside a river. The bank is narrow and populated

with pilgrims who write their troubles, write
you on their skins, in rooms,
on the edges of postage stamps, the spaces between
letters blown down airshafts.

From my room, the street promises
            in frightening songs and
                        your voice is in that radio,
                        is lips against the bitten sky,
is the hand pounding at my door.

labor day

Sean Thomas Dougherty

A morning without work is a morning to breathe, to watch the rain clear and walk inside the passing voices of strangers, a dog's barking, students with their bouncing knapsacks of books, baseball hats worn backward, as I walk headed toward nowhere important, which is, of course, the most important place of all—the trees dazzling with light, the dog laps a puddle reflecting the sky, drinking the shimmer, his belly a puddle of sky, and my feet beginning to glide down the block, children skipping rope on the sidewalk, hip hopping to hop-scotch calls and Double Dutch dance steps, scrawling their names in wet chalk, running colors like a clown's extravagant tears—the minor miracle of my job, this gathering and giving of details: A woman's perfume, lilacs and lemons, the breath of a baby's hair.

babies

Alice Fulton

born gorgeous with nerves, with brains
the pink of silver polish or
jellyfish wafting ornately
through the body below.
An invertebrate cooing
on the mother
tongue shushes and lulls them into thinking
all is well. As they grow they learn

salvage: tear-out
guides to happiness say apologies can outshine
lies, guilt be lickspittled from their lives, bad
glycerined to good. Like a child's first school pencils
in their formal brilliance
and sharp new smells, they lie

as lovers. Maybe one cries
the wrong name and the night skinning
them pleasantly alive
leaps away in shards.
Then it's time for restitution:
a tin of homebaked,
holding gingham safety, fetal
as the light through mason jars of beets and brine,

or jewelry, clasping and unclasping
aisles of fluorescence from great department stores,
a distracting plenitude, and tempting.

Still, the beloved may stay bitter as an ear
the tongue pressed
into, unwanted.
And the word *end*: spiney, finally-formed,
indents them and is
understood. They learn

the hard way as hurts
accrue, and the brain is cratered as a rock
by rain that fell ages past
on unprotected mud. An insult keeps
despite apologies. When it vaporizes at last,
its space fills with grains that harden
to a fossil shaped exactly
like the insult.
They grow up when they know that

sometimes
only a gesture responsive as a heart-
shaped parachute above a jump
a life depends on
to be perfect
the first time will ever do.

the blank notebook

Valerie Wohlfeld

I CAME TO THE SEA OUT OF SEASON. The December sea a cold and lonely misfit who believed only in ancient burials' shiftings of sand; in waves curling and uncurling, an infant tirelessly opening and clenching its fists; in the bridal havoc of drifting foam's unending sleeves of lace. I brought with me a new journal to write in, covered in a print of miniature roses, portraits of unspeakably tiny blooms forced into being under a weatherless glass climate favoring scrupulously selected cuttings. I walked the beach each day, with the fabric-covered notebook in my gloved hand. The sea lay robed, a woman dressed in layers of somber colors, a faded mauve under something black fastened with glints of pewter buttons; the light penetrated the folds of these clothes as if entering an alembic where, clouded in distillation, it never found a way out again. Half obscured by afternoon shadow, as if one eye patch strung across a face, the sea compensated with the brilliant remnants of the remaining eye, which grew sharper and fiercer and circled and dipped in the mantle of its mate's lightless profile, scintillating voraciously as the gulls above. Sea, pugilist ringed against December's winds, flurries, sleet, rain: but even when all the adversaries quieted and fell and left empty that little box for warring, so that all was again temperate as those unnaturally small roses, growing against their heated panes of window, even then there must be movement under the mirrored waters as even the bones inside the newly dead, the hair and nails, are said to restlessly continue their activities of growth. The sea was all rumor, voices upon voices, meddlings and woes. Then temporary death: the sea turned to the paint and glass stare of a shelf of false eyes, brown-gold blue-irised eyes waiting to be fitted into cavities of skull. Many eyes, the bee's great oracular eye built up of all its little lesser eyes. The flat sea, cheap mirror forged by marriage of tin and mercury, was as the afterlife, the smile left on the Cheshire cat: approaching exile, some different frequency remained among the buried bone. The sea was as the last words rooting themselves in our mouths from out of our dead bones, the dead making sense only to the dead when, before dying, one says, "I have enjoyed lighting the wick of a certain hurricane lamp," and the skeletons in their graves remember the quality of light such a lamp gives, the smell of the cotton wick eating itself away in flame and oil, while the newly dead drops to death through the coffin's oubliette, still occupied in blind vain search for the treasured lamp. Miraculous sea, mechanical as a player piano, rolls out again chords and waves with ghostly hands, invisible, depressing scrolls of ivory, all the keys moving, reels wound and rewound, forever the same songs sung out of the lacquered case. Sea, clock of figurines circling through a narrow door all day to represent the hour, the cuckoo who's abandoned for a moment its sonorous voice for the darkness of the little box retreated to: does the bird dream, between chimes, a field with its own lost voice above the cut-down crops? The sea not a snake but the skins the snake sheds, built of scales as sequins and beads of a reticule held one to the other by unseen elastic threads. Sea, impatient mortician who lies down upon his own table. Grotesque sea, the unbeautiful arms of an elderly woman striated with veins and white ribbons of stretch marks, flank marbled with lines of fat, while, quarantined between wrist and elbow, bracelet after bracelet of jewels and gold and silver. Sea pacing its prison yard, back and forth riding parameters of barbed-wire walls while the gulls, silver and white overlaid with white and silver as snow on birches, utter strange purposeful barks and moans whose origins seem wolf, seal, dog, and woman as well as gull; the pigeons, unrequited love (boomerang homing back to the hand that sends it), return again to their same sentries, while the gulls, by chaos or design, take up new posts on each reentry of flight. Sea performing tricks and obsessions, autistic rites and violences, behind clinical observers' one-way mirrored falsity. Sea, brain's old rot of coral, waters sipped like some immortal Socrates his cup of hemlock. What do the drowned dead dream?—they penetrate into sleep as if laborious sea creatures building the corridors of shells, singing breaths through a barnacle of lung. Sea, deck of cards shuffling endlessly tiny, ornamental icons of red and black. Text of ink's purest blue tingeing the central axis of the mostly-white morning glory. Sea of winds and spirits, dragons, dots and cracks, bams and flowers of the mah-jongg. Cell scraped from the single cell of some ancient antecedent deity rising out of the flickering elements of a universe of water. Waves unraveling and pulled taut, herded into the brass and silver holds of the blades of death of Atropos's scissors. Cicatrix erased in a welter of waves. Sea no less a nest than that ancient womb of sticks made out of ransacked tatters: laced improbably with various-colored cast-off foils, wattles and mud and cord wedded to the detritus of housewives' discarded threads and scraps of paper lists and hair culled from sweet-soaked broths of washed brushes, even sometimes the ephemeral wand of a dragonfly's dead wing stitched to the bowl of the nest. The sea's odor not its own, instead all its hapless carried ornaments' and creatures' odors as if vanilla-permeated cardboard of an empty bakery carton. Sea, subterranean memory of a mother's fragrant milk-stained body still leaking lacteal haze and the union which will not come again. Slipped from the tongue's diversions, the mouth's benedictions, the plunge to exile begins with this banished breast. Sea, mother me back to mother. Waves' faux-grained illusions of sponges mopped in vinegar and oils, feathers pulled through wet paint creating artificial marble and stone. Crests, scattered scripts, marginalia written in manuscript borders. Petroglyphs, incisions cut on white walls of wave. Crashings and undertows creating a little manual of chaos. Placed between the leaves of many pages, all the gathered drift and wreckage and sea wrack of tiny animals and plants pressed between endless blotters. Sea, colossus reading his colossal book: As if the sea rose up and took the shape of Goya's mystery and monster: a fisted, bearded, naked giant veiled in clouds above the world's exodus: each hand of the immense man creating and destroying all in one stroke: Or was the creature really Goya, old, deaf, writ too large, his own creations running from him? Everywhere grit and sand fell out of the sea's opened pages. I bent to pick up pieces of the strewn sea: a bottle cap transformed to burnt sienna, a piece of clouded and softened glass small as a cataract, a host of purple stones glossy from being wet whose vivid colors incrementally extinguished themselves as they dried. There were no fishermen, the sea would not favor them this year. I picked up a shell dripping salt water out of its open mouth, too perfect for the litter on this beach. I sorted my treasures, winds rustling a curtain of dust over me. The wind seemed to blow with particles of flame. For a moment I wondered if the strange wind might be fleeing out of the large, wonderful shell I held. The wind extinguished all its fires, the little tropics sequestered inside my beautiful shell would not save me, as again rages of winds assumed their icy temperaments. The storm swept down rains and I raised my arms to shield myself. The sea, pickpocket, put all its fingers in all my pockets. My hands were empty, I had lost the book covered in diminutive roses. I had never meant to write inside it: Chaste page after chaste page, planet inhabited only by snow, each crystal naming to itself as it dies the new vocabulary of a new world: earth, map, bookmark, aniseed; I remembered the rules of blue lines, inked so poorly they moved across the page quivering, almost like seawater, almost like rain.

E.E. Cummings

when faces called flowers float out of the ground
and breathing is wishing and wishing is having—
but keeping is downward and doubting and never
—it's april(yes april;my darling)it's spring!
yes the pretty birds frolic as spry as can fly
yes the little fish gambol as glad as can be
(yes the mountains are dancing together)

when every leaf opens without any sound
and wishing is having and having is giving—
but keeping is doting and nothing and nonsense
—alive; we're alive, dear:it's(kiss me now)spring!
now the pretty birds hover so she and so he
now the little fish quiver so you and so i
(now the mountains are dancing, the mountains)

when more than was lost has been found has been found
and having is giving and giving is living—
but keeping is darkness and winter and cringing
—it's spring(all our night becomes day)o, it's spring!
all the pretty birds dive to the heart of the sky
all the little fish climb through the mind of the sea
(all the mountains are dancing; are dancing)

a note on the type

Timothy Geiger

We chiseled them to fill our need to see
ourselves thinking, summon a voice to tell
lines from letters, occupy the empty.
Lao-tzu called the space inside the vessel
its usefulness. What of the alphabet?
Was it the dust the stonecutter removed
or the granite he left behind that let
those Trajan capitals be defined, used
to represent the law, the known
voice of reason? It's not any one thing
that gives the "U" its use—arc of the bowl,
the serif's curvature. Holding nothing,
it causes lips to pucker, tongues to rise,
then humming, speaks up and is recognized.

country wisdoms

Maggie Anderson

"Rescue the drowning and tie your shoe-strings."
—Thoreau, *Walden*

Out here where the crows turn around
where the ground muds over and the snow fences bend
we've been bearing up. Although

a green winter means a green graveyard
and we've buried someone every month since autumn
warm weather pulls us into summer by the thumbnails.

They say these things.

When the April rains hurl ice chunks onto the banks
the river later rises to retrieve them.
They tell how the fierce wind from the South

blows branches down, power lines and houses
but always brings the trees to bud.
Fog in January, frost in May

threads of cloud, they say, rain needles.
My mother would urge, be careful what you want,
you will surely get it.

More ways than one to skin that cat.
Then they say, Bootstraps.
Pull yourself up.

the eighteen dream-words that afoukal gave him

Patrick Chamoiseau

It is through them that Pipi went back into his own memory cleft open like a calabash by oblivion and buried in the farthest corner of himself.

1. The Kongos, captured in more profusion than fish fry. Each wave out at Pointe-des-Nègres is one of their souls. In your tree, they branch out in the densest foliage. But there were also: the Nagos, the Bamanas, the Aradras, the Ibos, and the Minas. And those frequent maroons, the Riambas, the Sosos, the Taguas, the Moudongos, the Kotokolis. They were all so different that they created the beginnings of your language to bind us together. In those days, the evil tides beached these thousands of jellyfish who had to reinvent life brutally, without any water save that of memory.

2. There were three names. The one from the Great-Country (lost through futility or force), the one on the boat (given by sailors during sea-water showers and the exercises that loosened up our muscles), and the one in the fields. That last name bespoke your certain death: you died with it and left it to children who had already forgotten you. So for us names no longer mattered. When the master named you Jupiter, we called you Crickneck or Big-Butt. When the master said Telemachus, Remus, or Mercury, we said Syrup, Afoukal, Pipi, or Tikilik. Has that died out?

3. Before the piping of the pippiree, the overseer whistled. His whip often cracked. In the distance pealed the bells of the big plantations. Still stiff with sleep, lines shuffled to the rhythm of the steward's roll call. Then we moved on to morning prayer and the break-fast. The foredawn and the lingering chill of the wind kept our voices low.

Imagine not misery or anguish, but well-trained reflexes for which there was no reason at all to Exist. We would set out for the fields without even raising our heads. The Long-beasts knew how to bring us down when, bent over the soil, we combed out the long, burning hair of suffering. Imagine not grief (that was too absolute to be constant), but the slow vertigo of absence. At noon, old-granny would bring us salt meat, boiled plantains, manioc, and harsh *guildive* rum. We'd eat hot food, and talk would well up (new words forged there in the fields). That was when the body sank into pain: hands were raw, singing with scratches from saw grasses. The overseer, with whip or whistle, would cry us back-to-work. And the field swallowed us up until the anus of nightfall. Think of that, repeated times without number, with those incomprehensible cutlass blows among ourselves, the poisoned deaths dealt by the Long-beasts, and the death suffered each hour in the almost fatal acceptance of this slow drowning.

4. Imagine this: you disembark, not into a new world but into ANOTHER LIFE. What you thought was essential breaks apart, dangling uselessly. A long ravine cuts its way through you. Now you are no more than gaping nothingness. In truth you had to be *reborn* to survive. What unholy gestation, what uterine hell, aie-aie-aie!

5. At the mill, it was best to be the one who slipped the fresh-cut sugarcane between the grinding wheels, the stiff cane that you shoved from a distance into the mechanical maw. But think of the second man, the one who for endless days gathers up the already crushed cane, flat, shredded, too limp to catch well in the wheels, so that it must be pushed by hand as close as possible to the rollers. A moment of fatigue, or a daydream, or the wrenching cry of a loved one in the far-off country, or else a touch of sunstroke, a trickle of sweat into the eyes, a slight dizziness ... Oh a finger's caught! The beast awakens in an inexorable slushing of ground-up bones and flesh. The hand is tugged in before your helpless eyes. Then the arm. The shoulder.

You can barely cry out. The cane juice turns rusty with blood and marrow. The water of your soul is squeezed out and gushes down into the tubs. What greater horror than a sugar press jammed with the stubborn, grimacing head of a nigger? (So, there it is: the second man started carrying a cutlass. If his finger got caught and he had enough courage, he had to hack off his arm. That was better, after all, the master said. Surely. Besides, at the mill, there were double rations of salt meat and all the *guildive* you wanted. It was better, after all, the master said. Surely.)

6. We moved backward for the holes and the planting. Forward for the weeding. Our row stretched across the field. Behind, the field-crier raised the Kongo in song. Backs endured blows, and heads lolled. The sun beat down during those hours. The earth was beautiful and touched us on the shoulder. Some of us knew how to talk to her. She was, it seems, quite surprised to see us there. Heavy rains stuffed us under our bags in groups of three. Heads down between our knees, we'd watch the ground spit the water back between our toes. Snails and worms came out. Impossible to count them, because the raindrops put us in a trance. The overseer's footsteps slopped through mud, back and forth, as he counted our huddles: troops of hunched-in tortoises, shivery-chilled by sorrow. Does that still happen, that spell cast by the rain?

7. On Sunday, we rose early. Without whistle or whip. While the steward checked the cleanliness of the huts, we lined up in front of the store for the weekly rations. The steward's assistant kept watch, discouraged pushing. We would move forward, not as solemn as ants, but fairly patient and orderly. The salt meat or fish was put in the small calabash-*coui* in the left hand. The larger one in the right hand received the manioc, plantains, millet, dried beans, the slices of yam, calabaza, sweet potatoes. Not all that all at once all the time, but a bit of one of them sometimes. We'd go stash everything away in the huts

before catechism. The rest of the day, while sunlight lasted, we'd speak to the earth of our own gardens or, depending on the season, go off to hover around crossroads, selling our produce. That brought in enough to buy *guildive*. The militia would check our passes, but they rarely shot at us. *Guildive* was our passion. Dice, cards, dancing as well, dancing, dancing, dancing ... Zat changed?

8. The most faithful of our yawings was starvation. The cane, that grass of calamity, lent us its roots. Can you imagine such a mooring? We sucked on it constantly. Sugar turned our lips rosy. And when times were hard, we'd chew even the tender bagasse of the violet stalks down to that fibrous paste we swallowed in one gulp. It made a nice weight in the stomach and kept us properly cleaned out. Can you see us, cane-suckers, drugged on sugar, dreaming all day long of the crusty salt on a dried codfish?

9. God. The Trinity. Redemption. Eternity. All that was spoken of in a mystery language when we disembarked. An old catechist drilled us in those words morning and night. The white priest lobbed them at us in sermons every Sunday before the long story of Mass. They were the first things to slip from our lips outside our own language. The black catechist was our godfather at baptism. He accompanied us, one hand resting on our shoulders as on the horns of a sacrificial goat. Glowing himself with a grace that fed upon the baptism of each one of us. In the evening, shunning the dancing and storytelling as the priest demanded, we would stay in our huts, listening silently to ourselves, watching for the awakening of the whites' magical power we were now certain of possessing. We gave ourselves wholly to this new God, hoping to partake of his white strength to understand, if not vanquish, this life, this country, this bewildering mess. The old catechist, flush with the souls brought that morning to the God of this country, would get dead drunk, dance the wrong way round from his skeleton, and leap unscathed onto ten cutlass blades. But we,

trembling from this baptism, would seek a slumber wherein we might dream of this newly tamed God, now ever so slightly in our power, who would help us to defeat the master. We didn't know, you see, that this God could not be swayed. That the master did not fear this God: ticks from the same *chien-fer.* Has this mirage faded away?

10. From the boat we brought with us scabies, scurvy, dysentery, smallpox. They doused us with mustard, vinegar, lemon, and sorrel tea. What they truly feared from us were scaly leprosy, madness, and the epilepsies that rendered even the oldest sales void and devalued all relatives of the afflicted slave. But more than elephantiasis, lockjaw, fevers, ticks or fleas, the irresistible craving for red clay, more than crabs or sores, more than the Siamese fever-evil, venereal diseases, headaches, merciless diarrheas, it was *sorrow* that beat us from the branches of life with the most efficient of misfortune's switches. Neither live-forever syrup, nor palma Christi oil, nor *sagon*-herb, nor the rarest emollients from whales' brains, nor althaea ointment, nor cochlearia water, nor calaba balsam, nor Kaiser's pills in their sacred boxes, nor cinnabar, nor mercurial honey, nor litharge, nor tartar emetic, nor *aillaud* powder and sarsaparilla for endless decoctions, nor even Venice treacle could rival our elders' knowledge of ancient herbs. We would have given a salt-cod tail for some wild purslane or American sage, both eyes for some fine peppergrass, blue vervain, or stink beans. And nothing could keep us from dreaming about wild pimpernel, verbena, and cresses. Is it still like that?

11. The women had learned how to expel all life from their wombs. They had command over tetanus, which carried so many children of the light off into the sky. Distraught, stripped of life like those palm trees bent so low over desolate waves they refuse to dream about clusters of coconuts, the women were trapped. Can you imagine how much love and despair it takes to kill your flesh and blood? We men were wrestling with our own misery and cared little for their

suffering, which was twice as ferocious as ours. We'd tumble one of them every night. We were trying to break their backs, to make them heave the most strident sighs. Each humping reinforced our own existence, straightened our backs a bit, and like true dogs, we'd leave them in the infinite anguish of a fruitful womb. In the torture of loving for nine months a life that must be rejected. In the lonely tragedy that left them more bruised than fallen mangoes: giving birth and having to kill in the darkness of the hut and the suddenly yawning chasm of the soul. As for us, you know, always far from them at that moment, we'd be wallowing in thoughtless rum and joyful dancing. Do you think they have forgiven us?

12. Telling stories at night, we'd speak of the Caribs' great leap from the cliff. There the sea opened up the most beautiful of graves for them. A splendid trail that confounds the mastiffs of slavery! But we kept silent to recall more truly our own dashes toward death: on the boat or after coming ashore, at the first hut or in the middle of harvesting. Do you know that some, at the moment of suicide, had white hair? Do you understand the strength and patience needed to swallow your own tongue? We would count up the dead: the army of their spirits marked down each *béké* for the most savage vengeance, as a viaticum for their return to the homeland. Meanwhile, the *papas-feuilles,* the bush-medicine healers who knew all about plants, would poison the plowing and carting oxen, the horses, the mules at the mill, so the whole plantation staggered along like a crab without a shell. They would also poison the master's favorite obedient slaves when they began giving us the looks one darts at dogs. Soon the master was regarding us askance, sometimes with the stunned eyes of a storm-soaked bird. In daylight, our submission in the fields; at night, the clandestine power that could do so much. It took us several generations to send the poison directly to the master, tainting his jars of rainwater, infecting the bamboo gutters. The chambermaids would

sprinkle the strength of our plants inside his boots, his underwear, along the edge of his chamber pots and the mauve enamel basins for his morning ablutions, on the sweatband of his hat where it stuck to his forehead, and in each end of his pipes. The kitchen women put it in every dish, on the tines of the silver forks, in the sparkling bowls of the spoons. It was amusing to see him afflicted afterward with relentless diarrheas, spasms, hiccups, reddened eyes, and a puffy face. His skin became transparent and we could see his veins. Our first heart-in-the-mouth came when we surprised him consulting one of our *papas-feuilles,* he was so sick. Can you imagine, him, a petitioner before our bush doctor? The second surprise was to find him dead one morning in the stable, swollen and unrecognizable. Can you understand? So, they could die like us!? But we didn't have time to dance our fill. Two months later a letter of appointment from the owner in France restored the master to life. That was when we learned they were eternal.

13. Think first of all about marooning to the edge-of-the-woods. That's what we turned to most often. You just took off, spurred on by some heartache or a flash in the brainpan, to run full-pelt into the free *raziés.* You got drunk cutting endless capers, daydreaming on beds of warm grass. But soon night was all around you. You drifted irresistibly toward your plantation and lurked nearby for several days. Living by stealing. Drinking from a freedom powerless to cut that umbilical cord tying you to the womb of your sufferings. This usually lasted six months. Then you went back. The master, who had always known you were around somewhere, whipped you on principle. As for the steward, he hadn't even struck you off the list. Anyone still go off on little maroonings these days?

14. Real marooning took more heart than I had in me. All those years of setting your dreams root-high—they rob you of your understanding and love of lofty foliage and even the wind. Ah, freedom isn't

a broody hen! First she leaves you misery and the cold rains of sinister woods. Your heart hurls cusses at the silence. You must cling fast to a beeline, hitched tightly to the Star, or else you soon start to swerve round, and at dawn you stumble into the dogs. You must fast find those who are already there. They will not call to you. You will have to ferret them out to prove worthy of their band. You live like a *manicou.* Moving little by day. Distrust. Vigilance. Escorting the women into the most distant ravines to gather roots and healing plants. Retreating before roving militias, packs of wild dogs, solitary bounty hunters who haunt the shadowy undergrowth with those white lizards the Caribs called *mabouyas.* But, you know, a few of those men have told me of the intoxication of night attacks. The savage rush at the plantation! Not some petty plunder, quiet and quick, to fetch away chickens, a few tools, manioc, salt, oil, sweets, black girls. No. The true shrieking charge on the master's house when the militia is far away. The cascade of torches. The wicked cry of the flames. The windows you can shatter at last. That world of gleaming furniture, of rugs, paintings, napkins, carafes, mirrors, that you can finally invade, touch, destroy. And those white women you absolutely must rape to really live ... But you know, face to face with the master, there is also the sudden numbing of your body. The old fear raising its head. Supreme moment to learn if you are a black-maroon or not. Either your cutlass strikes or the master calmly kills you. Do you know he often did just that?

15. You have to experience genuine marooning off alone, far from the bands of runaways. Those who had been hamstrung spoke of this during the long evenings by the fire. Ah, those black-maroons of silence! Planted like trees at the back of beyond, they stayed so still that spiders encircled their domain with long, creamy curtains. When you met them in the woods, their smiles were sad, their movements slow, their eyes wild from not seeing any sense in what was happening

to us. The silence enabled them to listen to the earth. To understand the leaves. They tended the wounds of the maroon bands and warded off the yaws. They seemed as solid as *baume*-wood, as rugged as a rocky shore, sturdy, but adrift. Theirs was the most noble of sorrows. Disquieted and stirred, maroon girls loitered outside their huts or sat nearby waiting to be called, to be made pregnant. The bands of maroons took in their children, whose dark and stricken eyes harbored a gaze keener and more distant than a memory of the Great-Country.

16. I left the fields behind because I knew how to talk to horses. How many maddened stallions, after escaping into the woods, came willingly to my furrow to dry my sweat with their muzzles? How many times did they come clustering around my hut when the steward emptied the stable to clean and air it out? When old Prêl-Coco (Coco-Fuzz) the coachman died, hoary with age and scurf, they naturally offered me his place. I thus put a little distance between misery and me. I was responsible for the horses, mules, oxen. The only animals I didn't take care of were the dogs. What's more, as the master's coachman, I traveled around through all the parishes. I knew the ferrymen, innkeepers, coast sailors. Once even, oh la la how wonderful, I spent a day in the port of Saint-Pierre. My only misery in those times was having to keep quiet when the animals died, sacrificed in our name by the *papas-feuilles.* Then the master would see me so sad that he never suspected I saw anything amiss.

17. I hated the whites and our misfortunes, but I had learned to love the master. I watched him live every day. I knew his friends, the freed black women he frequented. I saw his distress when the harvest was late, his quivering excitement when the steward's report was good, the way he sat up respectfully when letters from the owner in France were opened, which he had read by the accountant. His fate seemed linked to those papers from France. They determined the life of the

entire plantation for months, come to that. After they arrived, he would decide to step up the pace, have us spend nights out in the fields. Or else slow everything down and put half the field slaves to repairing buildings, tools, and thousands of padlocks. It's true, I'd find myself liking him. I was attentive to his wishes. He often spoke to me about his Brittany of mists, green plains, dark little farms (his coarse, common voice still rumbling with peasant accents almost unchanged by exile). Each time he died (poisoned by the *papas-feuilles*), I would grieve as if for my best horse. Then I would sink into torpor like a crab until a letter from France brought him back to life. It would all begin again. First our silent company, side by side, lulled by the horses. Then the subtle complicity of routine, and the meshing of our habits. I would begin to speak up, to advise him on decisions regarding the fields and stubborn slaves. He would listen to me, touch me on the shoulder. Some evenings, in fact, despite his wife's disapproval, he invited me to have a drink on the veranda. The aromatic liquor sent me into raptures. Can you understand these little sips of pleasure in that vast calamity?

18. I was so bound to the master that I could no longer envisage life without him. When abolition came, I was more dismayed than a column of ants in a downpour. The master loved me the way he loved his mules, his fields, his boots. I understood this when he split my skull open on that jar. But even today, I remember him almost with affection. With that shudder one still feels when recalling a friend who has proved treacherous. Or who was never a friend at all. Can you understand that dead image I had of my life if it had to go on without the master? Does that still happen today? *Those were the eighteen Dream-Words that Afoukal gave him.*

false leads

Yusef Komunyakaa

Hey! Mister Bloodhound Boss,
I hear you're looking for Slick Sam
the Freight Train Hopper.
They tell me he's a crack shot.
He can shoot a cigarette out of a man's mouth
thirty paces of an owl's call.
This morning I glimpsed red
against that treeline.
Aïe, aïe, mo gagnin toi.
Wise not to let night catch you out there.
You can get so close to a man
you can taste his breath.
They say Slick Sam's a mind reader:
he knows what you gonna do
before you think it.
He can lead you into quicksand
under a veil of swamp gas.
Now you know me, Uncle T,
I wouldn't tell you no lie.
Slick Sam knows these piney woods
& he's at home here in cottonmouth country.
Mister, your life could be worth
less than a hole in a plug nickel.
I bet old Slick Sam knows
about bloodhounds & black pepper—
how to put a bobcat into a crocus sack.

venus's-flytraps

I am five,
Wading out into deep
Sunny grass,
Unmindful of snakes
& yellowjackets, out
To the yellow flowers
Quivering in sluggish heat.
Don't mess with me
'Cause I have my Lone Ranger
Six-shooter. I can hurt
You with questions
Like silver bullets.
The tall flowers in my dreams are
Big as the First State Bank,
& they eat all the people
Except the ones I love.
They have women's names,
With mouths like where
Babies come from. I am five.
I'll dance for you
If you close your eyes. No
Peeping through your fingers.
I don't supposed to be
This close to the tracks.
One afternoon I saw
What a train did to a cow.
Sometimes I stand so close
I can see the eyes
Of men hiding in boxcars.

Sometimes they wave
& holler for me to get back. I laugh
When trains make the dogs
Howl. Their ears hurt.
I also know bees
Can't live without flowers.
I wonder why Daddy
Calls Mama honey.
All the bees in the world
Live in little white houses
Except the ones in these flowers.
All sticky & sweet inside.
I wonder what death tastes like.
Sometimes I toss the butterflies
Back into the air.
I wish I knew why
The music in my head
Makes me scared.
But I know things
I don't supposed to know.
I could start walking
& never stop.
These yellow flowers
Go on forever.
Almost to Detroit.
Almost to the sea.
My Mama says I'm a mistake.
That I made her a bad girl.
My playhouse is underneath
Our house, & I hear people
Telling each other secrets.

the man who wouldn't plant willow trees

A.E. Stallings

Willows are messy trees. Hair in their eyes,
They weep like women after too much wine
And not enough love. They litter a lawn with leaves
the butts of regrets smoked down to the filter.

They are always out of kilter. Thirsty as drunks,
They'll sink into a sewer with their roots.
They have no pride. There's never enough sorrow.
A breeze threatens and they shake with sobs.

Willows are slobs, and must be cleaned up after.
They'll bust up pipes just looking for a drink.
Their fingers tremble, but make wicked switches.
They claim they are sorry, but they whisper it.

from the passion artist
the martyr of la violaine

John Hawkes

A bright red dragonfly on a half-sunken post, the claw of the small yellow earth remover clutching the air, the rusted treads of the abandoned machine resting partially on the torn soil and partially in a pool of clear sun-filled water, his thin black shoes appropriate only to city streets but already bespattered with the mud of the marsh: thus he paused in that area of contested desolation where both marsh and city met, faltered, struggled, flowed, and ebbed in the rhythm of natural infestation. For all his walking, he had never before stood exactly here, though the yellow machine was a familiar monster and the dragonfly, its transparency gleaming with the color of blood, was catching the light and quivering as if adorning not the rotted edge of the tilted post but the black surface of the back of his gloved hand. Never had he stood beneath such a distant sun; in the brightness of the ferns at his feet he saw only the strangeness of vegetation that grows in the wake of a holocaust, while in the shell of the small upturned automobile that lay nearby in a bed of silt he recognized the remains of the vehicle Claire had spent her life desiring. Everything was here and nothing. A wire dangling from the iron claw contained the power of electrocution; an empty concrete conduit emerging from a lip of clay had been meant for sewage; a black shoe cupped in a clump of marsh grass might have been his own. With every breath he smelled the salty fetid smell of air that is always fresh, never confined, always stagnant, forever drifting in random currents between layers of water, layers of light. He stared at the marsh that receded in all directions like an immense pebbled sheet of purple glass. He could see nothing of hut, barn, haystack, cluster of young naked trees, yet these too were embedded in the distant glass. Konrad Vost was alone and unable to move in a landscape without shape or meaning, belonging to neither city nor countryside: it was worse than bearing his disfigurement through the dawn streets and indifferent crowds. For him there was only sun, emptiness, the smell of salt and putrefaction.

But then the air around him, vagrant, powerful, cut adrift from tides, earth, light, shifted its fetid currents and brushed aside the grass, rolled aside the still marsh water, and exposed momentarily what otherwise he could not have seen: the curling iron rails of some anomalous narrow-gauge railway track long ago destroyed and long unused, long buried in the flat and shifting marsh. Through the parted grass and water shone the deep orange light of the bent and splintered rails that now consisted of nothing except the splendor of rust which even while he watched was flaking, burning, as the iron itself continued its slow process of disintegration in the light of the sun. But a severed train track across an empty marsh? Rails and bone-like ties rising into sight from beneath blankets of sand, sludge, drifting water? He shaded his eyes and smiled. The sight before his eyes was unaccountable, but suddenly he remembered Claire and understood what previously he had merely feared: the unaccountable is the only key to inner life, past life, future life. From the silence of the purple distance came the rattle of couplings, the sound of gunfire, the chugging of a locomotive that did not exist. Air, rust, water, grass: had he not once ridden a train on these very tracks? And hidden himself in village streets now buried beneath the city streets at his back? He listened. Here, now, alone at the edge of a marsh, suddenly he knew that he had once been a child in flight. The sounds of the locomotive were coming no closer. But he was comforted.

He nodded to himself, compressed his lips, and without hesitation stepped into the water that lay between the shelf of mud where he stood and the section of railway track, once again hidden beneath the water, behind the grass. The tracks were gone but he had seen them; they were there, for his own use if not for the use of any actual train.

The water rose to midcalf and, as he could not have expected, was as cold as a blade. It dragged at his trousers, he felt the mask of his face reflecting the shock in his legs. The water eddied away from him as he pushed on toward the brackish spot where he had seen the tracks. Silt, water, algae clogged his shoes, his socks, his trouser bottoms, his nakedness. He would never again be dry or free of the dead smell of the marsh. But what did it matter? The inner landscape had become externalized. He would cross it with the ruthlessness of a police patrol following leashed dogs.

At precisely the moment when the smell of natural decay and artificial decay was strongest, and when behind him the dragonfly quit the safety of the rotten post and disappeared, leaving in its place only a droplet of shimmering water, then simultaneously he found his footing and climbed aching and dripping onto the all but concealed bed of ancient tracks. Again he shaded his eyes, waited, felt the water descending his calves inside the trousers now heavy and shapeless from his wading. The horizon was empty. He knew that he was becoming more gaunt than ever; he knew that behind the steel shutter of La Violaine, the shutter that was still down and would remain so until calm was again restored to the prison across the street, the silent figures of those men loyal to the rebelling women were gathered already for morning coffee or beer. He knew also that there was no longer a chair for Konrad Vost in the closeness and darkness of the café. So much the better, he told himself, and started off down the tracks that led, apparently, to the deepest easterly recesses of the marsh.

The tracks had been constructed on a roadbed nearly level with the deceptive surface of the marsh, so that occasionally he found himself again walking through sheets of water. Now he was totally exposed to the sun and was, he knew, an all too visible target to anyone lying prone and watching him from no matter how great a distance out there in the purple or deep green spaces; now he was well hidden behind walls of yellow and undulating grasses that rose higher than his head and whispered like thin blades sharpening each other. As he progressed, stumbling and adjusting his stride to the ties, it became increasingly apparent that the marsh was not merely flat. Shallow ponds concealed the wide mouths of wells that dropped downward for immeasurable distances; stands of pale trees suddenly sprang up from the mud; he could see the vestiges of an immense canal undulating through ribs of sand; off to his right lay a geometric arrangement of wet stones where primitive buildings, long since dissolved, had sheltered both men and animals. More fence posts, the rotten ribs and backbone of a small boat, brightly colored marsh plants festering in sockets of ice, the fragments of a shattered aqueduct gray and dripping where moments before there had been only flatness and emptiness, abrupt discolorations that revealed quicksand or underground rivers: it was all an agglomeration of flashing mirrors, the strong cold salty air was impossibly heavy with the smell of human excrement and of human bodies armed and booted and decomposing under the ferns, behind piles of rocks, in the depths of the wells. Had it once been a landscape of nighttime skirmishing? Was it then the terrain of at least some kind of history? At any moment an iron ship might loom before him, or the vast trench of a communal grave.

He stopped, wiped his face, looked back in the direction from which he had come: the city was now only the faintest line of little concrete teeth littering the horizon. Soon when he turned again to look there would be nothing. He felt as if he were walking on the crushed or broken bones of the world's dead. His shoes, socks, lower trousers were still damp and dripping; his upper body was growing warm in the sun. When he again paused and looked backward down the length of track at the distance he had already come, the city was gone.

Not a bird. Not a scurrying animal. Not a fish to leave bubbles or ripples on the clear or purple glass of the water. No insects. Nothing but the light, the swollen breath of life in decay, the muddy plains and fissures of the deceptive topography.

Toward midmorning he heard the unmistakable sounds of men's voices. Later, before he had time even to conceal himself within the shelter of a growth of high yellow grasses rising suddenly on his left side, he watched as three men, who were wearing the familiar kepis and dark blue uniforms and carrying weapons hung from straps on their shoulders, passed in single file across the line of his vision far down the tracks. In another moment they were gone, these representatives of the Prefecture of Police, disappearing abruptly as if into a tilted mirror. But he had seen them. He was not alone in searching the marsh. Again circumstance had borne him out, again he had been proven correct: where else to hunt down the fugitives of La Violaine except in the marsh? Still later, from a different direction, came the faint snarling of brutal dogs baring their teeth and straining on their leashes of black leather. Then again there was silence, with only the sounds of his own breathing and walking to scratch in his ears.

How long it had taken for the sun to climb directly overhead he did not know. But the hour of cessation had arrived; the light of the marsh was stronger, more evenly diffused than ever, as if it could not possibly intensify or fade; and in this hour of midpoint he felt suddenly safe, disarmed, stiff and fatigued from his walking, curiously freed from the purpose that at dawn had impelled him to enter the muddy, crystalline, uncertain reaches of the marsh. He rested, sitting on the edge of the track with one knee drawn up and the black hand lying inert at his side. He was on top of a low embankment from which he could see on an island of black soil a stone hut oddly intact, a threadlike road that might have been made with the tip of a finger, a long glassy stretch as of the sea. He clasped his raised knee with his active hand; he was conscious of the breath of decay that was in his clothing and the pores of his skin; he was at peace with the incongruity between himself and all this low wilderness. In face, neck, arms, chest, his muscles and tendons were slackening, coming to rest. The smell in his nostrils was like that of a naked human shoulder green with mold. He felt himself in a waking sleep, suspended between clear sight and silence: this was the landscape that had swallowed legions; everything and nothing lay at his feet. It was then that he heard the one sound that even he, in all this wet or spongy vastness, could not have anticipated: laughter, the shrill tones of what could only be an old woman in the grip of laughter. He listened, he held his breath. For the first time since leaving the hospital he was on his guard. The pleasures of the high sun had evaporated. In this place what could be more alarming than the sound of an old woman's laughter?

Carefully, propping himself on his left hand, disengaging his right from a circlet of thorns that had sprung up beside the rails, slowly and quietly he descended the embankment and entrusted himself to the shadows and sudden light of a thicket he had failed to notice from his vantage point above. The earth was silent beneath the wet soles of his shoes. He moved between the slender white trees with all the stealth he could summon, and despite fear and urgency he was entirely conscious of how the tall young trees dispersed and focused the light so that now, all at once, the thicket was warm and filled with star-shaped patterns of bright flashing light. Again came the sound of the laughter, high-pitched, close, trembling with the broken music of an old woman long confined among other old and laughing women. He knew without thinking that it was a sound to fear, that loud sounds of unreasonable pleasure were not to be enjoyed vicariously but to be feared. But he could not have imagined that within this thicket of flowering warmth and whitened light he himself could be so violent.

Her back was to him in the narrow clearing, and yet he recognized her at once. Despite the deceptive clothing, the black gown and, on the head, the black shawl holding the hair, still he recognized at once the same old woman who, from her barred window, had stared down happily at the chaos of men and women in the yard below. Now she was laughing to herself, without reason, here in the gentleness of shadows and light, as if she were not one of those condemned long ago to La Violaine.

He reached the small black figure in a single stride; she turned; the astonished face was staring up at his own. Now they were so close together, he and the old woman, that they could have clutched each other's clothing with angry hands, and though she was bent and though her face was far below his shoulder, still it was shockingly upturned toward his own in one of the brightest rays of light to pierce the leaves overhead, so that every feature was thrust upon his consciousness and sealed there in heat and light. He and the old woman were stock still, he tall and at the mercy of his fury, she bent and twisted in her attitude of vanished laughter. The two of them might have been about to embrace or to grapple together in unequal contest there in the new growth of trees. Within easy reach the ancient face was turned up to his own and brought alive, though unmoving, by the focused light. He stared down at the warmly tinted expression of fear and surprise, and there could be no question of identity: it was she, the old woman who had savored the chaos of La

Violaine as a private spectacle. The open mouth with its three amber-colored teeth and the breath of a great age, the small twisted ears that appeared to have been sewn to the sides of the skull with coarse thread, the skin that was shriveled tightly to the bone beneath and cured in sun and salt until the wrinkles were deep and permanent, the soft facial hair that flowered around the lips and on the cheeks like a parody of a bristling beard, and above all the yellow eyes, which alone reflected the ageless crafty spirit in a face that otherwise was only a small torn mask of leather: these were the elements that made his recognition a matter of certainty, and that inspired in him a rage which, even to him, bubbled and frothed in excess of what the emotion, the time, the place, or the old woman herself might have justified. But the very texture of her age affronted him, as did the cleverness that burned so youthfully in the yellow eyes of someone who should have been confined to an iron bed or rickety chair in a prison for women. He was appalled by her disguise, her freedom; he was infuriated that someone so old was still a woman. But in this instant, when warmth and speckled light cushioned the proximity of gaunt bony man and shrunken woman, suddenly he understood that the old creature's eyes were telling him that she knew full well that in her he despised the pretty bud that has turned to worms.

When he raised his arm he had no intention of letting it fall. He had not even meant to lift his arm, but when he felt his right arm moving upward and backward until it was higher than his head, he did so in the knowledge that he intended only to frighten the old woman, nothing more. Yet he too was shocked at the length and breadth of the gesture that carried the arm that had been inert at his side to the top of its arc so that the black hand was poised at its summit, prepared with greatest strength to strike its blow or fling a great weight to the ground. In the extremity of his vision he had seen the upward passage of the black hand, and when it was no longer in sight, raised at arm's length above and behind his head, still he saw the uplifted hand as did the old woman: black, clawlike, murderous, some interminably heavy and destructive weapon that would travel at a great speed down the terrible distance from its place in the air to her own small weightless self, at which the blow was aimed. But he intended none of it. He did not in fact swing down his arm.

For the old woman, however, it was otherwise. Before he could move and while the black hand was quivering high in the air, at that very moment she must have felt that the black hand would fall and must have felt the inevitable rush of air and the breathless pitiless impact of the blow itself. In that instant his own body was as unwieldy as an awkwardly drawn bow; his black hand was still in the air; he stared down and in disbelief as the old woman's eyes squeezed shut and the face gradually changed its expression from fear to girlish supplication to the pinched and luminous grimace she had saved for her doom. Death lit up the old woman's face as from within. She dropped at his feet.

Slowly he lowered the black offending hand to its place at his side. He heard a voice shouting and noticed, a short distance beyond where the dead woman lay, a great pile of fagots tied with a rope. He could not move, his scalp was bristling, he felt as drained of blood as was the small deflated body in its heap of rags. Obviously the old woman had been carrying the fagots on the little saddle of her bent back; obviously in this sunny spot she had decided for no reason to throw down her burden meant for the hearth. It was for this that she had been laughing to herself in the speckled light. Now the querulous voice was calling; now he felt as if he had been seized from behind by powerful bare arms locked around his waist. He thought of himself as that Konrad Vost who had again been wrong. He turned and fled.

For Konrad Vost, he told himself, the world was now in a constant state of metamorphosis, duplication, multiplication; figures deserving existence only within the limits of the dream now sprang alive; the object of least significance was inspired with its secret animation; no longer was there such a thing as personal safety; in every direction there rose the bars of the cage. What could be worse?

He gained the tracks and immediately, without wiping his face or glancing backward and downward toward the tranquil stand of trees where he himself had committed an act that had erupted only from his own contemptible imagination, and without waiting for a glimpse of the old man who was now discovering the sack of rags in the clearing, he broke into a clumsy run which defied his characteristic bearing and which he was able to sustain until his pained chest brought him again to a walk. He forced himself along, despite shortness of breath, the swinging arm, the clamminess of his legs and feet. As he hurried down the lengthening tracks, not in flight from evildoing, as he reminded himself, but only in pursuit of legitimate or even heroic ends, still he formulated what he had learned in the grove of laughter: that whatever his own previous misconceptions, nonetheless age never obliterates entirely the streaks and smears of masculine or feminine definition. Never.

He longed for water. Slowing his pace but walking on, he found it ironic that he who was making his lonely and treacherous way across a marsh, which was nothing if not the residence of a retiring sea, that in such a place a man as determined as himself should suddenly be compulsively concerned with drinking cold cups of water, immersing himself in water, when there was none. The hut where the old woman had lived with the querulous man would have had its well, its ladle, its ancient bucket on a length of dripping chain; even here, now, the light through which he moved was like a bright clear fluid which he could almost cup in his hands and drink. But it was light, not water, and for some reason the vista now surrounding him was dry, murky, muddy, barren, without any trace of water that might cleanse him, quench his thirst.

Now the light was changing, the mirrors were tilting, the tracks were lying exactly at sea level, and now the light that had so filled his eyes was spread in a miragelike sheet of water across the entire landscape, which, before, had consisted merely of parched grass or mud. The level of the roadbed so perfectly matched the level of the surrounding water that now the way of his journey appeared to be carrying him through the water itself.

Again it was a sound that brought him to a dead standstill in the midst of the emptiness. Suddenly his perspiration disappeared in a cool breath; the brightness of the light diminished to normal intensity; the air became clear; the mirrors of the marsh were again adjusted so as to be conducive to the ordinary sight of his eyes: still water, islets of crab grass and, to the left, a frieze of tall thin pale green trees aligned exactly parallel to the rusted tracks which lay now like broken lines of fire across the water. Behind the trees something was wetly gleaming. But also, and more important, the sound he was still listening to was coming from behind the trees.

Small but unmistakable, it was the sound of splashing. It reached him faintly, musically, yet without rhythm, like a bell deliberately tinkled to destroy rhythm and prevent anticipation. Again it came to him, the sound of water disturbed, water tossed into the air, water set randomly and sweetly in motion behind the trees. But dare he risk again leaving the solidity of the tracks? There was no way of knowing, for instance, the depth of the water between himself and the tall green trees that were spaced evenly and closely together like the stakes of a fragment of a gigantic fence. Yet here, after all, was the substance of what he himself had been desiring: the calmness of green trees, the freshness of water.

Abruptly and with a few awkward movements he hid his right hand from view in his suit coat pocket, attempted to judge the distance between himself and the trees, and then decisively and silently entrusted himself to the flat water. He felt as if he were gliding toward the screen of trees; underfoot there was firmness, the water rose only to his midshins. The splashing sounds drew closer, the structure behind the trees was brightly shimmering. The trees appeared to be clothed in pale green skin and, as he approached them in haste and silence, revealed the webbing of white vines that, never climbing more than a meter from the water's surface, laced the trees together trunk to trunk. His thirst was intolerable, he was surprised at his eagerness to see beyond the trees which, he knew full well, were watery replicas of those other trees, which had proven to be a grove of death.

He stooped, held his breath, with his left hand seized the green thinness of the nearest tree, and then bracing the side of his head against the tree, and crouching like a phantom in the still water, he stared at the spectacle that some master stroke had surely fashioned only to feed the needs of his own psychological function in this instant of suspended time. The crumbling remains of the old mill, for such was the structure that had gleamed through the trees, consisted of a high partial wall of jagged and blackened stones and a great iron wheel rusted into the antithesis of motion, and stood before him at a small distance like a dripping theatrical backdrop before which a single young naked woman was enjoying the water. The enormous wheel could not turn, could no longer bear water to the top of its arc, and the air itself was a dry transparency, and yet both wheel and wall were, on all their surfaces, totally and freshly wet as if from some invisible but constantly replenished deluge of clear water.

But the small young naked woman? This childlike creature quite unaware of the dripping ruin which, behind her back, could only exaggerate her nakedness, her small size, her dripping skin? But even in the first glimpse he knew conclusively that she who was now splashing herself in the pleasure of natural privacy was the selfsame person whom he and Spapa had beaten into unconsciousness in La Violaine. He could not be mistaken: the very bruises that blurred his own elation in a flash of shame gave absolute identity to the young woman who had in fact survived the combat in the prison only to experience now the privilege of being herself in her skin. The black and blue welts were all too visible, the eye puffed shut gave him a stab of pain, in particular he recoiled from a star-shaped bruise on the little haunch. She was disfigured, more so than he, and on her body bore the livid signs of his own righteousness. But her beauty remained: the freely hanging dark hair, the sun-darkened tan and pink complexion of the wet skin, the shocking symmetry of a body so small that in its childlike proportions it exceeded the beauty of the life-sized woman it was intended to represent: in all this his powers of recognition were even more confirmed than in the physical evidence of her injuries, the sight of which so offended, suddenly, his proud and sentimental eye.

She was facing him, she was close enough so that he could study as if in the magnification of a large and rapturous lens the eye that was open, the scarred stomach he could have contained in his hand now clinging to the tree, the naked breasts which had somehow escaped the damage inflicted by Spapa's brutal stick and his own. Facing him, in the water that reached above her knees, and in silence, without either song or laughter, merely reaching down and splashing her hands against the water or scooping it up and allowing it to trickle on the shining hair, the oval face, the waist where the skin was tightening in the exertions of her self-absorption, on the wet thighs that, together, preserved her modesty. As for himself, surely he who had beaten her on head and body could now be allowed to spy on her innocent nudity; after the first violation, peering at her through green trees was nothing. So he watched as the hands fluttered, as a knee rose, as one thigh crossed the other, as the shoulders dipped, as the muscles played beneath the skin about the navel, as the water flew from the fingertips and the mouth smiled. Alone, turning toward him her diminutive naked profile with its curves freshly dipped in light, it was she who imparted to the sinister ruins behind her back a lifelike pastoral completion. The wheel might have been steadily revolving, the water might have been coursing in its productive fall, the grain might have been gathering in its stone bowl, while on the other side of the building the old men might have been lounging among their waiting donkeys, unaware of her who, naked in the millpond, was causing the wheel to turn, the grain to flow.

Not once did he blink. Standing fully clothed in the same water in which her nakedness was flowering, now he was suddenly aware that the object of his spying had turned her back to him and was bending down to stir the waters. The sight of her body bent down from the waist in precocious but unconscious self-display destroyed in the instant his tranquillity so that loathing the repetition of the sensations that had been aroused in his trousers only days before, and determined to preserve in his mind the vision of the bather, he loosened his hold on the tree, turned away reluctantly from his secret view of the pond, and crouching, silent, stealthy, waded back across the water to the dry tracks.

He paused once to hear again the splashing. He noted that his thirst was quenched. He told himself that he could not have harmed her person for a second time or dared to interrupt her bright bare immersion in air and water. Abruptly he set forth again and the sounds of splashing faded, his own unwanted sensations faded, while only the vision of honey, light, water, and dark hair remained. He could not have been more soiled in his dress, or in his blood, his bones, his tissues, and yet he carried with him the clear indestructible sight and, despite discomfort and weariness, was now increasingly animated by self-satisfaction: he had looked at her, but he had not harmed her.

If he had known the identity of the little martyr of La Violaine, as he soon came to think of her, he would have suddenly understood his own death the day it arrived; and if he had not allowed himself to be consumed by the vision of the bather he had spied on through the green trees, he in turn might have prevented her martyrdom.

As it was, he walked with a fierce exhausted pleasure, he walked while bearing the entire millpond inside his head, he had eyes only for the nudity of her whom he had spared, he towered and staggered along bemused and unaware of the dangerous tracks and making no effort to recall his dream: he who knew better and should have concentrated on the path of his journey. But it was of course too late.

The snarling of the black dog destroyed the vision as swiftly as the fangs of the beast would have seized his thigh were it not for the leash. The terrible lean creature lunged at him from no place of hiding that he could see, while the loudness of the weapon being prepared for firing came to him exactly as if the dog had not been snarling but had instead been frothing and straining at the leash in silence. They came from nowhere, the vicious dog and the armed unkempt man wearing the familiar blue uniform and, on his head, the kepi cocked at an arrogant angle. From nowhere, man and dog, yet suddenly his way was obstructed; the muzzle of the gun was aimed at his chest. The beast was straining so fiercely on its leash that its front feet were free of the ground and its snarling jaws were not a hand's length from the center of his own body where lay the living entrails the animal clearly wished to rip and masticate while still steaming in the heat of his blood. As for himself, he fell back from the murderous pair, he raised his left hand in self-defense, in supplication, and managed to restrain himself from flight. He could hear the dog's breath and the guttural wet tones of its lust and hatred; he could hear the creaking of all the wrinkles in the thick uniform of the man who was leaning his weight backward against the pull of the leash wrapped several times about his left wrist and leveling with his right hand the weapon suspended from his shoulder by a leather strap. The stub of a yellow cigarette was caught between the lips, the careless stubble of beard on the coarse face glistened with the exertions of his search through the hot marsh. Even while noting these details he, Vost, was thinking that in a moment or two he would be shot by the man and eaten by the dog.

In shocked and cowering haste he heard the sound of his voice in his rancid mouth: "But I have discovered one of them, there, in the pond behind those trees where she is in the nude. She's alone. She's yours for the taking…"

The silent yellow eyes of the thick man cloaked in his barbarous officialdom stared into his own wide eyes as steadily and ruthlessly as the eyes of the dog. The man said nothing, holding both gun and dog, while the animal continued to choke and gnash its teeth. Perhaps the escapee naked in the millpond was not enough enticement for this man who bore on his body the smell of his dog; perhaps he would take the woman captive and, even so, fire his weapon into the tremulous breast of himself, Konrad Vost. But the image of the naked bather seemed to form at last inside the thickness of the broad cranium; the man in his suspicious but slowly growing interest lowered his gun; he jerked once on the leash and gave the quivering animal an incomprehensible command. Darkly this cruel pair circled around him, where he stood crushed in his shame, and set off toward the screen of trees.

But what had he done? Was it possible? Had he sacrificed the purity of his vision and the freedom of his former victim merely for the sake of his own well-being? Or merely because he had been so taken by surprise by the brute maleness of the man and dog that he had simply collapsed in the stench of their intimidation? But there was no excuse. With a word he had snatched the bather from her clear pond and imprisoned her once more, in some makeshift cell in the city. And who could say to what further mistreatment she, who had already suffered enough, might be subjected by her wordless captor once he had tied the leash to a tree?

It was then that he heard the burst of shots. Not a single shot but several. A sound like the dog snarling. But they were shots from a gun. He heard them, they hung in the air, they faded, he swung wildly around and then, in the stillness of the echo, seeing nothing of trees or man or dog wherever he turned, then in the silence and failing light he stood alone to bear as long as he could his incomprehension, his complete understanding. He did not know what had contrived the terrible correctness of his knowledge. But it was true: he himself had killed the little martyr of La Violaine.

His shoulders sagged, his head was bowed, his grief was centered in the pain of the face he dared not expose to the darkening air. When at last he took his hand from his face, he found that the formerly brilliant light of the marsh had given way not merely to dusk but to fog. Gauzelike, thick, tinted here and there with a wet pinkness, it lay in strips or massive handfuls on the tracks, on the nearby water, between blasted stumps and hummocks of cold grass, covering the entirety of his now subterranean world wherever he looked. Two thoughts came to him at once: that he could not determine which direction led back to the city, or which away from it; and that now the fog was smothering the small naked figure as it drifted, face downward, in the pond. But she too was gone, the millpond was gone, while for himself there was only the sightlessness that resulted from the paradox of the increasing whiteness of the fog and the growing darkness of the approaching night.

consolation

Billy Collins

How agreeable it is not to be touring Italy this summer,
wandering her cities and ascending her torrid hilltowns.
How much better to cruise these local, familiar streets,
fully grasping the meaning of every road sign and billboard
and all the sudden hand gestures of my compatriots.

There are no abbeys here, no crumbling frescoes or famous
domes and there is no need to memorize a succession
of kings or tour the dripping corners of a dungeon.
No need to stand around a sarcophagus, see Napoleon's
little bed on Elba, or view the bones of a saint under glass.

How much better to command the simple precinct of home
than be dwarfed by pillar, arch, and basilica.
Why hide my head in phrase books and wrinkled maps?
Why feed scenery into a hungry, one-eyed camera
eager to eat the world one monument at a time?

Instead of slouching in a café ignorant of the word for ice,
I will head down to the coffee shop and the waitress
known as Dot. I will slide into the flow of the morning
paper, all language barriers down,

rivers of idiom running freely, eggs over easy on the way.

And after breakfast, I will not have to find someone
willing to photograph me with my arm around the owner.
I will not puzzle over the bill or record in a journal
what I had to eat and how the sun came in the window.
It is enough to climb back into the car

as if it were the great car of English itself
and sounding my loud vernacular horn, speed off
down a road that will never lead to Rome, not even Bologna.

and then there were the feet

William Kistler

And then there were the feet
showing their white bones beneath the long skirts,
and then there were the these and the and these,
such as the eyes behind the glasses

and the words of the mind behind the eyes
burning and attaching themselves to each thing
before the eyes, which also were burning
and becoming the life freed. And now

I'm off to hear the up and the down
of the unfolded wings of music where they lift
from the strings of instruments. And now
I'm at the station of trains where wheels

go turning through shrouds of steam and the sound
of iron rolling. Such a world is opening
its events before me. And my eyes are only
just beginning to see what they eat, and already

I am anxiously waiting for the sun to set
so that as in the many places and times
of lives past I can hold that fierce burning
out from the darkening body of evening.

in media res beginning

biographical notes

MAGGIE ANDERSON was born in New York City and moved to West Virginia when she was thirteen years old. In 1991 she edited *Hill Daughter: New and Selected Poems* by West Virginia poet Louise McNeill; she and Alex Gildzen edited the anthology *A Gathering of Poets,* published in 1992. Among her awards are fellowships for poetry from the National Endowment for the Arts, the Pennsylvania Council on the Arts, and the MacDowell Colony. She is currently teaching creative writing at Kent State University.

PATRICK CHAMOISEAU is the author of *Texaco,* which won France's coveted Prix Goncourt, *Creole Folktales, Solibo Magnificent,* and *Chronicle of the Seven Sorrows.* He lives in Martinique.

BILLY COLLINS is the author of six books of poetry: *Questions About Angels, Picnic Lightning, The Art of Drowning* (which was a finalist for the 1996 Lenore Marshall Prize), *The Apple That Astonished Paris, Pokerface,* and *Video Poems.* Collins' work has appeared in anthologies, textbooks, and a variety of periodicals, and his work has been featured in *The Pushcart Prize* anthology and *The Best American Poetry* for 1992, 1993, and 1997. He is professor of English at Lehman College, CUNY, and a visiting writer at Sarah Lawrence College.

E.E. CUMMINGS was born in Cambridge, Massachusetts, in 1894. One of the best-known American writers of the Twentieth century, his *Complete Poems* appeared in 1991. He died in 1962.

SEAN THOMAS DOUGHERTY is a former high school dropout and factory worker. A nationally renowned performance poet, he is the author of three books of poems, including *The Body's Precarious Balance* (Red Dancefloor Press, 1997). His work has also appeared in the recent anthologies *Identity Lessons* (Penguin, 1999), *Brooding the Midwest* (Bottom Dog, 1998), and *Poetry Nation* (Vehicle, 1999). He teaches at Syracuse University, where he is completing a Ph.D. in Cultural Rhetoric.

JOHN DREXEL's poems have appeared widely in magazines in the U.S. and Britain, including *The Hudson Review, Oxford Poetry, The Paris Review, Salmagundi, The Southern Review,* and *Verse.* A recipient of the Amy Lowell Poetry Travelling Scholarship and a Hawthornden Fellowship, he is a freelance writer, editor, and reviewer, and also directs a poetry workshop in Hay-on-Wye, Wales.

BARBARA EDELMAN is a Visiting Lecturer in English at the University of Pittsburgh and Poet in Residence at the Ellis School. Her work has appeared in journals including *Prairie Schooner, Cimarron Review,* and *Poet Lore,* and her one-act play *Charades* received a 1994 production at the Pittsburgh New Works Festival. She's the (grateful) recipient of a Pennsylvania Council on the Arts 2000 fellowship in poetry. Her chapbook of poems, *A Girl in Water,* is forthcoming from Parallel Press at the University of Wisconsin-Madison.

LYNN EMANUEL was born in New York and has lived, worked, and traveled in North Africa, Europe, and the Near East. She is the author of three books of poetry, *Hotel Fiesta, The Dig,* and *Then, Suddenly—.* She has been a recipient of the Great Lakes Colleges Association Award, two NEA Fellowships, the National Poetry Series Award, and three Pushcart Prizes. Her work has been featured in *The Pushcart*

Prize anthology and *The Best American Poetry* in 1994, 1995, and 1998. Currently, she is a Professor of English at the University of Pittsburgh and Director of the Writing Program.

ALICE FULTON's books of poems are *Sensual Math; Powers of Congress; Paladium,* winner of the National Poetry Series and the Society of Midland Authors Award; and *Dance Script With Electric Ballerina,* winner of the Associated Writing Programs Award. She has received fellowships from the John D. and Catherine T. MacArthur Foundation, the Ingram Merrill Foundation, and the Guggenheim Foundation. Her work has been included in six editions of *The Best American Poetry* series.

WILLIAM GASS was born in Fargo, North Dakota, in 1924. He has been the recipient of grants from the Rockefeller and Guggenheim Foundations, as well as the Academy and Institute of Arts and Letters Award for Fiction, the Academy and Institute of Arts and Letters Medal of Merit for Fiction, the Lannan Foundation Lifetime Achievement Award, and the National Book Critics Circle Award for Criticism (1985 and 1996). He has also won the Pushcart Prize (1976, 1983, 1987, 1992), and his work has appeared four times in *The Best American Short Stories.* He lives in St. Louis, where he is director of the International Writers' Center.

TIMOTHY GEIGER is the author of six chapbooks of poetry and the full-length collection *Blue Light Factory* (Spoon River Poetry Press, 1999). He is the proprietor of Aureole Press, a literary fine-press, and founding editor of *Whirligig: A Journal of Language Arts.* He teaches creative writing and letterpress printing at the University of Toledo.

Amy Gerstler's eleven books include *Bitter Angel* (North Point Press), *Nerve Storm* (Viking Penguin), *Crown of Weeds* (Viking Penguin), and the forthcoming *Medicine* (Penguin Putnam).

Michael Graber lives in his native Memphis with his wife and three children, works as an editor, and moonlights as a mandolin player and crooner, a teacher, and a reviewer. Many of his poems have been published in print magazines and on-line. Currently, Mr. Graber spends his free time finishing the libretto for a requiem and writing a novel in verse form.

Gabriel Gudding was educated at Evergreen College, Purdue, and Cornell. His work has appeared in *American Poetry Review, The Nation, Iowa Review, Seneca Review,* and elsewhere. He's a recipient of *The Nation*/Discovery Award, and lives in Ithaca, New York, with the Irish poet Mairead Byrne.

Sunetra Gupta was born in Calcutta. As a child, she accompanied her parents, a teacher and a historian, when they moved from India to live in Ethiopia, Zambia, and Liberia. She majored in biology at Princeton University and studied creative writing under Joyce Carol Oates. She lives in London, where she is a member of the Epidemiology Research Group at Imperial College. Her books include *Memories of Rain, The Glassblower's Breath,* and *Moonlight into Marzipan.*

John Hawkes was a member of the American Academy and Institute of Arts and Letters and the American Academy of Arts and Sciences. His many books include *The Beetle Leg, The Blood Oranges, Death, Sleep, & the Traveler,* and *The Lime Twig.* He died in 1997.

Terrance Hayes is the author of *Muscular Music* (Tia Chucha Press, 1999). His poems have appeared in *The Beloit Poetry Journal, Chelsea, Callaloo, Green Mountains Review,* and elsewhere. He has received a Red Brick Review Award and a Whiting Writers Award for his poetry. He is currently an assistant professor of English at Xavier University in New Orleans, Louisiana, where he lives with his wife, poet Yona Harvey, and their daughter, Ua.

Jack Heflin's first collection of poetry, *The Map of Leaving,* won the Montana First Book Award, and his poems have appeared in numerous magazines, including *The Antioch Review, Missouri Review, Poetry Northwest, Poetry East, Green Mountains Review,* and *Willow Springs.* He directs the Creative Writing Program at the University of Louisiana at Monroe where he is Associate Professor of English. In 1995, he was awarded a Fellowship from the Louisiana Division of the Arts.

William Kistler was President of Poets and Writers and was also a founding member of Poets House, where currently he serves on the Program Committee and is the Treasurer. He is the author of four volumes of poetry: *The Elizabeth Sequence,* which won the Oklahoma Book Award in 1989; *America February* (1991); *Poems of the Known World* (1995); and *Notes Drawn from the River of Ecstasy* (1998). In 1992, he co-edited and wrote the lead essay for *Buying America Back,* a collection of essays on America's social and economic problems.

Yusef Komunyakaa is a professor in the Council of Humanities and Creative Writing at Princeton University. He has published five of his ten books, including the Pulitzer Prize-winning *Neon Vernacular* (1993), which also won the Kingsley-Tufts Poetry Award from the Claremont Graduate School, *Magic City* (1992), and *Dien Cai Dau* (1988). In 1991, he won the Thomas Forcade Award; in 1993, he was nominated for the *Los Angeles Times* Book Prize in Poetry; and, in 1997, he was awarded the Hanes Poetry Prize. His most recent collection of poetry is *Thieves of Paradise.*

PETER LA SALLE is the author of the novel *Strange Sunlight* and two story collections, *The Graves of Famous Writers* and *Hockey Sur Glace.* His work has appeared in *The Best American Short Stories* and *Prize Stories: The O. Henry Awards.* He has taught at universities in the U.S. and in France.

JEFFREY MCDANIEL lives in Los Angeles, California, where he teaches poetry writing workshops at UCLA Extension and as part of Poets-in-the-Classrooms sponsored by PEN West. He has read his work at the Smithsonian Institution and on National Public Radio's *Talk of the Nation.* He has published two books, *Alibi School* and *The Forgiveness Parade,* both with Manic D Press.

SHARON MCDERMOTT lives and writes in Pittsburgh. She is a visiting lecturer in English at the University of Pittsburgh, and also teaches at Carnegie Mellon University. Her work has appeared in many journals, including *The Louisville Review, Southern Poetry Review, Poet Lore, Zone 3,* and *West Branch.*

KRISTINA MCGRATH's first novel *House Work* was published in 1994 and selected by *The New York Times* as a Notable Book of the Year. She is a recipient of grants in poetry and fiction from the New York Foundation for the Arts, a fiction grant from the Kentucky Foundation for Women, a *Kenyon Review* Award for Literary Excellence in Fiction, a Pushcart Prize, and a Writer's Voice Residency Award.

HEATHER MCHUGH has published several books of poetry, including *The Father of the Predicaments, Hinge & Sign, Shades,* and *To the Quick.* She is the winner of the Folger Library's 1998 O.B. Hardison, Jr. Poetry Prize, and was elected a Chancellor of the Academy of American Poets. McHugh is Milliman Distinguished Writer-in-Residence at the University of Washington MFA program.

MARJORIE MADDOX, an associate professor of English at Lock Haven University, has published five collections of poetry: *Perpendicular as I,* 1994 Sandstone Publishing Book Award winner, *Nightrider to Edinburgh* (Amelia), *How to Fit God into a Poem* (Painted Bride), *Ecclesia* (Franciscan University Press), and *Body Parts* (Anamnesis). Her manuscript *Transplant, Transport, Transubstantiation* has been a finalist at nineteen national competitions. The recipient of numerous awards, she has also published 200 poems in literary journals.

SUSAN MITCHELL's first collection of poems, *The Water Inside the Water,* was published by Wesleyan University Press. Her many awards for poetry include fellowships from the National Endowment for the Arts, the Guggenheim Foundation, and the Lannan Foundation. Twice a Claire Hagler Fellow at the Fine Arts Work Center in Provincetown, and a Hoyns Fellow at the University of Virginia, Mitchell grew up in New York City, and now lives in Boca Raton, where she holds the Mary Blossom Lee Endowed Chair in Creative Writing at Florida Atlantic University.

RICK MOODY is the author of three novels: *Garden State, The Ice Storm* (which was made into a successful film), and *Purple America.* He received the 1994 Aga Khan Prize for Fiction for the title novella in his collection *The Ring of Brightest Angels Around Heaven.*

MIKE NEWIRTH grew up on Long Island and now lives in Chicago. His essays and fiction received a Henfield Transatlantic Review Award and have appeared in *The Baffler, The Pushcart Prize XXII,* and *Personals: Dreams and Nightmares From the Lives of 20 Young Writers.*

A.E. STALLINGS's first collection of poetry, *Archaic Smile,* was chosen by Dana Gioia for the Richard Wilbur Award and published in 2000 by the University of Evansville. Her poetry has received the Eunice Tietjens Prize from *Poetry,* a Pushcart Prize, and the James Dickey Poetry Prize from *Five Points.* Her work has been included in many distinguished periodicals and has appeared in *The Best American Poetry 1994.* Stallings currently resides in Athens, Greece, with her husband John Psaropoulos and their cat, Marta.

CONNIE VOISINE has begun her first year as Assistant Professor of Creative Writing at the University of Hartford. She has been published in *Ploughshares, The Threepenny Review,* and other magazines. A devotee of the work of Frank Bidart and Anne Carson, she is finishing a collection of autobiographical narrative poems of which "Psalm" is a part. Her second book is a collection of short stories about waitresses.

BELLE WARING's first collection of poetry, *Refuge* (University of Pittsburgh Press, 1990), won the Associated Writing Programs' Award for Poetry in 1989, the Washington Prize in 1991, and was cited by *Publishers Weekly* as one of the best books of 1990. Her second collection, *Dark Blonde* (Sarabande Books, 1997), received the first annual Levis Reading Prize and the 1997 Poetry Center Book Award. She lives in Washington, D.C.

Edmund White, the author of eleven books including *A Boy's Own Story, The Farewell Symphony,* and, most recently, *The Married Man,* is a Chevalier de L'Ordre des Arts et Lettres, and the recipient of a Guggenheim Fellowship and the Award for Literature from the National Academy of Arts and Letters. His *Genet: A Biography* won the National Book Critics Circle Award and the Lambda Literary Award. He teaches writing at Princeton University.

One of the pre-eminent contemporary American poets, anthologized and collected into over a dozen volumes and famous for his beautiful long verse line, C.K. Williams has won numerous literary awards, including the National Book Critics Circle Award, two NEAs, and a Guggenheim. His latest book of poems is *The Vigil* (Farrar, Straus & Giroux). Currently professor of English at Princeton University, Mr. Williams lives part of each year in Paris.

Valerie Wohlfeld's 1994 collection, *Thinking the World Visible,* won the Yale Series of Younger Poets Award. She holds an MFA from Vermont College.

Dean Young was born in 1955 in Columbia, Pennsylvania. He has received a fellowship from the Fine Arts Work Center in Provincetown, a Stegner fellowship from Stanford, and two fellowships from the National Endowment for the Arts. He has published three previous books of poems, *Design with X, Beloved Infidel,* and *Strike Anywhere,* which won the Colorado Poetry Prize in 1995. Currently an associate professor at Loyola University, he splits his time between Chicago and Berkeley, California, where he lives with his wife, fiction writer Cornelia Nixon, and his cat, Minnow.

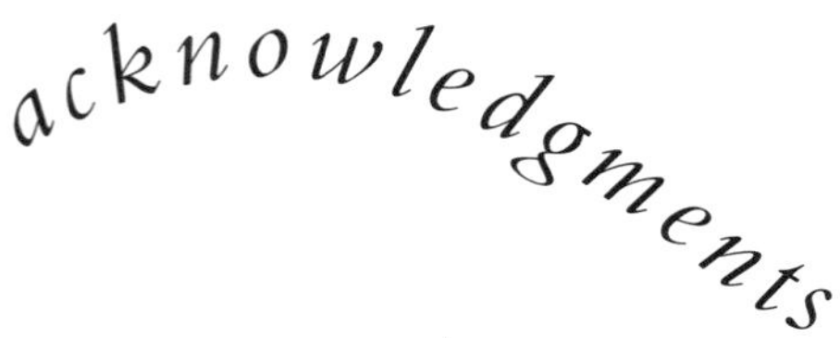

"Country Wisdoms" from *Cold Comfort* by Maggie Anderson, © 1986. Reprinted by permission of the University of Pittsburgh Press.

"The Eighteen Dream-Words that Afoukal Gave Him" from *Chronicle of the Seven Sorrows* by Patrick Chamoiseau, translated by Linda Coverdale, Reprinted by permission of the University of Nebraska Press. © Editions Gallimard, 1986. © 1999 by the University of Nebraska Press.

"Consolation" from *The Art of Drowning* by Billy Collins, © 1995. Reprinted by permission of the University of Pittsburgh Press.

"when faces called flowers float out of the ground," © 1950, © 1978, 1991 by the Trustees for the E.E. Cummings Trust. © 1979 by George James Firmage, from *Complete Poems: 1904–1962* by E.E. Cummings, edited by George J. Firmage. Reprinted by permission of Liveright Publishing Corporation.

"inside gertrude stein" from *Then, Suddenly—*, by Lynn Emanuel, © 1999. Reprinted by permission of the University of Pittsburgh Press.

"Who Is She Kidding" from *The Dig* by Lynn Emanuel, © 1992. Used with permission of the poet and the University of Illinois Press.

"Labor Day" from *The Body's Precarious Balance*. © 1997 by Sean Thomas Dougherty. Used with permission of the poet and Red Dancefloor Press.

"Babies" from *Palladium*. © 1986 by Alice Fulton. Used by permission of the poet and the University of Illinois Press.

"The Music of Prose." From *Finding A Form* by William H. Gass. Copyright © 1996 by William H. Gass. Reprinted by permission of Alfred A. Knopf Inc.
"Lucky You" from *Bitter Angel*. © 1990 by Amy Gerstler. Used by permission of the poet and North Point Press.

From *Memories of Rain*. Copyright © 1992 by Sunetra Gupta. Reprinted by permission of Grove Press.

"The Martyr of La Violaine" from *Humors of Blood & Skin*. Copyright © 1984 by John Hawkes. Reprinted by permission of New Directions Publishing Corporation.

"Boxcar" from *Muscular Music.* © 1999 by Terrance Hayes. Reprinted by permission of the author and Tia Chucha Press.

"And Then There Were the Feet" from *Notes Drawn from the River of Ecstasy.* © 1998 by William Kistler. Used by permission of the poet and Council Oak Books.

"Venus's-flytraps" from *Magic City.* © 1992 by Yusef Komunyakaa, Wesleyan University Press. Used by permission of the University Press of New England.

"False Leads" from *Copacetic.* © 1984 by Yusef Komunyakaa, Wesleyan University Press. Used by permission of the University Press of New England.

"The Latin Ice Kings" by Peter La Salle originally appeared in *The Virginia Quarterly Review,* Autumn 1998 (Volume 74, No. 4).

"Hunting for Cherubs" and "The Jerk" from *The Forgivness Parade.* © 1998 by Jeffrey McDaniel. Used by permission of the poet and Manic D Press.

"Language Lesson 1976" from *Hinge & Sign: Poems,* 1968–1993. © 1994 by Heather McHugh, Wesleyan University Press. Used by permission of the University Press of New England.

"The Other Hand" from *Perpendicular as I.* © 1994 by Marjorie Maddox. Used by permission of the poet and Sandstone Publishing.

"The Hotel by the Sea" from *Rapture* by Susan Mitchell. © 1992 by Susan Mitchell. Reprinted by permission of HarperCollins Publishers, Inc.

"The Mansion on the Hill." © 1997 by Rick Moody. First appeared in *The Paris Review,* issue #144, Fall 1997. Reprinted by permission of Melanie Jackson Agency, LLC.

"Give the Millionaire a Drink." © 1997 by Mike Newirth. First appeared in *The Baffler.* Reprinted by permission of the author.

"Baltazar Beats His Tutor at Scrabble" from *Dark Blonde.* © 1997 by Belle Waring. Used by permission of the poet and Sarabande Books.

"My Mother's Lips" from *Selected Poems* by C.K. Williams. © 1994 by C.K. Williams. Reprinted by permission of Farrar, Straus and Giroux, LLC.

"Ready-Made Bouquet" from *Strike Anywhere.* © 1995 by Dean Young. Used by permission of the poet and Center for Literary Publishing/University Press of Colorado.

the editors

Joe May

Kirby Gann is managing editor at Sarabande Books. His fiction has appeared in *American Writing, bananafish: short fiction, The Crescent Review, The Southern Indiana Review,* and *Witness,* among other journals. His work has received Special Mention in *The Pushcart Prize,* and is anthologized in *The Best of Witness.* Also a musician, he plays guitar in the band Jakeleg, whose CD is available on ear X-tacy records.

Leonardo Prada

Kristin Herbert has been awarded grants for her poetry from the Kentucky Arts Council and the Kentucky Foundation for Women. Her stories and poems have been recognized with an Academy of American Poets Prize, four Pushcart Prize nominations, and publication in journals including *Colorado Review, The Cream City Review, 5 AM, Kingfisher, Phoebe, Red Brick Review, New Delta Review, The Louisville Review, Controlled Burn, The American Voice, Green Mountains Review, Prairie Schooner,* and *The Antioch Review,* as well as in the anthologies *Present Tense: Writing and Art by Young Women* and *ChickLit 2: No Chick Vics.* She lives in Santa Monica, California.

Cover and text design by P. Dean Pearson.